Fire and Ice
Beyond Alchemy

A Detective Craig Rylander Mystery

By
George Arnold

EAKIN PRESS ✦ Fort Worth, Texas
www.EakinPress.com

This book is dedicated to Prashant Valangu, PhD, and the scientists of The University of Texas Institute for Fusion Studies. Also to my good friend Ken Squier, whose ideas led to the creation of this story

Fire and Ice is a work of fiction. Characters, places and events are the products of the author's imaginations or are used in a fictitious context. Any similarity to the reality of actual persons, living or deceased, is unintended and purely coincidental.

Cover design by Matt Arnold

Illustrations by Jason Eckhardt

FIRST EDITION

Copyright © 2015
By George Arnold
Published By Eakin Press
An Imprint of Wild Horse Media Group
P.O. Box 331779
Fort Worth, Texas 76163
1-817-344-7036
www.EakinPress.com
ALL RIGHTS RESERVED
1 2 3 4 5 6 7 8 9
ISBN-10: 1-940130-82-4
ISBN-13: 978-1-940130-82-8

Readers' comments about
Fire and Ice: Beyond Alchemy

- "When nature coughs up a chunk of Plutonium that outweighs a Buick, the race to recover it is on between the usual suspects. And a few unusual ones."

- "Suspense, action, rumor! All wrapped up in a story of international intrigue."

- "The cleverness of the author never ceases to amaze or to entertain."

- "Fire and Ice: Beyond Alchemy is an exciting and totally engaging story. Greed, politics, science and technology play roles in this delightful book that focuses on high-stakes international competition."

- "Fire and Ice is very thoughtful and made me think."

- "This was a fun read, with craziness galore, although some of it was the kind of crazy that scares the pants off you. Clearly a lot of research and atlas-reading went into this story."

- "One of the best. Fast paced. Kept me on edge looking forward to the next chapter."

- "If Tom Clancy, in a fit of whimsy, wrote a movie script similar to the movie "Rat Race," it might look like this far-fetched but fun take on world events, major players and egos. Added bonus: cultural and physical geography lessons. Good fun. Read it!"

- "This is the story of a bunch of bad people chasing a prize for bad reasons. It is certainly surprising how the solution came about."

- I laughed at the foolishness and excesses of each group as they tried to find ways to get to the Plutonium first, Most of all, I like the interplay of time, suspense and human comedy between the characters of the story."

- "'I liked the strong women's roles."

- "The calendar/date of each chapter kept the suspense alive; the reader needs to remember the problem needs to be solved in days, not months."

- "I could definitely see this storyline in a Netflix mini-series. The story would translate very well to film or TV."

- "I'm impressed. The book is well written, entertaining, and where in the hell (did the author) come up with these story lines?"

- "Craig, Gady and Greycloud get pulled into another adventure—this time to save the earth. Follow the action as three unlikely heroes work together to keep Plutonium out of the hands of nefarious billionaires and rogue governments."

- ". . . a page turner. Lots of research to get all the science details."

Author's Notes

I have diligently tried to avoid taking liberties with the science, and particularly the chemistry and physics, in the descriptions in this book. With the help of a well-known and –respected physicist, what I have described is admittedly simplified. But it is scientifically possible according to the laws of physics known at this time.

The element Plutonium is a heavy metal, normally found as a by-product of energy production via commercial nuclear reactors and as a fissionable material for producing both energy and weapons of mass destruction. While it is most often isolated by a centrifugal process from combination with Uranium-235 and Uranium-238, it does appear in nature in its pure form on occasion. To date, the occurrence of pure Plutonium in nature has been confined to very small amounts. The amount of Plutonium described as discovered in nature in this book has not, to date, been observed. But science cannot say it is an impossibility. In short, the amount of the heavy metal "discovered" in Siberia in this story is possible, though not probable. But . . . it could happen. And one day it may.

The fusion-fission process and international patents described in the narrative both exist today.* The reduction to harmlessness of spent nuclear fuels, which to date has been a long-term problem given the extremely long half-lives of Uranium and Plutonium, remains only a matter of time and financing.

In appropriate hands, Plutonium is a major source for good. In the wrong hands, it can lead to wholesale disaster.

---

* See "Nuclear Fusion-Fission Hybrid Could Destroy Nuclear Waste and Contribute to Carbon-Free Energy Future." The University of Texas Institute for Fusion Studies, January 27, 2009.

Meet the Major Players

The Rogue Scientists

- *Haji G. Kahn*—Iranian nuclear physicist bent on producing dirty suitcase nukes to destroy Western infidels. But is he really a jihadist? Or is he just totally insane? Or, even worse, both? Nobody knows for sure.

- *Mahmood Bijahn*—Al Qaeda apparatchik and political advisor to Kahn. Or is he?

The Rich Business Interests

- *An unidentified cabal*—a handful of some of the richest people in the world, whose intentions include turning their billions into trillions by stealing international patents to control the world market for reducing spent nuclear fuel to harmless "dirt."

- *Number Four*—Technologically-gifted computer wizard and contract operative to the international cabal.

Off the Grid International Investigators

- *Monica Skrabacz*—former field operative recently appointed head of the Russian Desk at the U.S. Central Intelligence Agency. Monica, frustrated by the CIA's seeming paralysis to deal with what she sees as an acute international emergency, goes rogue, off the grid, to enlist the aid of the only person she knows for sure can prevent a worldwide travesty of terrorist destruction.

- *Detective Lieutenant Craig C. Rylander*—of the Austin, Texas Police Department. Craig is summoned into clandestine service for his country to prevent a unique discovery from falling into the wrong hands. But he's skeptical of Monica. Will he help her?

- *John Greycloud*—renowned Navajo Shaman and tracker of people and objects for Western intelligence services. Known as Hosteen Greycloud, a title of honor among the Dineé, his people.

- *Sanjay Pradeet, Ph.D.*—nuclear physicist and technical advisor to Craig and his small team. A practical scientist with a keen sense of humor.

- *Alfredo "Lobo" Diaz*—recently retired captain of the Texas Rangers, recruited because of his extensive ties to the underworld. He has worked with Craig, Greycloud and Monica Skrabacz before. Like John and Craig, he is very suspicious of Monica and her motives. Fluent in both Spanish and French.

- *Gady Esparza*—Lt. Rylander's young protégé, newly recruited to the Austin PD from her previous job as a rookie detective in Tucson. She is John Greycloud's god-daughter in the Navajo culture and, with Craig and John, helped track down Felix Pavlovich, head of a 200 year-old assassination ring and the killer of her identical twin sister, Gloria.

- *Amanda and Josef Reynosa*—half siblings to Monica Skrabacz, the three of them having the same father—Felix Pavlovich. Amanda, known to friends as Nana, heads Pavlovich's former international gas and oil consulting and production company. In that role, she has become a billionaire. Josef, her much younger half-brother, is finishing his studies in international commerce at The University of Texas in Austin.

The Politicians

- *POTUS*—President of the United States—A man with enough on his plate already who really doesn't have time to deal personally with what's happening. But can he trust his National Security Advisor and the DCI, head of the CIA, to actually accomplish anything?

- *Vladimir Putin*—President of the Russian Federation—Like POTUS, he finds what's happening a pain in the butt; who can he turn to deal with the situation? The FSB, Russia's Federal Security Service, successor to the KGB?

- *Kim Jung-Un*—First Chairman and head of the Supreme Peoples' Assembly —in the Democratic People's Republic of Korea. His subordinates know he's totally insane, so they fear telling him what's happening. But they fear even more having him find out that they didn't tell him. Maybe it's time to defect.

- *Kwak Pum Ji*—Minister of People's Security for the Democratic People's Republic of Korea—North Korea.

- *Chang Sung-taek*—Vice Chairman of the National Defense Commission for North Korea. Chang and Kwak take on an assignment sure to end in their deaths. Or do they?

- *Madam Park Geun-hye*—President of The Republic of Korea—South Korea. She deals with defectors from the North in unorthodox ways.

- *Supreme Leader Ali Khamenei*—Grand Ayatollah of the Islamic Republic of Iran. The Supreme Leader remains hell bent to develop nuclear weapons to advance Iran to the international status that he believes ancient Persia has earned.

- *President Hassan Rouhani*—is skeptical, having given his word to the Western powers that Iran does not seek to develop such weapons. Will there be a power struggle? What would Allah say?

Cameo Players

- *Alex Garza*—garrulous chief of the Austin Police Department. Alex is a cop's cop, a leader who respects and protects the 1,600 or so sworn officers under his command.

- *Ships' Captains of the USS Josef and the USS Pavlovich's Folly*—an ice-breaker and shallow-water drilling rig owned and operated by Van Pelt Industries, international oil and gas exploration and production company.

Diverse groups, each with its own strategy.
All after the same target.
For very different reasons.
Which will prevail?

Table of Contents

Fire and Ice
Beyond Alchemy

"Some say the world will end in fire,
Some say in ice.
From what I've tasted of desire
I hold with those who favor fire.
But if I had to perish twice,
I think I know enough of hate
To say that for destruction ice
Is also great
And would suffice."

Robert Frost

Introduction

Two figures sit at a round table in the dark.

"What the hell is that?" The head of the CIA's field operations stared at several projections on a wall in a darkened room in the CIA headquarters—the executive floor.

Monica Skrabacz, now heading the Russian desk at the Company after 15 years in the field in such lovely places as Beijing, Mogadishu and Moscow, looked with disdain to the questioner, the assistant DCI for field operations. After all, he'd never been in the field. Didn't have a clue what intelligence gathering out there in the real world is all about. A former analyst and desk-jockey whose greatest risk had been traffic on the Beltway for 26 years. In the dark he couldn't see the raw disgust on her face.

"What do you think it is?" she asked, curbing her inclination to add, "Dumbass."

He answered, "It looks like an egg on an ice field with a tiny yolk and a huge white that's dark. How far across is that egg-white thing?"

"Figure a diameter of 60 yards. The yolk, as you call it, is the size of a basketball. And it's on an ice field."

"Where?" her one-man audience asked.

"Siberia. Seven degrees north of the Arctic Circle on the edge of the Laptev Sea and the Arctic Ocean. The northern tip of the Central Siberian Plateau."

"Coordinates?"

Monica sighed. *As if this asshole could read a map.* But she answered, "Seventy-four degrees North, one-oh-five degrees East."

"That's way up there, huh?" he said.

"Technically speaking," she said, rolling her eyes, "it's way the fuck up there."

1

Her audience stood up as if to leave. "Well, Monica, are you going to tell me what the hell this is all about? Or are we going to have to play 20 Questions? It's Christmas Eve, and some of us have families."

To Monica, who had only a half-sister and half-brother in Texas, that comment was the last straw. "Listen you jerk, get your ass back in that chair and shut your mouth and listen. Or this may be the last Christmas Eve either of us has, with or without families."

"You're insubordinate."

"Fuck you. I don't report to you any longer, thank God. And you're a joke in the field. If you don't want to hear what I have to say, I'll grab the DCI and we'll interrupt the President's and the national security advisor's Christmas Eves."

"You wouldn't dare."

"Try me. You watched me in the field for 15 years. Do you really think there's anything I'm not capable of pulling off?"

He sat back down. "Cut to the chase."

"No," Monica said, "I'm going to paint this picture for you, number-by-number, because the entirety of field operatives knows you can't follow anything slightly complex. You either sit there and soak this in patiently, or leave now before I call the DCI."

"Go ahead." He knew Monica would carry through with her threat. No, he knew Monica didn't threaten. She promised. And if she did, his butt might become cultural affairs officer in Antarctica next week. If not on Christmas day.

Monica began, "Here it is, then. That dark egg white, as you call it, is a melted snowpack. Around the circumference of that circle, the un-melted wall of ice is 12 feet tall. What has melted that circle of ice is a physical anomaly."

"What could do that?" He was still in a hurry to get home.

"A lot of things could do that," Monica said. "But in this case, that yolk, as you called it, is a chunk of almost pure Plutonium, with a trace of Uranium-235 and, maybe, a tad of Uranium-238. It's about the size of a basketball."

"Who told you that?"

"One of our scientists. After he had one of our satellites zero-in. Don't argue. That's what it is. QED."

"But you have to have centrifuges to make Plutonium, don't you?"

"Personally, I've never 'made' Plutonium. And neither has anybody else. It's an element. A very heavy metal. And before you say something else stupid, yes, it does occur naturally. But up until now, only in very small amounts. This chunk must have made its way up to the surface over billions of years."

She had her audience's attention. "Who else knows about this?" he asked.

"Right now, just me, you and Dr. Evans. I've sworn him to secrecy."

"Do the Russians know?" he asked.

"My replacement in the Moscow embassy is checking for rumors; he doesn't know the potential subject. But, look, they're not stupid. That's something I tried to tell you for six years, but you never believed me. Once more, Russians are not stupid."

He stood again. "Well, Monica. This can wait a few days. Let's get back together on Friday. I'll think about it in the meantime. And don't you do anything crazy before then."

"I won't be here Friday."

"Why not? Where will you be?"

"Not that it's any of your business, but I'm going to see my brother and sister in Texas for a couple of days. I have family, too."

"Good," he said, "then we'll talk about it when you get back."

Monica, exasperated, said, "Do you have any idea what the consequences might be if this much weapons-grade Plutonium falls into the wrong hands? Even a clue?"

"Monica, I'm going home. Nobody's going to get it before next week. No more discussion."

And with that, he walked out the door, slamming it behind him.

Monica looked at the projections once again. She thought, *That much Plutonium must weigh more than 5,000 pounds. And it takes how much to produce a bomb? Forty or fifty pounds? Twenty pounds for a dirty suitcase bomb?*

With the resolve she'd become famous for in the Company, she reached for the phone on the edge of the table. "Get me the DCI. This is Monica Skrabacz on the Russian Desk." She paused. "I don't care where he is or what he's doing. This is a national emergency. I have to talk to him. Right now!

"And while I'm talking to him, run down the president's national security advisor. The DCI is going to want to talk to him right away."

She paused, then added, "And, thanks. This is more important than anything you've ever done. Or ever will do."

The Prize

SIBERIA

FIRE AND ICE
BEYOND ALCHEMY

Sea of Okhotsk

Hokkaido

Lake Baykal

MONGOLIA

Gobi Desert

Sea of Japan

Beijing

N. KOREA

SOUTH KOREA

JAPAN

Yellow Sea

CHINA

Eckhardt '14.

Part One

Lights!

Chapter One

Auld Lang Syne

Detective Bureau—Austin Police Department—December 30

My regular Monday morning detective staff meeting had just ended. I had asked my two most junior associates to stick around a few minutes. They didn't know why, but I wanted to do some one-on-one training with them. I guess, accurately, that's one (me) on two (them).

Today was Tom Sellers' first day as a detective. He'd had almost three years on the streets in uniform, and I thought he had the makings of a police chief one of these days. God knows that's not a job I ever want. For the past 18 months, Tom has been my uniformed shadow on three of the strangest cases I ever expect to see. He's a former NFL free safety— Green Bay Packers. At six-five and 240 pounds, he carries around less fat than a 12-ounce jar of peanut butter in his size 15 shoes.

The ultimate team player. And leader.

Gady Esparza, fresh from a year as a rookie detective in Tucson, has been more than my shadow for the last year. No, it's not what you're thinking. She's the identical twin to her late sister, Gloria, the brand new detective I'd mentored until she was brutally killed by an international terrorist, Felix Pavlovich. That's another story, but Gady joined me and her mother's brother, her "Little Father" in the Navajo culture, Navajo shaman John Greycloud, to track down the sonofabitch across five continents. We found him. But only Gady, John and I and a couple of others know when and where.

And we're not talking.

While John, Gady and I were continent hopping following Pavlovich all over the place, Tom made it his job to protect my new wife, Dr. Amy Clark-Rylander. Pavlovich had told me he would kill her.

And I believed him.

I can tell by the way you're looking at this page that you don't know who the hell I am or what in the world I'm talking about.

So let's clear some things up.

My name is Craig C. Rylander. The C stands for nothing, although some folks around here will tell you it's for "Crazy." I prefer "Committed."

I joined the Austin PD 10 years ago, fresh from a criminal justice degree from Sam Houston State University, in the shadow of Texas's maximum security state prison in Huntsville. I had an option: to sign a minor league contract with the Texas Rangers Baseball Club. I was handy with a bat, glove, arm and had some fast legs. Only one out of 50 or so signees ever get to the majors, though.

Besides, since I was a tyke, I've always wanted to be a detective. My mother said I was a natural. "Nondescript," she would tell me. At five-eight and totally unremarkable in any physical aspect, I'm the kind nobody will ever notice—on the sidewalk or in a room—big or small. It took me five years in a uniform to make the grade, but I'm here now. Three more years as a sergeant and, as of six weeks ago, I've inherited command of the APD detective bureau.

Besides "crazy," plenty of people around here would also call me "anal." I prefer "organized" and "disciplined." Maybe even "detailed." But I've never gift wrapped the garbage.

Yet.

Before I begin to tell you the rest of still another bizarre episode in the life of an everyday keeper of the peace and protector of the populace, you need to know a bit about the last two years in my life. Not about me, personally. But about those bizarre escapades I mentioned earlier.

So let's get that on the record. Judges say that a lot. Lawyers, too. Even interrogators like me, from time to time.

Twenty-eight months ago, seven girls between the ages of 10 and 15 disappeared from the streets of Austin in September and October. Each was either on her way to or home from school. The girls had little in common. Different schools. Different neighborhoods. Different ethnicities and different economic statuses. There was no pattern. They left home or school and just never arrived at their destinations. I recruited a specialist from Family and Protective Services, a state agency, to help me find the girls. Dr. Amy Clark, a nationally-known child psychologist (who is now my bride), and we set out to do just that. But wouldn't you know it? We got some help—a lot of it—from two places we didn't need or want help from, and from two sources who really didn't want to help, anyway.

Evelyn Baskins, the district attorney running for re-election in November, got on our case. She made some wild-ass accusations and then, and this is unforgivable, released the name and address of her idea of the prime kidnapping suspect, a totally innocent young man who ended up murdered in an arson fire within hours of Evelyn's dramatic announcement. She didn't give a rat's ass about finding the girls. But she was sure she could up her vote count by her gratuitous grandstanding.

Evelyn was hated by everybody who puts his or her life on the line every day when they strap on their Smith & Wesson 40-caliber sidearm. But she wasn't our only helper.

Before you could add a pejorative adjective to Evelyn's name, another band of yahoos chimed right in. I'm referring to the talking heads on talk radio and the fake "news" assholes on cable television. We knew, and so did they, that their only interest in the case involved creating a controversy where none existed, and then stirring the pot and riding that controversy to a bigger name and higher ratings for themselves. You know who they are. The likes of Gracy Nann and Geraldo Loquaz.

Neither Evelyn nor the entertainers-cum-pseudo news reporters cared a fig about the harm they might be doing with their . . . what shall I call it? How about "malicious, irresponsible bullshit?"

We found the girls, in spite of the interference that we had to face to get to them. But it wasn't what Evelyn or the talking heads had speculated, pontificated and evangelized about. Still, the damage had been done. An innocent 31-year old with the mental development of a pre-schooler ended up roasted when some vigilantes, seeking vengeance based on Evelyn's complete misinformation, chose to get him by burning down the home whose address Evelyn had released.

Before I could figure out how to get even with Evelyn Baskins, she was re-elected, and then she was immediately roasted, herself, when those same vigilantes, pissed at her for giving them the wrong culprit, blew the limo she was riding in to her election victory celebration into a ravine off Bull Creek Road. The limo, a stretch Lincoln, ended up in about a quintillion pieces. Evelyn was thrown free of the wreckage but not of all the 30 gallons of gasoline that burst from the limo's tanks and ignited. We call those kinds of bodies "crispy critters." Crude, I know, but in the case of Evelyn, we didn't care. A half full bottle of Jack Daniel's melted to her right hand. How she held onto it through all that chaos remains a mystery, but she had her damn-right priorities, all the way to well done.

The arson murder and the terrorist-like car bombing gave us two more local (we thought) cases to solve. None of us cared much about Evelyn, but she took four other people with her in the tumble down the ravine. However, all of us had a special intense interest in finding the arsonist who had killed Timmy Van Pelt, the innocent betrayed by Evelyn for maybe 30 votes.

Her 30 pieces of silver.

In the midst of solving those two cases, we were warned by the FBI, Interpol, the Texas Rangers and (it turns out) the CIA, that our investigations were likely to lead us into the crosshairs of the aforementioned international assassin, Felix Pavlovich. And his gang of merry torturers from around the globe. Turns out their warning, to which I refused at first to give any credence, was spot on.

We solved the two crimes, but came up close and personal to Pavlovich, bastard grandson son of Princess Alexandra and the mad monk Rasputin, last of the Romanoffs in Russia. So this Pavlovich would today have ascended to the throne of the monarchy in Russia if a few chaps named Lenin, Trotsky, Dzerzhinsky and Stalin hadn't had other plans for the mother country.

Those Russians. Always making trouble for somebody or other. Only this time, it was for me, my team and all our families.

That brings us to the final episode that began with the girls' disappearances. Gady, John Greycloud and I were dispatched to find Pavlovich. To bring him back. Or lose him somewhere permanently. We tracked him and his lap-dog lieutenant from Austin to Mexico to Beijing to Buenos Aires to Mogadishu, to the Italian Alps, to Paris, Moscow and back to Austin.

Trust me. He's as gone as Jimmy Hoffa.

Getting him gone wasn't painless. I missed with a 12-gauge shotgun, having just been hit in the left shoulder by a .223 military steel-jacket fired from the end of his fake cane.

The FBI's had 40 years to track him down. They're still looking for him. Why spoil their quest for more outrageous publicity? Besides, it'll keep them busy and out of the hair of local PDs. We don't like them much. No, we don't like them at all.

Why hold back?

It took me two months to recover physically and another two months to get my head back together, figuratively, you see. I came back to work in July after being shot in early March

For a change of pace, we had a short, but very interesting, case involving a group of senior women too clever for their own knickers, in my opinion. But I must say, as we worked through the evidence, I thoroughly enjoyed watching them deal with a far-right radio talk show host, an itinerant street guitar picker, a shady wrecker-repo queen, and a three-times-fallen evangelical televangelist who had his eyes on their hefty bank accounts, but ended up another of their conquered. That was the funniest case I've ever worked. And nobody threatened or tried to kill me.

For a change.

So now you know what I've been up to for two-and-a-half years. And that's all you need to know to hear the rest of the story I'm about to tell.

Stand by. As incredible as this tale is about to be, I promise you it's true.

My promise to you on the hiding place of Felix Pavlovich.

Chapter Two

Should Old Acquaintance Be Forgot?

Back In Craig's Office—A Half-hour Later

I haven't had this job as head of APD's detective bureau for more than six weeks. My former boss, Captain Wally Williams, retired just before Thanksgiving. APD Chief Alex Garza, my new boss, offered me the job. No, he told me I was going to take it. He did concede that I could have the freedom to work a few cases myself. After almost six years as a detective, the thought of a desk job, totally administrative and covered in paperwork . . . well, as we say around here, I didn't "cotton to" the idea.

On the upside, one of the great joys of the job is the time I have to find and mentor new detectives. Take Tom Sellers and Gady Esparza, for examples. I just finished a good 30 minutes sharing with them the finer points of interrogation. Things I had learned the hard way. They soaked it in, and I could tell they both wanted a subject to practice on.

That'll happen. Maybe before the day's out.

This is the part of the job I love the most.

Following my session with them, I had grabbed a cup of coffee—brown swill, really—from the machine down the hall—the one we all hate. And I was reflecting on how pleased I had been with Tom and Gady's rapt attention and smart questions.

My reverie was to be short lived.

I should mention that detective's jobs are not as glamorous as TV shows make them out to be. Budgets are tight, and rightfully so, I suppose. We drive the cars the uniform guys and gals have driven into the ground—the ones no longer considered safe for high speed pursuit. And we put our payroll dollars into sworn officers on the street. Administrative help, a little more of it, would be nice, but my budget only allows for two admins for all of us.

Share and share alike.

And speaking of admins, the newer of our two just stuck her head into my office, breaking my reverie, and bringing what would quickly become mixed news.

"Lieutenant," she said, "you have some visitors out front. A woman and a young guy."

"Who are they?" A natural question.

"The lady said to tell you they're the Reynosa family. Said her name was Nana, and that you knew her. She said they're expecting someone else to meet them in a few minutes."

"Yes, I do, for a fact, know them. Put them in the Interrogation Room, fix them up with some coffee, and tell them I'll be right in. And, Merilee? Thanks."

"You're welcome, Sir."

"Remember, Marilee? It's Lieutenant, or Craig? We're a family inside these walls."

"Yes, Sir. Er, Lieutenant."

Amanda, or Nana as we've come to know her, Reynosa is one of the daughters of Felix Pavlovich. The young man with her is likely her half-brother, Josef. Two of my favorite people. Key players in my life lately. Good people. It's going to be great to see them again.

Then again, sometimes I'm wrong.

I put away some paperwork and locked my S&W in its indoor resting place, the right top drawer of my desk. We don't "carry" on the premises. Too many chances for an accident to happen. If only the right-to-carry nuts would understand that message.

Not going to happen, though.

As I left my office, I saw Merrilee step into the Interrogation Room with a pot of real coffee and some cups. So I tossed my swill into the first wastebasket I passed. Half a cup of that stuff is too much, anyway.

Nana Reynosa is a lawyer, the youngest person ever to pass the Bar in Texas—at barely 20. Her biological father was Felix Pavlovich in one of his incarnations, although she didn't know that until recently. She hated him so much she put up six million dollars and a private Gulfstream 550 jet for John, Gady and me. To track him down. For years, as Pavlovich faked death after death and moved on, Nana took over as CEO of Van Pelt Industries, oil and gas exploration and production worldwide. Van Pelt was one name he used coincidental to Nana's birth 36 years ago.

After he'd raped her mother. Repeatedly.

FYI, Nana's a genius. IQ off the charts.

Her half-brother, Josef, just turned 18. He's finishing up his degree in international commerce this year at The University of Texas here in Austin. He, too, is a Pavlovich offspring. Felix went by the name of Conde in Argentina, where Josef was born. Another higher-than-me IQ. Josef, too, wanted Felix dead, and we actually used him as bait ... sorry, I can't tell you any more.

Didn't even tell that much to the FBI.

Nana hit me with, "Craig, we need your help," as I stepped into the room where the two of them had settled in. Merrilee was just leaving, having poured them both coffee and left the pot and two empty cups behind.

"What?" I said. *"Not even a 'Hello, how are you? How are Amy and your baby? Did you have a good Christmas?' Just, 'Craig, we need your help?'"*

Neither of them smiled. This was not going to be the reunion I'd expected.

"What's going on?" I asked, assuming their somber demeanor. "What can I do for you?"

Josef stood as if to make a statement. Apparently he'd been elected to be the primary spokesperson. Or at least the opening speaker. He began, "Craig, what we want to talk about is absolutely top secret. National security to the max. Is there any chance the recorders might be on in this room? Because they just can't be."

The three of us all remembered an earlier meeting that was taped. One that shouldn't have been.

"You have my attention," I said, sitting down across a table from them. I picked up a phone on the table and dialed Gady's extension. "Be sure, please, that the recording in this room is off—O-F-F," I said to her. Gady, I knew, wouldn't ask questions. She would do what I asked and wait for me to explain to her later. If I chose to do so. That's the Navajo way, and Gady's half Navajo and half Mexican. Steeped in the traditions of the Dineè, her Navajo tribal ancestry. And, by the way, she's a 12 on a scale of 1 to 10. Absolutely gorgeous.

We exchanged more normal small talk while we waited for Gady to report the results of her mission. Turns out Josef, who had sat back down., had finished his class work for his BBA degree in international commerce, and had been offered a good entry-level job at the US State Department. Liaison with the Commerce Department folks specializing in Latin America. He would be based, starting in mid-February, in Buenos Aires, his old home town.

Within less than two minutes, Gady stuck her head in the door. "I unplugged the tape machine," she said, "and I took it and put it on your desk." Seeing Nana and Josef, she smiled and said, "Hi," and retreated to whatever she was doing before I interrupted. Again, the Navajo culture kicked in. She and Nana had become close friends on the hunt for Pavlovich. A biligaana, Navajo name for white people, would have more likely barged right into the room to give Nana a hug. But she hadn't been invited to this meeting. She knew I would tell her what I wanted her to know.

Idle curiosity is a foreign concept to her culture. Right along with minding one's own business.

The room now secure, I asked, "Who's the fourth cup for?"

This time Nana spoke up. "It's for someone you know," she said, a frown appearing on her forehead. "She's waiting in the ladies' room for me to come to get her." She paused. "Or to tell her you refuse to meet with her."

She unfolded her hands and took a sip of her coffee. Nana was waiting for me to react. I had a pretty good idea who was hidden out down the hall, but no clue as to why. I decided to wait Nana out. So I just looked from her to Josef as if to say, *"What the hell are you talking about?"*

Josef came to her rescue. "Craig, you know we're talking about our sister. Monica wants to tell you an incredible story that only seven of us in the world know about, including, I might add, the President. At least we hope nobody else knows. But Washington's a sieve when it comes to secrets, so time is critical. And it may very well involve the survival of civilization on this earth as we know it."

Before I could react, Nana spoke up. "Craig, it's about an incredible risk to our country. And at least half the world. Won't you please just listen?"

My occasionally anal mind kicked into warp speed. I looked at my visitors. *How the hell do I answer that question? I'm a local police officer. Where are the Joint Chiefs? Where are the Marines and the ICBMs? This is crazy.*

But I knew these two people. Solid as a rock. Especially Nana. Smart as hell, and always calm. Not given to histrionics.

They both looked at me. I could see and feel the sincerity and hope oozing out into the room.

Finally I got my voice back. "You both know that Monica and I have had our differences. She's a shadow. A spy. Accustomed to subterfuge. Even trickery. And we all learned through some snooping by Lobo Diaz that she's headstrong, unpredictable and, in the eyes of her CIA counterparts, sometimes unstable."

Lobo is Captain Alfredo Diaz of the Texas Rangers. Stationed in McAllen in the Texas Rio Grande Valley, Lobo, who speaks Spanish and French fluently, has not only been involved in some of our most bizarre cases recently, he also spends a lot of time in Mexico and Latin America, undercover, posing as *El Patrón*, a big-time drug capo.

He is, in fact, retiring tomorrow, and I plan to attend his retirement party at the Texas DPS headquarters out on North Lamar Boulevard.

I paused, looking at the ceiling as if thinking, considering. I went on, "But I know and trust the two of you. I've trusted you, Nana, with my life. And you saved it. How can I refuse you when I know you're serious and not blowing smoke?

"Go get her. I'll listen, but no promises."

I headed for the door to get another pot of coffee. What I really wanted right now was a cold bottle of Shiner Bock.

"I'll be right back."

Chapter Three

*Déjà vu, All Over Again**

Small Conference Room Next to Craig's Office—December 30

Marilee will take care of the coffee or whatever's needed in the interrogation room. I want to slip into my conference room to flip on the video recorder to take a peek at what I'm about to walk into.

The three of them are sitting. Talking in whispers during the coffee pot exchange. Nana and Josef are spitting images of one another. She could almost be mistaken for his mother. The differences? Nana's Mexican heritage includes coal black hair, black eyes and a medium-dark complexion. She's attractive, as I find most young Hispanic women to be.

Josef's blond hair and blue eyes, both inherited from his Argentinean mother, are the only differences. The two are about the same height. Josef is slight, probably weighing little more than Nana. Both are fit, clear eyed and eager looking.

Then there's Monica. She looks nothing like her siblings. Red hair, green eyes, and a tall five-ten or so, likely inherited from her Philadelphia-born mother. A thicker build than Nana or Josef, yet still not overweight. She has a tube with her—one that might be used to mail a rolled-up photograph or painting. Aside from physical differences, Monica is different in yet another way, probably a much more significant way. You'll see what I mean when I go back into the room with them.

Gady stuck her head in my door and asked, "Do you need anything?" She's obviously seen who I'm looking at, and she knows the trio well.

"Not right now. Thanks."

"I'll go back to my rat killing, then," she said, showing no curiosity at the monitor I'm studying.

---

* Yogi Berra

19

I laughed. "Stand by. I might need some help with my own rat in a few minutes."

"Monica?"

"Yep."As I switched off the monitor, I saw Josef had spotted the camera up on the wall near the ceiling. He gave a wave of his index finger, knowing I'm watching. Or, at least, somebody is.

Back in the Interrogation Room

Josef waited for me outside in the hall. "We can't have that camera on while Monica's in there," he said.

A caveat, not a command.

"It's off," I said. "I just wanted to get a quick look at Monica. She hasn't changed."

"Give her time," he said. "She's a chameleon, you know."

An apt description. Spot on.

As Josef and I walked into the room, Monica stood. She said nothing, instead giving me the blank stare of a catatonic person, detached from reality. *Dead-pan* is not strong enough.

To be sure Monica couldn't get in gear first, I took charge as I sat down. "Monica, I've agreed to hear what you have to say. But you need to understand upfront that I have no reason to trust you or believe anything you say."

"Why would that be?" she said. "I thought we'd gotten past that by now."

"Let me be specific, then," I answered. "You came to us first almost two years ago representing yourself as an Interpol operative from Warsaw. Not true. Oh, there was a Monica Skrabacz at Interpol, and in Warsaw. But she was 60 years old. A clerk, not a field operations specialist."

I paused, thinking about how to finish my response. "Few of us really bought your story. Lobo did some digging, and we found out you, in fact, were the Cultural Affairs Officer in the U.S. Embassy in Moscow, using the name Alice Something-or-other. And a long-time CIA field agent. A field agent with a reputation within Langley as a potential loose cannon."

She said, "In my position with the Company, what would you have done, Craig? Marched in here and boldly announced, 'I'm a spy in Moscow?' I don't think so. Since I joined the Company 15 years ago, I've been many people. Had many identities. That's how one survives in my business."

She had a point.

Nana and Josef sat silently. Stoic.

"I understand that," I said. "But let me tell you what really bothers me. There are two things in this world I'm particularly good at doing.

"One is forensics. That wouldn't help me to deal with you.

"The other is reading 'tells' on people's faces and body-language reactions. Whether I'm grilling a suspected mass murderer or chatting at a cocktail party, I know when somebody's lying. Exaggerating. Feeling guilty. Afraid. I can read the signs—facial expressions, tics, body language."

I paused for emphasis. "Monica, you're the only person I've come across in the past 10 years who completely baffled me. You're unreadable. You give away nothing."

She interrupted. "That's why I'm still alive after 15 years in the field. Those 'tells,' as you call them, will get you on a cold slab in somebody's morgue. Damned fast."

She paused. I waited. Seeing no response from me, she added, "I'm trained. I'm proud of those skills. They kept me alive when torturers worked me over in Somalia. They got nothing from me, even after they shot me to the moon. So you're picking at one of my strengths."

I had lost this argument. She easily had trounced me. My objectivity--something I'm known for-- obliterated.

Time for me to say "*Uncle.*"

She claimed her win. "I'm sorry you have such a low opinion of me, Craig. I'm here because you're the first—and only—person I know I could go to. Two years ago, I came here to warn you about an international menace. Our father," she glanced at Nana and Josef, "though we hardly knew that at the time. I didn't think much of you at first, but I quickly admitted I was wrong. For 40 or more years, the FBI, Interpol, the Mossad, MI6 and every other credible authority in the free world had been trying to find him—Felix Pavlovich—a psychopath beyond redemption. He had more aliases than I've ever had. Not even the old KGB could get a bead on him."

She sipped some coffee and then went on. "It took you, John Greycloud and Gady Esparza, with some help from my little sister and brother here, only three weeks to run him down. You may not believe this, but I now see you as someone who can finish a job nobody else can. You know why?"

The question wasn't exactly rhetorical, but I sensed she didn't expect an answer. She told us her answer herself. "All these high-powered organizations are self-defeated by their own incredible bureaucracies, egos the size of Jupiter, budgets and paperwork and internal competitions so full of intrigue, they trip all over themselves and end up chasing their own tails. The FBI is the worst. Tell me you disagree with that."

She stared at me; this time she waited for an answer.

"Monica, I'm not going to disagree with you. The internal political battles among the FBI, CIA, NSA, even Congress, are nothing short of outrageous. The only one you named that might be a bit more effective is the Mossad. They seem to get things done."

"Here's my point, Craig. Your team—an expert, by-the-book investigator; a Navajo shaman known and respected as a tracker—a finder of people and things; a young detective with a burning desire to avenge the death of her identical twin; and ample funds from my sister—and, shazam--you get results.

"You, Craig, get results. Right now, our country needs results. The world, in fact, needs results. And I don't think we have the fucking time to sit around while the CIA, the NSA, Congressional oversight committees and bureaucrats and politicians dither and squabble and claw and scratch for turf.

"The problem needs to be solved, and to hell with the system and chains of command and who's on first, who has what authority, and who's afraid of the big bad wolf. Let the ditherers wring their hands and call meetings and argue among themselves. By the time they pull their heads out of their collective asses, we can solve the problem. And maybe prevent a nuclear holocaust.

"Do I have your attention?" she asked.

She pulled a 20-inch by 30-inch satellite photograph from its tube and spread it out on the table.

Now I know a little about chemistry as it relates to forensics. Quite a lot as a matter of fact. My knowledge of physics comes from high school and the legends of the Newtons, Einsteins and Max Plancks of the world. I even recall reading about the Manhattan Project and its outcome that ended a world war long before I was even born.

When she told me what we were looking at in the photo, I confess my mind was boggled. First thing, I called a brief recess and walked to our (limited) crime lab for a periodic table of elements. That's chemistry. I'm comfortable.

Plutonium is a heavy metal with the atomic number 94. Okay, I began to see a bit more of the picture. That blob she said was the size of a basketball must weigh at least a few tons.

Back in the interrogation room, periodic chart in hand, I said to her, "Tell me what this means. It can't be good."

"It means," she began, "that we're seeing the unbelievable. Plutonium, as an element, occurs occasionally in nature. But always in small amounts—measured in grams, not pounds. And certainly not tons. It means there's enough plutonium in that one blob to produce 125 large nuclear bombs, each many times more powerful than the ones that dropped on Hiroshima and Nagasaki. It means," she continued repetitively, "that, in the wrong hands, that Plutonium could be quickly turned into maybe 250 dirty suitcase bombs—enough firepower to wipe out almost every city on the face of the earth with a population of more than a million people."

She took another sip of coffee, grimaced at its now-tepid temperature, and said, "It means, we don't have time to sit around and wait for the system to act. We need to grab the bull by the tail and look him straight in the eye."

I wanted to laugh at that visual description, but Monica, in her mood, might just come over the table and emasculate me.

Literally.

She sat down. Folded her arms across her chest, then thought better of her body language and reached to warm up her now-tepid coffee, signaling it was my turn to say something.

"How did you get your hands on this?" I said, pointing at the satellite photo.

"I'm head of the Russian desk at Langley," she said. "Everything Russian is my bailiwick. It came to me late the afternoon of Christmas Eve— six days ago.

"Let me add something" she said. "Nobody in Washington, and not that many in Moscow, know as much about Russia and the Russians as I do. Aside from the fact that I'm half Russian, I spent several years in the heart of the internal intrigues that, to this day, are the modus operandi of the Russian government. I know more about Putin than his wife does, let alone the average Russian on the street. And the fact that this Plutonium popped to the surface, by random chance, on Siberian soil, will turn out to be the worst luck Europe has seen since Ivan the Terrible didn't die of infection when he was circumcised."

"What have you done about it?" I asked. "Officially, I mean?"

She told me about showing it to the head of field operations at Langley and his lack of concern, emphasizing she didn't think he had the IQ to grasp its significance. She told me that, out of concern for national—even worldwide—security, she had contacted the head of the CIA, the DCI, clearly her prerogative and duty as head of the Russian desk. She had even had the company's operators track down the president's national security advisor.

"What happened then?" I asked.

"The DCI was cordial," she said. "Even thanked me for making him aware so quickly. He said he would talk to the national security adviser and, if necessary, accompany him to the White House to brief the President. He asked me to have copies of the satellite shots messengered to his home ASAP, and then told me to stand by. Said he would get back to me as soon as possible."

"Did he?" I asked. "Get back to you? How quickly?"

"Oh, yes, he called me the day after Christmas. Thirty-six hours later. He said he had talked by phone with the national security advisor and—get this—they had decided this revelation—his word—didn't merit interrupting the President's holiday with his family. Apparently the two of them spent all day Friday huddled to concoct some sort of recommendation that they plan to present to the President this morning. The regular weekly national security meeting."

"Looks like they don't agree with your sense of urgency." I said.

"That's just it. This is just another wrinkle to the two of them. They simply don't get it."

"Do you have any idea what they've told the President this morning?"

"Oh, yes. The DCI had the courtesy to email me the bones of their pitch. Craig, it's nothing more than a cover-their-ass paperwork clusterfuck. It never occurred to either of them to alert the joint chiefs or even the President's chief of staff. They're low-keying it to the level of a footnote."

"Do you know why?" I knew that was a loaded question, and I girded myself for a frantic response.

Instead, Monica sat back, resigned. "Yes, unfortunately. The DCI told me they were concerned about the already tense relations between Putin and POTUS. Didn't want to add to the President's burdens. Or give Putin some obscure reason to rattle his sabers louder in the former Soviet satellite countries. DCI said he would be speaking personally with his counterpart, the head of the Russian Federation's FSB, Federal Security Service, in mid-February at a planned three-day conference in Geneva. He saw no reason to accelerate that schedule."

"What about the national security advisor? What's his plan?"

"He's also protective of the President. But he is putting up a satellite over the area 24/7 in case any 'unsavory agents' decide to grab off a few hundred suitcase bombs."

I sat back, stared at the ceiling and tried to think. *If she can't rustle up any more urgency than she's seen so far, what does she think I can do about it?*

I had another question before I ended this bizarre meeting. "Monica, do you plan to go off the grid on this one? Take matters into your own hands in spite of what you know you should do legally?"

"Only if I have to, Craig. Only if the threat gets too big and the prevention remains too small. And too slow."

"So what do you want from me?"I asked, not wanting to hear the answer.

"What you did last time. Either get that Plutonium to safe ground, or make it disappear."

"I need some time to think, Monica. Tomorrow, 7:30 a.m. Right here in this same room. I'm going to involve some others in this discussion."

She frowned. "Who?"

"John Greycloud, Gady Esparza and Lobo Diaz. See you in the morning. I'll bring the donuts."

Chapter Four

Follow the Money

Three men sit around a rectangular table in a suite on the fourth floor of the luxury hotel built in the 1880s next to Lake Louise in Banff National Park.

For purposes of this meeting and their new, joint project, they would be known only as One, Two and Three. Each knew the others' names, of course. But names were not to be used.

They had much in common, and also little in common.

All three should appear on any list of the 25 richest people in the world. But each had been circumspect enough to avoid any list, anywhere. That anonymity, and an insatiable greed for even more wealth—those were their two commonalities.

By contrast, they looked nothing alike, and each had come from a different faraway place to this meeting.

One came from the Middle East, though he dressed as a Western businessman in Savile Row style. Tall and dark with black eyes, black hair, his prominent nose hinted at his Arab roots. His personal wealth was the least of the three at $475 billion. Educated in the U.S. at Stanford and MIT, he held a doctorate in nuclear physics though he had never worked in that field. He, in fact, had never worked at anything except managing his extended family's immense wealth—wealth gained from sucking petroleum out of the ground and selling it to the highest bidder. He, however, was not lazy. Far from it. He had hobbies, and the particular hobby he came to this meeting to pursue involved the knowledge he'd gained in California and Massachusetts as a student. His criminal past had begun with a little cheating—screwing his country out of most of the depletion taxes he should have been paying on the recovered oil. From there, he had found it easy to push his cheating to ever higher lev-

26

els. Short of murder, One had a past that would preclude him from living in an industrialized nation.

Two had Asian roots, though his eyelids immediately ruled out Korean ancestry. Aside from the obvious Asian features, Two could best be described as 'invisible." In an international setting, Two would blend into any crowd, totally unnoticeable. Short, with graying hair and brown eyes, he too dressed as one might expect of a well-to-do businessman. His tailor would come from Hong Kong. Literally come to him to measure and fit, returning to Hong Kong to make the suits, shirts and ties that Two ordered regularly. Two's wealth came from the illicit drug trade, although he had never so much as touched a grain of heroin or handled any transaction personally. No, he'd kept his hands seemingly clean while exporting heroin and nose candy to the children he knew would get hooked, making him ever richer. Like One, he had been educated in the U.S., with BS and MS degrees in mechanical engineering from Rensselaer Polytechnic Institute in upstate New York. He claimed a Ph.D. from MIT, but in truth he had been expelled from that University and deported. Flagrant cheating took its toll on young Two. But he had learned from the experience.

Three made his money in mining. Diamond mining, to be precise. A true human chameleon, Three's ethnicity and roots could not be determined by looking at or listening to him. A Caucasian, along with a few billion others, Three had mastered several languages, each of which he could mimic in the pronunciation style any of the others. He spoke English with a British accent. Spanish with a Jamaican lilt. Speaking French, he could sound Russian. You get the idea. Three had no formal technical training. Years ago, he had met One at Stanford, but as a waiter in a restaurant rather than an enrolled student. His wardrobe varied day to day—from Australian Outback, to Wyoming western, to Mexican serapes and pantalones.

A man for any occasion. A man who made his wealth on the backs of black miners. Miners who might have as well been slaves, for all he paid them for their backbreaking work.

This meeting had originally been scheduled for three months from now, in mid-March. Fate had intervened via a satellite photo recorded and reported to the trio by Four, an unofficial appendage to the three. Four had no particular wealth. And he claimed no competition existed to his silent persona as the world's best hacker. No code, no firewall, no encryption could keep him from any file he wanted to see. On any computer system. Anywhere. Four's real claim to fame lay in being a wanted man in several countries on three continents. For espionage, for commercial spying. Even for treason. His skills had brought him to Banff, though not to the suite where One, Two and Three met. No, Four waited in the bar, perfectly happy with his drinks, two laptops, and the Wi-Fi the Banff Springs provided so accommodatingly.

The group's combined resources formed an almost perfect collection for the job they had in mind—turning their billions into trillions. Among their maze of international companies, they could cover civil engineering and architecture, heavy construction, the manufacture of both raw construction materials and technical instrumentation. They owned trucking companies, shipping companies and mining operations. The only resource they had lacked until Four appeared was that of a fission-fusion process.

Four had that, or ready access to that.

And now, Four had found what seemed to be an immense supply of a rare fuel they would need to feed their project and accelerate its schedule. Exponentially.

And allow them to become the world's first trillionaires.

Their long-term plan had just become immediate. They had to act quickly, before someone else found what Four had found on a northern Siberian plain—a few tons of pure Plutonium.

Getting reservations on New Year's Eve on short notice had not been easy, even for billionaires. The Banff Springs had been sold out for this week for several months until Four cracked the hotel's reservation system and found a few guests willing to give up their reservations for $25,000 each, the funds supplied by the trio upstairs.

No hill to climb for the hacker.

Back upstairs in the suite, the three principals pored over a photo that Four had lifted from a U.S. National Security Agency satellite. Two said, "If it's what Four claims it is, and he can get the blueprints, we're in business."

Three said, "Let's get him up here. Before we touch that stuff, I want to be damned sure he can get into the International Patent Office's computers. Without the plans and blueprints, that Plutonium is nothing to us but too hot to handle."

Snickering and rubbing his hands together, One added, "But if he can get what we need, we've got the energy world by the balls."

In the bar that overlooked Lake Louise and the slowly-melting gla-ciers beyond, a waiter walked to the table where Four sat, leaned down and whispered to him. The hacker closed down both his laptops, left $20 Canadian on the table from the $1,000 U.S. a day retainer he was collecting, and strolled to the elevators in the lobby. As he pushed the UP button, he thought, *A million each isn't greedy. They want what they want. And I have the prize. Three million's chump change to these yahoos. Whatever the hell they have in mind.*

He boarded an opening elevator door and pushed 4, smiling.

Chapter Five
Death to Western Infidels
Addis Ababa, Ethiopia—A Small Apartment—December 31

Iranian ex-patriot and nuclear physicist Haji G. Khan stared in disbelief at the satellite photo his alter ego, Mahmood Bijahn, had laid on the kitchen table. *Can this really be?* he thought. It would take 10,000 centrifuges dozens of years to separate so much Plutonium. It's a miracle! he thought in his native Farsi.

The middle initial G stood for Genghis, a little humor his practical-joker parents had saddled him with 37 years ago at his birth in Shiraz in southern Iran near the Persian Gulf. Not wanting to raise children, they had ignored young Haji, leaving him to do as he pleased during his formative years. Fortunately for Haji, a maternal uncle took the lad under his wing, encouraged his obvious intelligence and curiosity, and financed a first-class technical education at California Institute of Technology. There, at Cal Tech, Haji became nothing short of a brilliant nuclear physicist.

His peculiar upbringing, contrary to the Persian culture, however, had begun to take its toll. His technical brilliance, on the one hand, became challenged by an ever-increasing fanatical devotion to Mohammed and the Muslim faith. Nowhere in the Koran could he find any references to his passion for physics, and—having had a shaky youth without foundation—he soon developed mental conflicts. Conflicts so severe that his behavior slowly became more and more irrational.

He was in Ethiopia for two reasons: First, his own country had stripped him of his scientific credentials and put a price on his head. Iran had been joined by the entirety of the international scientific community in labeling him the Persian equivalent of a loose cannon. He freely admitted selling nuclear insights to the North Koreans, who had managed to produce a bomb, and to Yemini jihadists who wanted to develop nuclear bombs. His second reason involved being closer to like-minded

Muslim radical groups in Somalia, a short distance southeast of Ethiopia's capital—Addis Ababa. A place where he could continue his work without exposing himself to too much international scrutiny.

And possible capture or arrest.

Haji's mind fought an ongoing battle between passion and reason. Had he become a dedicated soldier of Mohammed, a vessel to carry out the prophet's commands? Or had he simply gone insane?

His own government and the international scientific community had already answered those questions. And the answers were "Yes" to both.

He found himself, more and more, standing in front of a full length mirror in his bedroom looking at a man he could not identify with. The result of poor nutrition as a child left to his own devices, he remained small in stature—just over five feet tall. Bad diet and too much time in the sun had left his skin leather-like and wrinkled well beyond its age. The stress of the battle in his brain had made him prematurely gray.

He looked like an old man. He felt like one, too, when his brain sided with the insanity verdict.

Other times, when the soldier of Mohammed prevailed, he felt youthful, invigorated, ready to take on the infidels.

Today, he wanted vengeance.

After all, had not Christians, sponsored by the Popes, themselves, sent crusaders to kill Arabs, Persians, anybody who followed the prophet? Too many centuries had gone by. The 21st century was his time. He knew it. And his special knowledge was his gift from Mohammed. The knowledge to annihilate infidels with dozens, hundreds even, of suitcase bombs. Dirty bombs, each capable of being infiltrated by one messenger, and each capable of destroying a major city in Israel, Europe and the United States. Or anywhere else he decided to send them.

On the eve of another new year, he was convinced . . . he knew . . . what he was going to do. And he now knew where the raw materials he would need would come from—Siberia.

Today Haji was ready for his destiny. Until his mind changed again. Against his will. That must not happen. He would fight it. And his friend Mahmood Bijahn, whom he considered a fellow Iranian ex-patriot and a devoted jihadist soldier, would help him.

I will build them in the desert, and Mahmood will deliver them to our soldiers in Somalia, he thought.

31

Death to Western Infidels!

Khan turned to his fellow warrior of today. "Mahmood, we are ready. Can you go tonight to Mogadishu and find the help we'll need to retrieve this gift from Mohammed and bring it to the desert? There surely may be others who will discover what only we know today. Time is short, but Paradise awaits our success."

"Haji, count on me," Mahmood said. "I'll be back in two days. In the meantime, rest, don't think; please do not think. Just remember that we must avenge the Crusades. And claim the waiting virgins."

With that, Mahmood pointed to the object in Siberia with one hand, while the other slipped a small pill into Haji's thick, sweet coffee, knowing the scientist whom the cause needed would sleep deeply for at least two days.

And he left, apparently for Somalia. Ostensibly to contact both Al-Shabaab and Al Qaeda for Dr. Khan.

Death to all the Western Infidels!

Chapter Six

The Road Less Traveled By

APD Detective Bureau—December 31

After yesterday's meeting, I asked Gady to get in touch with her little father, John Greycloud, to see if he could join us this morning. In the Navajo culture, John Greycloud was Gady and Gloria's uncle—her mother's brother. That made him the biligaana equivalent to a godfather, more or less.

Nana had sent one of her company planes to pick him up last night in Tucson. And I had caught up with Lobo Diaz at his retirement ceremony at the DPS headquarters last evening.

The four of us—Lobo, John, Gady and I--had decided to get together at 7:00 so I could fill them in on what it is that Monica apparently wants us to do. And apparently thinks we can do, although I'm still skeptical about that.

And I remain leery of anything Monica proposes.

As I had promised, I brought in 18 donuts, one of my own coffee-makers and a pound of Starbucks Italian roast. I'm tired of brown swill from the dratted machine, and Amy and I had an extra Mr. Coffee just sitting in a closet, anyway.

So the three newcomers were up to speed when Nana, Josef and Monica arrived about 7:25. We also had a head-start on the pastries and coffee.

Lobo, newly free of a 30-year career in law enforcement, mostly as a Texas Ranger, began the discussion. "So, Monica," he said, "why do we need to get involved in something that by all rights should be up to the government of Russia first? And the international community second? What makes you think there's a need for outside interference . . . that's most likely dangerous, illegal, and stupid?"

Before Monica could pounce with an answer, John Greycloud asked more questions. One of them apparently nobody else had thought about, and one that stumped Monica. "If one of these 'blobs' of Plutonium has made its way to the surface, what assurance do you have that others might not follow? How do we know they won't continue to pop up regularly? And how do we know where they may pop up? It's one thing to find one on the frozen steppes of northern Siberia, quite another if the next one shows up in Iran, or North Korea. Or Peoria."

Clearly, Monica was taken aback. I guessed that international spies like Monica train to deal with the here and now. What's down the road, during what they think of as an emergency situation, will have to wait until the current fire's put out. At least that seemed logical to me, having never been a spy.

Stalling for think time, Monica retrieved the satellite map from its tube and spread it out on the table, anchoring the four corners with note pads and a couple of cups. "First, John," she said, "we have no way to know the answer to your question. Since it's never happened before, I think we have to consider it an isolated incident. If it's not, then we'll be setting a precedent with this first one as to how to handle future appearances."

She turned to Lobo. "I explained to Craig yesterday my thoughts on the answers to your questions. It's just like tracking down Felix Pavlovich. Right now, we don't know who besides the few of us and a handful of bureaucrats in Washington even know that Plutonium's out there. I tried to sound the alarm through channels, and the response I got was a big yawn. The President himself may have just found out about it yesterday—if the DCI and national security advisor haven't decided to wait for another chance to fill him in."

She continued to think as she walked to a sideboard and refilled her coffee. Then she went on, "Look, I know how the system works. Or more likely, how it doesn't work. All these players who've never been in the field have no clear idea of what's outside the Beltway. They will go on believing that nobody knows anything about the Plutonium except me and a handful of them. They've forever thought the Russians mostly stupid and incompetent. That's after they got over thinking the Russians had to be advanced scientific geniuses during the cold war. Whatever description fits their agenda at the moment is the one they'll attribute to the Russian Federation, or any other country or group that crosses their vision.

"I spent fifteen years in the field. Under cover. Being somebody I never was, and hiding my real agenda successfully. From Asia to Africa to the Middle East to Moscow, I tried to tell the desk jockeys at Langley how much they continue to underestimate both friends and enemies, except at budget time when they do their best to scare the hell out of Congress.

"They didn't buy it. They haven't bought it. And they never will buy it. "

Lobo spoke up. "So what you're suggesting is that we go out there and either capture or neutralize two or three tons of lethal radioactivity On our own? Secretly?"

He turned to John Greycloud. "John, how's your experience in nuclear physics? Are you up to speed with this kind of assignment?"

"I'll tell you what I've been doing for the past couple of weeks, Lobo. I've been in New Mexico at a little Navajo village on the Checkerboard Reservation. Goes by the name of Church Rock, New Mexico. I've been helping with an effort to simply evacuate and abandon the entire small town. Know why? Because it's contaminated with radioactive waste. Piles of refuse from a dozen uranium mines all around the town. And there are literally hundreds of these mines scattered all over the Checkerboard. That's an area about the size of West Virginia."

"Big problem?" I asked.

"No, Craig, the radioactive refuse is not a problem that couldn't be solved by just removing it. The problem is the bureaucracy. It's mind boggling. You've got the Bureau of Indian Affairs, the Environmental Protection Agency, the Nuclear Regulatory Commission, the uranium mining industry, and that's just federal. The State of New Mexico jumps in, and the various Navajo tribal councils. And we've ended up with what the Italians would call Zuppa Inglese.

"An almost unsolvable mess.

"The EPA has spent $100 million on our lands in the past six years. Energy companies have spent another $17 million. And now they tell us Church Rock won't be habitable for another eight years. All it takes to make it habitable is for the polluted soil to be removed. Because of the bureaucracy, that's going to take eight years! Unbelievable!"

Monica said, "I think you've just made my point, John. There's not enough Ex-Lax in the universe to get the federal bureaucracy to produce a good movement."

I said, "Monica, he did make one of your points, but he didn't answer Lobo's question. I'll ask again, Who among us knows squat about handling highly-radioactive materials? I don't see anybody in this room. Do I?"

For the first time in two meetings, Nana had something to say. "You all remember my fiancée, Chad Brauman? Doctor Brauman? We met when you, Craig, recruited him from the Linguistics Department at The University of Texas to help crack Pavlovich's code. He's not only a linguistics phenom, but also a mathematics genius. You will remember that, too, I hope?"

I nodded. Chad had helped us, not just by cracking Pavlovich's code, but also, in the process, he had become the first man intelligent and humorous enough to attract Nana's attention. Amy had mentioned a June wedding to me last week.

"But he's not a physicist, too. Is he?" I asked.

Nana answered, "No, I don't think so. He's a lot of things, but physicist isn't one of them. However, he serves on a committee at UT that's made up of representatives from several departments. And he's become good friends with one of the physicists in UT Austin's Institute for Fusion Studies. That group has patented, in the name of UT-Austin, a process called Nuclear Fusion-Fission that will render spent nuclear fuel and other nuclear waste harmless. I'm sure we can find a physicist to give us the guidance we need to handle the Plutonium."

"Handling it is one thing," Gady said, "but getting to it without being considered foreign invaders is quite another. With all the satellites in place, ours and theirs, we can't just stroll up and wish the Plutonium a happy new year."

"We have resources," Josef said. "My sister runs an international oil and gas exploration and production business. How does that help us?" he asked rhetorically. "I'm not exactly sure, but I do know Van Pelt Industries has lease arrangements in the Arctic Ocean. And ships. And submersibles capable of going down to a mile or more. And drilling equipment. And drilling engineers. We can find a way to get to that Plutonium and disappear it."

He turned to Nana. "Am I exaggerating?" he asked her.

"It could be a bit tricky, but we've climbed bigger hills to get to gas fields. And who has bigger gas fields than Russia?" She looked at me. "We can do it. I have no doubt of that."

I had the panic-stricken thought that our legs had suddenly begun to outrun our heads. We had begun to talk ourselves into something as if we had Superman, Batman and Spiderman on our team and Albert Einstein as our consultant. I needed think time. Enthusiasm is contagious, and this group's optimism had begun to run amok.

"All right," I said. "Without any commitment from the four of us," I indicated Lobo, John and Gady, "I'm willing to continue to investigate the possibilities. Here are the first two steps: Nana will produce Chad who will produce a consulting nuclear physicist. Then Nana and Josef will blueprint the materials, equipment and resources that Van Pelt Industries can provide for a clandestine trip into Siberia."

I paused, thinking. "And Monica, get in touch personally with your replacement at the U.S. Embassy in Moscow. Let's be sure if the Russians are onto this Plutonium, we know what they're planning to do. Maybe they'll take care of it, themselves."

"Can we get back together this evening?" Monica asked.

I shuddered. "First, I don't think all we have to do can be accomplished by this evening. Second, this is Amy's and my first wedding anniversary, and it's New Year's Eve. If we want a psychologist on this team, there can be no meeting tonight. For that matter, if we want a detective on this team besides Gady, for sure there can be no meeting tonight."

"How about tomorrow? In the morning?" Monica said.

Nobody had an objection, so I said, "Ten o'clock at my apartment. You all know where it is." This same group had met there several times while we tracked down Felix Pavlovich.

I asked Lobo, John and Gady to come to the little conference room next to my new office. The time had come for an honest, objective assessment.

My thoughts included, *What the hell am I even thinking about this for? I've been head of detectives here for exactly six weeks and two days. Now I'm supposed to take another leave of absence and get involved in something that might very well kill us all? Monica's middle name is Trouble—in any language, under any alias.*

Craig, get a grip.

Chapter Seven

Prove It

Banff Springs Hotel – December 31

Four stepped off the elevator on the fourth floor and rapped lightly on the door of the suite where his benefactors were apparently plotting. Three opened the door and motioned him in with a nod of his head.

"Four said, "What can I do for you?"

One answered. "Your claim to be able to access to the files of the International Patent Office and the computers at The University of Texas is the only thing between us and our goal—the one unknown. How can we trust you?"

Irritated, Four thought, *Oh, you will trust me. You will learn of the need to protect me with your very lives until I have delivered the prize.* Instead of showing his aggravation, he calmly said, "So now you doubt me, huh? You're worried that I won't be able to deliver the golden egg, right? But what choice do you have? Which of you can do what I have said I'll do for you?"

He paused, looking from face to face, not expecting an answer. Then he said, "No volunteers? I didn't think so."

"Show us," said Two. "Sit down with your computer and steal five million dollars from the U.S. Treasury. Then we will know you can do what you say you can do."

Four laughed. "You are hopelessly naïve. I could steal five million dollars for each of you, have it transferred secretly to your own accounts. And then, within three days, you would each have a knock on your doors and a voice calling, 'FBI, open up!' Stealing from the U.S. Treasury is a fool's game. They would never find me, but the three of you would be in the hoosegow in short order. If I were to steal five dollars for myself, I would join you there. No, we are not raiding the U.S. Treasury. Their firewalls, encryptions, and redundant systems are no challenge for me.

38

But their law enforcement is among the best in the world. You would be lucky if they didn't take you to some remote place like Namibia and torture the shit out of you."

One said, "So how can we know you're not just blowing smoke up our pants' legs? What proof can you give us?"

Four smiled. "Rich people are not only greedy, but also untrusting and afraid of anything they can't do or control personally. I expected this little faceoff. I came prepared. So, now, pay attention. I want each of you to go, right now, to your computers. Just check your balances on your largest Swiss accounts." He smiled. "I'll wait." He folded his arms and nodded to the three laptops on the table across the room.

"Why are we doing this?" Two demanded.

"I guess you won't know until you follow directions, will you? Just do it!" Four said.

As the three busied themselves, barely able to contain their curiosities and anticipations, Four laughed quietly. Of course, he knew what would happen. Two days ago, he had gone online and arranged this little demonstration because he was sure the three assholes would demand some magic trick to prove his *bona fides*. *And there they are, he thought, about to find out how vulnerable they are to people like me.*

Two was the first to see what had happened. "Holy shit!" he said, "How did you do that?"

Four answered, "Let's wait until all are properly shocked, and then I'll tell you."

One banged his palms on the table just as Three jumped from his seat. All three began talking at the same time, creating a shrill cloud of indecipherable noise.

"Quiet!" Four shouted. "Sit down and look at me."

Curiosity won out over fear, and the three did as he asked.

"Now," Four began, as soon as he had their attention, "be quiet for a minute and I will tell you what each of you saw. One," he began, "you saw that one billion dollars was withdrawn from your account and, two hours later, a different billion was deposited. So your balance remains unaffected. Am I right?"

One nodded. Four went on, "And Two and Three, you each saw the exact same thing, correct?" Again, both nodded.

Four continued, "So all of you have the same balances you expected to see. I could have taken a billion from each of you and just kept it. But, after all, we're partners. Correct?"

Seeing no response, Four spoke more loudly, "Correct?"

All three nodded.

"Now," Four went on, "if you were to sit down to compare the times of each withdrawal and deposit, you would see the following pattern: First, I took a billion from One. Then I sent it to Two. I then took a billion from Three and sent it to One. So his account was back up to snuff. Then I sent a billion from Two to Three, and—voila—everybody lost and gained exactly a billion. No harm, no foul. Am I right?"

"But how did you do this?" Three asked. "You may not even know our names. Or anything about us."

Four laughed. Loudly. "In this world, there is no such thing as anonymity, my friend. I know more about each of you than your wives, One and Two, and your four mistresses, Three.

Want to know how?"

"Yes!" In unison.

"Very simple, for me at least," Four said. "This meeting was arranged by One. He sent me an email. Fatal mistake. I then knew who he was and could read his messages as if I held them in my hand. Your messages from one to another told me the rest of the story. Then I began checking databases and public records in your respective countries."

He paused, gave the group a little smile, and said, "You have no secrets. Only I can get you the information you want and leave no trail. Absolutely no way anyone can trace the hack back to each of you."

With that, he opened one of his laptops and said, "Step away from the table, please. Stay clear of your computers." As the three moved across the room, Four typed commands into his open laptop, taking about 15 to 20 seconds.

Then, looking at his curious benefactors, he uttered the famous line, "Watch this!"

He hit a command key and began counting down from ten—aloud. Before he got to five, all three laptops on the table simply exploded and began pouring nasty-smelling smoke into the room.

Their owners gasped in unison. Two began to complain loudly. Four cut him off, saying, "Computers are cheap. And each of you is rich beyond belief. You can buy new computers."

Three shot back, "But you've destroyed all our records. Everything's lost!"

"Au contraire, amigo," Four grinned. "The entire contents of each of your hard drives and remotes? I saved it into the cloud while I was having a drink in the bar downstairs." He paused, looked individually at each of them, then said, "I will return it all to each of your new laptops . . . for a price."

He gave them a wicked grin. "And that price is," again he paused for effect, and then continued, "$1 million each. Three million dollars, total. Chump change to each of you."

"What about the plans in the patent office and the notes in Austin?" Two asked, seeming unconcerned at the $ 3 million ransom demand.

"Once I've received your payments, then I'll deliver what you ask. Be sure you have everything you want from me right then."

"Why?" said One.

"Because I will immediately disappear, taking the $ 3 mil with me, never to be heard from again.

"Consider me retired.

"And set for life."

Chapter Eight

Are You Still Sleeping, Brother Khan?

Addis Ababa – Late January 2

Back late at night from his trip sooner than he expected, his mission accomplished, Mahmood Bijahn found Haji Khan still sleeping, just as he had expected. Tossing a pitcher of water onto the sleeping scientist, Mahmood shouted, "Wake Up, Haji! I have news from Somalia."

Haji stirred, rolled over, and began to snore once again.

Mahmood considered letting him sleep until morning, but quickly dismissed the thought. *We have no time to waste, he thought. How do we know others haven't stumbled on the prize as well?* This time, he brought a small bowl of very cold water to Kahn's bedside and carefully plunged one of the scientist's hands into it—an old trick known to dormitory dwellers across the world.

Haji sat straight up, urinating all over himself and his cot. The strong potion Mahmood had given him two days ago had kept him sleeping almost 48 hours. Meaning his bladder was over-full. Haji made no move to get up or to stop the flow for a long time as he continued to empty his bladder. Instead, still dazed, he began to remove his soiled clothing, finally wrapping it in the equally soiled sheet and shambling to his tiny bathroom, not much more than a hole in the floor and a small washing tub.

Slipping into a fresh izzar and thowb, Khan returned to greet Mahmood as if he had just arrived. Or hadn't left yet. He made no mention of accidentally soiling his bed. "You haven't left for Mogadishu yet, Mahmood?" he asked. "Why are you delaying?"

Mahmood thought, *The fool has no idea that almost two days have passed. But, he is our fool, and we must keep his jihadist mindset to the forefront.* He replied, "Haji, my friend, I have gone to Mogadishu and returned already. You must have slept for a long time. And I bring excellent news from our Al-Shabaab camps in Somalia."

Kahn shook his head rapidly as if to make his brain wake up. "What day is it?" he asked, clearly confused by the lost time.

"It is January second, Kahn," Mahmood said. "Late at night. In fact, in a few minutes, it will be early January third. You have been well while I was gone?"

"Well? I must have been unconscious. But you said you have excellent news. Tell me."

"Yes, excellent news," Mahmood said, thinking *I must keep the idea of punishing Western infidels before Haji so the scientist wouldn't be tempted to lapse into his less violent, more forgiving frame of mind.*

He went on, "I have met with all three camps under the command of the general, and we are making much progress."

"Tell me!" Khan insisted.

""First, a complete precision machine shop has been set up in two trailers. Everything you will need to craft suitcase bombs. The trailers are to be moved to the site of our choice in the desert by day after tomorrow. Expert machinists are standing by to follow your every command. Two more mobile-materials vehicles will accompany the machine shops. They are to be filled with the metals and materials you have specified. And, best of all, one of the Al-Shabaab teams has a vessel near the Bering Strait—one with a helicopter on board. The ship will be fitted tomorrow with snow-worthy power movers and dispatched to the Arctic Ocean. Four or five days from now, it will be in international waters off the northern Siberian coast, waiting for decisions from you. How much of the Plutonium do you want to retrieve? How much will you need to fashion each device, and how many devices will we need?"

Haji, finally fully awake, said, "We have much to think about and decide on. First, though, I need a target date. When do we want the Western world to feel the wrath of Mohammed?"

"Mahmood smiled. "That date, Haji, has been set. The fireworks will commence at sundown on June 27—the beginning of Ramadan. Can we be ready?"

Haji became excited. "I will fashion the first device personally, teaching two others exactly how to do the job. Then the three of us should be able to complete at least two per week."

"That means we could have 20 to 25 ready by mid-June?" Mahmood asked.

Haji's face took on a dark, evil look. "Mahmood, if you can get the Plutonium here by Mawlid al-Nabi, Mohammed's birthday, we will be ready by sundown on June 20. When do we leave for Siberia?"

"You expect to go yourself?"

"I demand to go," Haji said. "And one more thing, Mahmood. Pick your targets. Begin with the 25 most prominent, and select a backup site for each one.

"We must not fail," Khan said.

Khan must not go, Mahmood thought.

Chapter Nine

How to Confuse a Physicist

New Year's Day—Craig and Amy Rylander's Apartment

Nana's fiancée, Dr. Chad Brauman, true to her expectations, had produced a nuclear physicist from the University of Texas's Institute for Fusion Studies. A somewhat confused Sanjay Pradeet, Ph.D., had been introduced by Chad, who promptly left, leaving him in my company, along with Lobo, John, Gady, Josef and Monica. Nana had left with Chad, her parting comment, "Josef can speak for me . . . and I'll have my cell phone with me if you need me. Or Josef needs me. The entire resources of Van Pelt Industries are yours, and Josef knows, mostly, what they are."

Their host, my bride, Dr. Amy Clark-Rylander, served coffee and rolls, and then promptly announced she was taking our four month-old son, Timmy for a little air in his new stroller. She left me in charge of a pot of coffee and whatever else the group might need.

Amy was not anxious to see me get involved in any further activities, or "schemes," as she called the things Monica seemed to be able to cook up. She didn't like Monica, didn't trust her and, frankly, was wishing this morning that Monica would just disappear. Go away and never come back. *She plays fast and loose with other peoples' lives, Amy thought, and I don't want to see Craig become one of her casualties.*

Sensing Dr. Pradeet's unease, Lobo suggested the members of the group should introduce themselves—individually. "We know each other," he said, "but Dr. Pradeet just got dumped here in our midst, and we surely must seem like an odd group, to say the least." Sanjay gave him an appreciative nod.

"Chad didn't tell me much at all," Sanjay said. "He just said he didn't know what's going on, but that this group, whom he would trust with his life—and had trusted with Nana's life – is involved in a major international project that requires some expertise from a physicist." He looked

45

around at the group, still wondering why he was here, and then added. "Well, I'm a nuclear physicist. So . . . what can I do for you?"

Monica spoke up. "Let's introduce ourselves to you first, Doctor. We'll have some questions, and, maybe then we'll go into the specifics of this 'project,' as Chad called it, a bit later this morning." She looked to me and John; we both nodded. This was the right approach. No need to go into details unless the physicist seemed amenable and cooperative.

Lobo looked at Monica. "Why don't you begin, Monica. Once again, you're the reason we're together. This is your project." He turned to Sanjay. "We're all in the same boat here, Sanjay. Trying to determine if we should get involved and, if so, what we can do, and how we are going to do it."

He nodded at Monica.

She began. "The name I'm using these days is Monica Skrabacz. I've had many identities and aliases over the past fifteen years and, to be truthful, my birth name is a reminder of things I never want to think about. So call me Monica.

"The reason I've been known as so many different people? I have worked for the Central Intelligence Agency for the last decade and a half. Fifteen years as a field agent. An intelligence gatherer. A spy, if you prefer. In such places as Beijing, Mogadishu, Moscow, and others you don't need, or want, to know about. Josef and I have the same father. So does Amanda. The one we call Nana. Each of us was born to different mothers who, along with some siblings, were destroyed, killed, by that father."

She saw Sanjay's face turn dark. He looked to John and me as if wondering if this wild tale could possibly be true. Monica reassured him, "That father's not going to bother any of us again. Don't worry about him. Those of us in this room have seen to that problem. And that's all I need to say about it."

She went on, "The reason I'm here is simple. We can talk about the specifics later—if you're interested." She directed that comment to Dr. Pradeet. "Let me now just say that in my official capacity as the head of the Russian Desk at Langley, I'm confronted with a serious international issue that I fear . . . no, I'm dead sure . . . is not going to be dealt with properly through routine channels. I'm proposing, and all of us here are considering, whether we can, or should, take some rather unusual unilateral action."

Lobo said to Sanjay. "We know you're confused. Stick with us, though, please. You need to know who each of us is and why each is here before you even consider whether you want to help us. Fair enough?"

Sanjay nodded. He'd decided to stop trying to connect the dots. Those dots were still running around, too mobile to even allow for a guess.

"I'm still here," he said, adding, "I'll stick around and wait to hear what the hell you're all talking about. Then I'll either call a cab, since Chad left me here without wheels, or I'll stay to hear the specifics. Is that fair enough?"

The introductions of Josef, Lobo, Gady and me went quickly and seemed to be taken in by Dr. Pradeet without much confusion. Last, though, to introduce himself was John Greycloud, and John's backgrounder clearly puzzled the physicist. He asked if he might ask a question or two, and we told him to "shoot."

"Okay," he said, "everything seemed to be somehow connected, though I don't know how, up until John Greycloud introduced himself. Then you lost me. It's like one of those puzzles where you're supposed to figure out which part doesn't fit with all the others, like a circle in an array of squares, triangles, rectangles and trapezoids. You're all connected somehow with either law enforcement or international intelligence. Two police detectives, a newly retired Texas Ranger captain, a CIA agent. A mysterious young man with a wealthy sister."

He paused, looked at Greycloud, and added, "And then there's a Navajo shaman, a medicine man. What does this group need with a medicine man? Or a nuclear physicist, for that matter? I need more information. I'm a scientist looking for solutions through relationships, and this group seems to as much resemble a random collection of subway riders in Manhattan as any other group I can think of."

I nodded to Monica. This was her show, her confusing assemblage. She said, "Sanjay, it will all make sense in just a few minutes. Let me just say two things right now: first, this group has experience working together in the past in the international arena. Successfully. And, second, before we pull you into something you might not want to be a part of, we need to ask you a few questions . . . questions to help us understand the dilemma we're facing." She looked at the physicist.

"Go ahead," he said.

I spoke up. "Dr. Pradeet, you need to know that none of us is a scientist. We have some questions, but we may not know enough to even ask the right questions. That's why we invited you here this morning."

Sanjay looked around at the faces staring at him. He said, "I've never heard so much double-talk before. You folks sound like a computer salesman—telling me how great this new hardware is going to work, once you get it built." He shrugged. "Look," he went on, "I have no idea what you're planning to do. Or thinking about planning to do. Or how any of it relates to me or a need for a nuclear physicist. So can we please just cut to the chase?"

He gave a small smile. "Ask me your questions. And then, if you're so inclined, tell me why we're here and what this gathering is really all about."

So Monica asked, "If you were going to approach and transport a chunk of heavy metal, say Plutonium, and it's the size of a basketball and weighs maybe 5,000 pounds, what would you be most afraid of?"

Sanjay laughed. "That's easy. I would be terribly afraid I had lost my mind. That I was in need of a strait jacket and a padded cell. Such a concentration of Plutonium simply doesn't exist outside strict laboratory conditions. And not in one place. Or one piece. Anywhere." Suddenly his eyebrows shot up. "You're not contemplating breaking into a military arms facility, are you? Stealing weapons-grade Plutonium?"

"We're not thieves," Lobo said. "We're the good guys. Just play along with our question. Consider it hypothetical. What would you be concerned about? Just tell us about being around Plutonium."

I added, "And keep it simple, please. We're not scientists."

Sanjay leaned back, elbows on the table. His fingers steepled tip to tip, and he took on a serious face. "There are several things to know about Plutonium," he began. "First, it is very heavy. You said," he turned to Monica, "about five thousand pounds for a chunk the mass of a basketball. That may be a bit heavy, but it's close. Where is this chunk? Inside? Outside? In a controlled environment?"

Monica answered, "Assume outside in nature. In an extremely cold, remote environment. Latitude far north. Above the Arctic Circle."

"I assume this is not some kind of a joke," Sanjay said. "But what you have described is extremely unlikely. Plutonium in nature is usually measured in grams or ounces. Certainly not pounds or tons."

He looked around for reassurance. Finding none, he began to answer the question.

"This hypothetical mass of Plutonium will give off several forms of energy. I'll keep it simple, as you asked. There are *Alpha* rays. *Alpha* rays are relatively weak. Likely they would not penetrate even one layer of clothing. Certainly they would not penetrate bare skin and so are relatively harmless in small doses.

"Then there are *Beta* rays. These are somewhat more powerful. No, 'powerful' is the wrong word. They are stronger than *Alpha* rays, but not so strong as to be particularly dangerous in short doses."

He paused, looked around, and then turned serious. "The ones that will get you are the *Gamma* rays. Are you familiar with how a microwave oven works? Well, *Gamma* rays will cook you from the inside out, just like a microwave oven will cook a chicken. And *Gamma* rays are stoppable only by lead-lined suits. If there's a pinhole anywhere in that lead shielding in the suit, your goose will be cooked. The *Gamma* rays will pour in to a hole no bigger than the point of a needle. And that's your Waterloo. Stick a fork in you. You're done. It doesn't matter whether you're in a remote ice field or in a laboratory under strict safety controls. *Gamma* rays will boil your blood.

"Does that answer your question?"

Monica said, "So what we would need for protection would be lead lined suits?"

Sanjay frowned. "You said to keep it simple. If you're thinking about getting anywhere near a chunk of Plutonium, you need some training first, and then a lead-lined suit. A perfect one without a pinhole in it anywhere. And more than a little good luck."

Josef spoke for the first time since introducing himself. "What about equipment? Heavy equipment needed to move a mass that size into some kind of a safe container? What would be the long-term effects on, say, a Caterpillar tractor? Or a heavy-duty backhoe?"

Sanjay answered, "The equipment could be decontaminated. But if you're in any kind of a hurry, my advice would be to build a big fire under it and let it sink into the ice. We are talking about an ice field, aren't we?"

Josef nodded.

I interrupted. "Who's ready for some fresh coffee?" As I refilled cups and passed around sugar and cream and creamer, our visiting physicist spent the time staring at the rest of us, one at a time.

When the coffee service was complete, he spoke up with a tone that told us he'd figured out a few things. "You people have somehow come upon a highly-unlikely find. And, for reasons I cannot imagine in my wildest thoughts, you're planning to go somewhere cold and remote and actually retrieve a couple of tons of Plutonium. Am I right?"

Monica nodded.

He looked around and then spoke slowly, "You are all crazy. Certifiable lunatics."

Then he broke into a big grin and said, "Count me in!"

Part Two

Camera!

Chapter Ten

Delayed Reactions

The Oval Office—White House—January 2

The President of the United States, standing, peered closely at the large map prints spread across a sofa in his office. He spoke to his National Security Advisor. "So you think this basketball-sized blob in Siberia is mostly Plutonium?"

"Yes, Mr. President," the head of NSA answered. "We've run it through every analysis we have available for satellite images, and it's clearly a very heavy metal and highly radioactive."

The President turned to the Director of the CIA. "Tell me again where you got this—how we came on this, this . . . what shall I call it? *Anomaly?*"

The DCI said, "It was Christmas Eve, Mr. President. I received a call from the head of our Russian Desk advising me of the satellite images and their apparent content."

"And you've waited nine days to bother to tell me?" The President clearly was not pleased.

His National Security Advisor came to the DCI's rescue. "Mr. President," he said, "we need to take this slowly. Measured steps. We're monitoring the site around the clock. So far, there has been no activity anywhere in the area. We don't know if the Russians are aware of the Plutonium. In fact, we don't yet know if anybody besides the three of us and a couple of CIA personnel know about it."

The DCI spoke up, "Any effort to retrieve, claim or move the Plutonium is going to require a major effort. Not only does it weigh maybe 5,000 pounds, but its *Gamma* rays will fry any living organism that gets near it without adequate protection. Look, Sir, you can see how the ice has melted for maybe 30 yards in all directions. That's right up to the shoreline of the Arctic Ocean. Short story, Mr. President, nothing's going to happen quickly. And we face all kinds of international, scientific, and political pitfalls with any action we might take."

"Tell me the pitfalls. All of them," the President said.

The DCI, head of the CIA, responded, "Let's just look at what we don't know because everything we don't know is liable to bite us in the butt." He turned and nodded to the National Security Advisor. "You start," he said, passing the monkey to his associate's back.

"Feel free to chime in," the NSA said, looking to the DCI. He continued, "We don't know if the Russians know about it. It's on their soil, after all. We need to determine whether they are aware and, if they're not, should we make them aware? And what are the political ramifications of some kind of joint effort? Even if they would allow such a thing?"

The President interrupted. "Putin has been particularly belligerent lately. I won't rule out a joint effort, but I'll imagine he'll say, 'What business is this of yours?' And that's hard to argue with. So, what business is it of ours?"

He looked to the two advisors, expecting an answer.

Both the DCI and the NSA were taken aback by the question. The President could see that that particular question had never occurred to them. The NSA stammered, "Mr. President, there's enough Plutonium there to produce scores of nuclear bombs of sufficient size to obliterate every city of more than 10 million population on the face of the earth."

The DCI, recovered somewhat from being taken by surprise, added. "In the wrong hands, that Plutonium could produce more than 200 dirty suitcase bombs—even more dangerous, Mr. President."

The President's Chief of Staff came into the office to remind the President it was time for him to leave by helicopter to Andrews Air Force Base where Air Force One waited to take him to an important meeting with the heads of several Silicon Valley tech companies. And, later, to a fund raiser in San Francisco. He turned to his two now-embarrassed advisors, "You have brought me some information. Frankly I don't know if I should be concerned or not. You're full of questions, but have not offered a single answer. I'll be back tomorrow afternoon."

He turned to his Chief of Staff, "Clear my calendar starting at 4:00 tomorrow." Turning back to the DCI and NSA, he said, "Be here. A lot fewer questions. Some serious situation analysis. And, for damn sure, some answers. But, for now, nobody else besides the three of us is to know anything about this. Is that clear?"

"What about Monica Skrabacz?" the DCI asked.

"And she is?" the President asked.

"Head of the Russian Desk at the Company."

"Absolutely not. Tell her whatever you want, but not the truth. Not yet."

"Mr. President, she can go off the rails. I'm not sure we can lie to her and not expect some unwanted behavior on her part."

The President scowled. "That's your problem. Lock her up if you have to."

With that, he turned and left the room through his small private library, leaving the head of the Central Intelligence Agency and the National Security Advisor with a hefty coating of egg on their faces.

The Kremlin—President Putin's Office—January 2

President Putin, elected head of the government of the Russian Federation, bent over a table in his office, studying a map and a printout of a Russian satellite photograph. He had only one visitor, the head of the Russian FSB, that country's Federal Security Service. Successor to the infamous KGB, and the Russian counterpart to the CIA.

"How did we discover this phenomenon?" Putin asked.

"Once again, Mr. President, our friends at the U.S. Embassy tipped us off. I don't mean they are really friends, of course. But they continue to think we're stupid, and we learn much from their clumsiness. In this case, Sir, their cultural affairs attaché, who is most certainly CIA, began snooping around trying to see if we knew about 'something going on in Siberia.' Actually, we didn't at the time, but his not-so-subtle and clumsy inquiries told us we might want to see if there was something going on out there. It's a big place, as you know, so it took us a few days to zero in on this particular image. What gave it away was the appearance of two U.S. stationary satellites suddenly sitting up there looking down. We took a look ourselves and, voilà, there's the prize."

"So, what do we do about it, Boris?" the President asked. "We already have more of this stuff than we want. Or need. You know that we even ship the radioactive remnants of bombs we decommission to the U.S. to finish off. Some place called Amarillo. In Texas, I think. So, if we don't want it, the only reason the U.S. might want it would be to keep us from having it. And to sneak it out of our country so they can snub their crazy noses at us."

"Well, Mr. President, it's on the soil of the Russian Federation. That makes it a resource owned by our country. Even if it is a liability."

"Oh, it's a liability, all right," Putin said. "But I suppose we have to deal with it."

The FSB director cleared his throat. "There is a larger liability, Sir. If this Plutonium were to fall into the hands of terrorists, the result could make our problems with the Chechens seem like a Sunday afternoon picnic."

"How bad, Boris?" the President asked.

"More than 200 conventional nuclear weapons, though the terrorists will lack delivery systems. But, here's the big problem. Maybe as many as 250 dirty suitcase bombs. Think of that! No city of any size in the world would be safe."

"Make that the Western world, Boris," the President said. "And that might just include us."

Boris spoke. It was a question, or perhaps a statement. "So we have to take action to secure this ticking time bomb?"

"Absolutely! I see no other choice."

Boris, with some trepidation, decided to offer a suggestion. "If we don't want it, then the U.S. doesn't want it. In fact no nuclear power today wants it. Then those who do want it are those seeking nuclear weapons."

He turned to a globe and spun it. Looking up at Putin, he said, "Suppose we do the unexpected?"

"And what would that be, Boris?"

"Suppose we invite the present nuclear powers to assist in the securing and disposition of this thing that's popped up on our soil? It would show a kind of cooperative spirit that would surprise most of the world . . . and shock the Americans into ceaseless investigations to try to figure out what we're really up to."

"And what would we really be up to?"

"Absolutely nothing. Except getting a dangerous nuisance out of our back yard."

Putin smiled. "I like it. Bring me a plan. For the time being, just you and me, Boris. We'll include others when they need to know."

Chapter Eleven

Who's on First?

Supreme Leader and Grand Ayatollah Ali Khamenei sat across a small table from Iranian President Hassan Rouhani. Together they sipped tea while they studied a large printout of a satellite photo of the northern Siberian plains.

"So," the Supreme Leader said, "you believe this is two and a half tons of pure Plutonium? How can that be? We have tens of thousands of centrifuges hidden in the mountains. And yet we cannot produce anywhere nearly this much Plutonium. Where did it come from?"

President Rouhani said, "Apparently it has just popped up to the surface over millions, maybe billions, of years. Allah has not seen fit for it to pop up on our land, and that is a shame. Think of what we could do with that much fissionable heavy metal. Think of the energy we could produce."

The Grand Ayatollah looked around, and then leaned toward the President. "Or, Hassan, think of Iran joining the nuclear nations, taking the rightful place Persians have earned in this world with our ancient civilization."

Rouhani looked startled. "You're talking about the bomb?"

"Yes, the bomb. We can spin those centrifuges until the Prophet returns and never get this much Plutonium. Who else knows of this? Why not just go get it?"

The President answered, "Perhaps nobody knows. Maybe everybody knows. But even with it, do we have the final technology to complete a bomb?"

The Grand Ayatollah snapped his fingers. "Where is that idiot nuclear scientist? The one we banned two years ago? What was his name?"

"You mean Haji Kahn? He's somewhere in Ethiopia. We made a big deal of kicking him out of the country to appease those who would interrupt our nuclear weapon development. He thinks he's hiding from us, but the Republican Guard knows exactly where he is. And we have attached our own agent to him—a chap named Mahmood Bijahn. Khan believes Bijahn is an agent of Al Qaeda who is helping him to create suitcase bombs to avenge the infidels in the name of Allah. He's a fool, and he's likely totally insane. But he knows his nuclear physics."

"Then get him. Grab him and bring him back. If necessary, bring him back tied up in a gunny sack. He has the technical knowledge to put that Plutonium to good use. No longer will the West, the infidels. and the Jews, be the only ones with the bomb. We will neutralize the threat of the Zionists and the Western imperialists. With nuclear power, we will, as a nation, once again command respect, the kind of respect due our ancient civilization."

President Rouhani pressed a button on his phone, and immediately the commander of the Republican Guard answered. The President said, "The Grand Ayatollah has a mission for you. Meet me in my office in 15 minutes."

Democratic People's Republic of Korea
Ryongsong Residence--Pyongyang—January 2

Chang Sung-taek, vice chairman of the National Defense Commission and reputed to be the number two or three official in North Korea, turned on a small portable white noise machine and slipped it into his coat pocket. He sat in a library of the Ryongsong Residence, also known as Residence No. 55, one of eight or nine official residences of Kim Jung-Un, first chairman of the Democratic People's Republic of Korea. No. 55 is the only official residence in the capital city of Pyongyang.

Satisfied that his conversation would be muffled by the little machine in his pocket, he turned and spoke softly to Kwak Pum Ji, the country's Minister of People's Security. "Do we dare tell him about this?" he asked. "You know what he's going to say, don't you?"

"He's going to demand we go get it," Kwak answered. "No question. But I'm almost as worried about interrupting him right now. He's at his favorite pastime down in the movie theater."

"What's he watching this time?" Chang asked.

"*High Noon.* Ever since that giant freak basketball player told him Gary Cooper was very short, he's been watching every Gary Cooper movie ever made. This is about the twelfth time for High Noon. You can guess why; he loves short people."

"Still," Chang said, "we have to tell him. If he finds out later, we're up against the wall. Maybe bullets will be too good for us, even. Our jobs are to keep him informed."

"And wait for his snap decisions. However bizarre they may be. So I say we wait until the movie's over, and then break the news to him," Kwak said

A half-hour later, Kim Jung-Un joined the two high-ranking officials and they carefully explained to him the sudden appearance of enough Plutonium to make dozens and dozens of bombs. Kim immediately wanted to know how many.

"If we make small bombs, perhaps as many as 120, Sir," Chang explained, adding, "with bigger bombs, maybe up to 95 or 96." Both Kwak and Chang waited for the expected reply.

They were disappointed, though not surprised.

"Then we must have it. All of it!" Kim said. "That will be your jobs. Go get it and bring it back to our scientists at once."

Should we try to reason with Kim? Chang thought.

Kwak was wondering the same thing. But he had a bit more resolve and either more courage or greater stupidity than Chang. So he said, "Sir, this is on the sovereign soil of the Russian Federation. The Russians would consider any such attempt an invasion. And that might bring the wrath of the Russians down on our country."

Kim was not to be dissuaded. "I didn't say 'attempt' to retrieve it. I said 'Go get it.' The Russian bear growls, but he has no fangs. With enough nuclear bombs, we will be invincible. Nobody will dare cross the Democratic People's Republic of Korea. Remember, China is our ally, and—together—we cannot be stopped."

As the two officials left Kim's residence, Kwak said as he turned off his white noise machine, "At least he didn't say by tomorrow. No deadline. I don't know about you, but I'm seriously thinking of defecting to the South."

Realizing what he had just said could get him shot, Kwak added, "That's a joke, Chang. This is a no-win for the two of us. If we succeed, too many bombs will be in the hands of a madman. If we fail, well, we're just a couple more corpses in his gallery."

Chapter Twelve

Go, or No-Go? Decision Time

At the end of yesterday's meeting at my apartment, the group had decided to sleep on the entire matter and reconvene the next morning at the Detective Bureau in the Austin Police Department. Each participant was asked to come prepared to say whether or not he or she wants to get involved, and why.

Nana and Josef had joined the group, bringing donuts. I provided the coffee, courtesy of APD.

Before Monica could take the floor, I began the meeting. "Speaking for myself, I have to say that any lengthy involvement by me is going to be impossible. Chief Garza is tolerant, but I've only been in this new job for a few weeks. He's not going to approve another leave of absence of any duration. That's not going to happen. On the other hand, I'm willing to do what I can to help create a successful mission. If our own government is willing to sit on its heels and watch some crazies grab that much Plutonium, somebody has to intervene. So I'm in--under those conditions."

Lobo spoke up. "I'm in, and I have time. But I think we need to spend more effort planning." Turning to Monica, he said, "You're asking us, in effect, to invade a foreign country. And not just any old country. Russia, for God's sake. The only upside I see is that the area is so remote. Uninhabited. And likely uninhabitable. I don't expect we'll find much resistance from the locals, if there are any. Polar bears, maybe? Monica, can you be sure we can get access to continuous satellite surveillance of the area? So we'll know if anybody else is coming around?"

Monica nodded. "Yes, as head of the Russian Desk at the Company I have access to any satellites over the Russian Federation—any time I choose to look in."

John Greycloud said, "I can help out there, too. Remember when we

59

were tracking down Pavlovich? I was able to monitor the NSA satellite surveillance system. I've done them enough favors over the years. They won't question me too hard. I'll figure out a plausible story. They won't need to know exactly what I'm looking at. They'll just clear me for their network, and we can see what we want to see for at least a few hours each day. And remember, that far north, there's not much daylight, anyway. The nights are very long."

Seeing a trend developing, I said, "Is there anybody who's not on board? Who doesn't want any part of this . . . this escapade? That's a good word, I think. Escapade."

Monica jumped in. "We're all on board, then. My replacement as cultural affairs attaché in the U.S. Embassy in Moscow is monitoring the politicos and apparatchiks on the ground there. So far, there's no indication the Russians know anything. At least nobody over there seems excited about anything in particular at the moment."

I turned to Dr. Sanjay Pradeet. "Sanjay, now that you know what's going on, what are your thoughts from a scientific point of view? Are we all crazy?"

Sanjay looked around the room. "The only way to answer your question, Craig, is 'Yes!' The whole idea is beyond crazy. And I use that term clinically. You're describing a ridiculous escapade, as you called it. Nobody in his or her right mind would even consider going forward with it."

Monica started to object, but Sanjay interrupted her. "Let me finish, please, Monica. I want to tell you the story of scientific progress down through civilized history. In fact, let's just talk about progress in any field: Science, music, art, you name it."

He stopped and looked around the room to be sure his listeners were tuned in. Because he intended to make a very important point.

Sanjay continued, "Down through civilized history, individuals or small groups of individuals often risked being burned at the stake as heretics, hanged as witches, and banned from their own city-states like Dante and Machiavelli.

"And why were they at risk? Because they dared to think about, talk about, and act on what *could* be rather than what *had been*. Every advance in any field you care to name came because of these people. I'm talking about the Platos, the Aristotles, the Virgils, Michaelangelos,

Martin Luthers, Newton, Einstein, Fermi, Madame Curie, Von Braun, and—more recently—Salk and Sabin, and even our astronauts."

He stopped and looked around to see if anybody was catching on to the point he was about to make.

Seeing only puzzlement, he continued, "These individuals and hundreds more you can name, dared to think about and act on what *could be* rather than what *had been*. That's the difference between creative thinkers and linear thinkers. Now, to be sure, there's nothing wrong with linear thinkers. They're just wired differently from creative thinkers."

He paused, then continued, " My point is this: there can be no progress by hanging onto what *has been*. Progress comes by thinking about what *could be*. And then doing something about it."

Sanjay went on, "Governments are bound up by what *has been*. Therefore, they're slow to act. And fearful of anything that they can't point to from the past. Real accomplishment comes only from those who are willing to go for it. So I say, let's go for it!"

He paused, seeing his point sink in among the wry smiles around the room. "Look," he continued, "the stakes here may be virtually nothing. Or, on the other hand, they may hold the potential for international Armageddon. Death and destruction like this planet has never seen. If we can sneak in and quietly pull the plug, or maybe better said, defuse the fissionable, we may just have done some real good. If we're really lucky, nobody will ever know. Only we can quietly celebrate the success of a dangerous and heroic, what was your word, Craig? Ah, yes, *escapade*."

Throughout the entire discussion, Josef and Nana had sat silent, only showing unusual interest when Sanjay got into his monologue.

Now Nana had something to say. "If we are going to go forward with trying to do whatever it is we're going to do with that mass of Plutonium, then Josef and I have the equipment and the potential pathway into that part of Siberia. My company, Van Pelt Industries, has a long-term contract with the Russian Federation and its major petroleum producer, Rosneft. Our contract calls for us to locate potentially large gas reserves in the Siberian plain. By contract, our activities are supposed to be limited to April through September. And they're for an area a bit south of the coast of the Arctic Ocean But it's just possible we might be able to approach the site as contract oil and gas producers . . . even out of season and, having gotten lost, ending up too far north."

Josef spoke up. "So here's what I propose. Can the three of us—Nana, Monica and me—meet with Sanjay, John, and Lobo, in our offices on Hamilton Pool Road this afternoon? Craig and Gady can go on today with their detective work. We can figure out what resources and personnel we need to put in motion and how we're going to move that Plutonium."

He turned to Sanjay, "Do you have any idea what we can do with the thing once we've got our hands on it?"

Sanjay scratched his chin as if considering the question. Then he said, "Maybe we won't have to move it or take it anywhere. I'm hoping there's a better solution."

Just as he spoke, APD Chief Alex Garza stuck his head into the room. "Craig," he said, pointing at me, "when you have a few minutes, we need to talk about a couple of your cases. I'm getting some pressure from the City Council and the local press, and I need some answers that will pass muster."

First seeing John Greycloud, then Lobo and finally Monica, Nana and Josef, the Chief came on into the room. "What kind of mischief could this group possibly be cooking up?" he said with a laugh.

Greycloud stood, took the chief by the elbow and led him back to the door. "Chief, you don't want to know what's going on in here. Don't you know the head man has to always maintain deniability? But I have a story you ought to hear. And since this meeting just ended, Craig and Gady will need a couple of minutes to check on things out there." He pointed to the Detective Bureau and its rows of cubicles, then added, "You're going to love this story."

And he led Chief Garza from the room.

Gady and I broke into laughter. Gady said, "My Little Father, my mother's brother, is always telling Chief Garza stories. They're supposed to contain sage advice from a venerable tribal elder, a *Hosteen*, as he's called."

She snickered. "But they never make any sense."

I added, "Garza hasn't figured that out yet. He just walks away, shaking his head and looking confused."

As the others agreed on an afternoon meeting time at Van Pelt Industries and filed from the room, Gady and I lingered just inside the door to try to hear Greycloud's latest story for Garza.

Greycloud was saying, "Chief, it's been said that what you don't know can hurt you. Right?" Garza nodded.

John continued, "But that's *biligaana*, white man's, wisdom. Navajos know better. In biligaana words, we call it deniability. For example, on the Checkerboard Reservation where we live in Arizona and New Mexico, we see lots of tourists. And those tourists are always very curious. Asking questions, asking for directions, and wanting to take a picture with a real Indian. It gets to be a bit of a nuisance. Know what I mean? But all those questions almost always contain the white man's word, 'Indian.' In Navajo, there is no word for Indian. Just doesn't exist. After all, most of us came from Mongolia across the land bridge to this continent many years ago. We don't know about India. Or Indians.

"So we just tell them, 'Sorry, we don't know what an Indian is.' That freaks them out.

"And that, my *biligaana* friend, is Navajo deniability."

We stifled laughs as Garza patted Greycloud on the shoulder, turned and walked toward the elevators in complete confusion.

Chapter Thirteen

Follow the Money. Again.

Fairmont Banff Springs Hotel—January 2

Four watched with amusement as One, Two, and Three opened Fed-Ex boxes and pulled out their new and powerful laptop computers. The replacements for their previous laptops he'd caused to explode in a demonstration of his unusual hacking skills. They struggled with the installation CDs and with those of all the data he'd returned from the hard drives of their now-exploded computers.

These guys have no idea how to reload their information, he thought.

"Here," he said, "let me help you with those. We'll be here all day at the rate you're going."

Gladly, the three billionaires handed him the job, and he quickly had all three computers downloading disk after disk.

One broke the silence. "How do we know you haven't kept copies of everything you took off our old laptops?" he asked Four.

"You don't," Four said, a smug smile on his face. "You don't know. And as long as you don't, I have my assurance the three of you won't renege on your promises to me. I get my millions, and then you'll get whatever I have. Or don't have."

Three said, "But you can just go into these three new computers and copy the hard drives whenever you want to." He looked worried.

"Yes, Three, I can do that," Four shot back. "And if you guys screw with me, that's exactly what I will do." This time he gave them a firm look with no smugness.

"Then how can we trust you?" Two asked. "Seems like we're at your mercy."

"Unless you follow through with your parts of the bargain, you are," Four said. He paused, and then added, "At my mercy. So don't even think about messing with me. I'm either a full partner in this gig . . . or the

64

three of you will be in deep doo-doo. Is that clear?"

All three scowled. But they nodded. What choice did they have? Without Four, they were on a fool's mission. And they knew it.

Four, reloading another set of three CDs, said, "Let me ask you guys a question. When we steal the blueprints and technical details from the International Patent Office, it's still going to take a year or more to build that fusion-fission gizmo, right? So what are you going to do with all that Plutonium in the meantime? Barbecue goats with it?"

"We have marketing plans," One said. "While construction is underway, we'll be quietly signing up customers in Europe, Asia, and the U.S.—wherever nuclear fuel waste is creating a problem."

Three chimed in. "We're already creating an animated demonstration film showing the top-line of the process. But we need to get those plans in hand ASAP so the demonstration will be credible."

Four looked confused. "And you think the powers that be are just going to accept what you're promising without looking into how you developed the technology? I don't think so. They're going to put you under a microscope. They'll pretty quickly know more about you than your wives, or your concubines, or soft young boy lovers. You're sounding delusional."

"Not at all," One said. "First, none of the three of us will be even remotely visible. All work and representation will be through several of the enterprises we control. And all of those enterprises we decide to employ to promote this offering are legitimate international companies, any one of which might have come up with the process on its own."

Four said, "So why spend your own R & D monies when you can just steal the process and blueprints from the Patent Office? Right?"

"Precisely," Two said. "Our enterprises are already on the cutting edge of this technology. But we're three or four years away from duplicating the process ourselves. Or so our scientists tell us. Eventually we would be able to compete on our own. But the appearance of this demonstration Plutonium makes it possible for us to get to market first. We can show, for the entire scientific world to see, the reduction of highly fissionable heavy metal to harmless dirt, a few ounces at a time.

"Those with nuclear waste stockpiles will line up to get rid of a bunch of highly-radioactive liability. Bet on it."

Four thought, *They don't know that the patent's developers are just waiting for funding. The funding they're about to provide.*

"Voila!" One added. "A few billion here. A few billion there. And before you know it, our business will be worth more than Exxon-Mobil."

"Or Microsoft. Or Apple. Or the U.S. Treasury," Three said.

"Sounds like you've thought this through," Four said. He paused, and then added, "But you have a major problem you seem to have over-looked."

One, the trio's main planner, looked startled. He glanced at Two and Three. "And what would that be?" he asked, showing his concern with a crack in his voice.

"Your problem, my filthy-rich compadres, is simply that I know ex-actly what you're up to. I have it all documented. Remotely, where you'll never find it. So I can bring your budding empire down with a few key-strokes. Have you not thought of that?"

Two said menacingly, "Then you have just become expendable. What are you to us once we have the plans? Nothing! That's what you are."

Four smiled, infuriating Two. "You take me for a fool, do you? You actually thought I would sit right here and hack the Patent Office's com-puters and hand you the plans. Then ask for my three million, and wait for one of you to kill me?"

He paused. "That's not how it's going to happen."

He smirked. "Let me tell you how we're going to proceed from here: First, so you know the ground rules, I have an encrypted email already prepared and addressed to both the International Patent Office and the patent holders. For good measure, Vladimir Putin is copied on it. I can send it off into cyberspace from any computer, iPad or smart phone. Any time I want to. You do not want to fuck with me, or I *will* send it.

"And by the way your names are included. In bold Italics."

Four looked at each of the trio and continued, "So here's what we're going to do. First thing in the morning, each of you is going to come up with ten cashier's checks, each for $100,000. That's the three million you've promised me. You will leave checks, ten each in three plain enve-lopes at the main desk of this hotel. Downstairs. And just so you know, when I walk out of this room, you will never see me again.

"I mean today. This afternoon." He nodded to reinforce his inten-tions.

"The Fairmont management at this hotel will send those envelopes, by special armed courier, to another of their hotels, where I will pick them up in two days. Once I have all 30 checks in my hands, then and only then will I go into the International Patent Office computers and provide the files you want."

Again, he looked directly into the eyes of each of the three. "You don't follow through exactly as I have just said, and two things happen. First, I trigger that email, spilling your whole scheme and naming each of you personally. Second, I forget about the computers at the International Patent Office and just go about my merry way."

This time he stared—a hard stare—into each of their faces. "Do. You. Understand?" Four bit off each word. Slowly.

The three looked at one another. Two shrugged and, in unison, they all nodded.

"We understand," Three said. "I would think less of you if you hadn't taken these kinds of precautions. But do not forget, Four. We know who you are as well."

Four said, "In two days, Sir, I will be someone else entirely, far away, retired, living the good life, and only hacking for my own amusement."

"Then we understand one another," One said.

Four nodded. "Now, if you will hand me my thousand dollar retainer for today, tomorrow, and the next two days, I will be on my way. I will know, as will the world, I suppose, if you three are able to pull off this scam without killing one another."

One handed him an envelope with his remaining four thousand dollars. Four put it in his pocket, picked up his laptop and headed for the suite's door.

"Aren't you going to count the money?" Three asked.

Four gave him a shame-on-you grimace. "Never count your winnings while you're still at the table."

With that parting advice, Four left. Out of their lives and control. Forever.

Chapter Fourteen

Inshallah—If Allah Wills

Addis Ababa, Ethiopia—Haji G. Kahn's Apartment—January 3

Mahmood Bijahn, Haji Khan's "political advisor," stepped from the crazy nuclear scientist's apartment to take an important call from Tehran.

Haji must never know of calls from Iran, he thought.

Bijahn answered, "Allahu Akbar, Allah is great," he said.

"Bijahn?"

"Yes, I am Bijahn. Who is this, please?"

"You do not need to know my identity. I call on behalf of the Supreme Leader Ali Khamenei and President Rouhani. Can that fool Khan hear you?"

"No. I'm away from him for the moment. How can I serve the Supreme Leader?"

"We have a new assignment for you. It involves liaison with the Republican Guard and a swift trip back to Niavarin Palace. You are to bring Haji Khan with you."

"Are you crazy?" Bijahn asked. "He will never go back to Iran. There's no way I can do this on my own."

"Relax, Bijahn. How about some help from the Republican Guard?"

"That might be possible," Bijahn said. "But do the Supreme Leader and President Rouhani know how far I've come in our efforts with Khan?"

"Probably not. Why don't you tell me, and then we can discuss the importance of getting him back to Iran. And, perhaps, how to do that while he thinks he's somewhere else."

Bijahn spoke to the caller. "A few days ago, I drugged him. Very easy to do. Then I made a quick trip to Shiraz, his former home, where I made every trace of him disappear. But I told him I had been to Somalia

68

to arrange for mobile laboratories and equipment with which he could fabricate suitcase bombs."

The caller said, "Good cover. Did he buy it?"

"As long as he trusts me, he's easy to fool . . . and to persuade. But surely you and the Supreme Leader and President Rouhani are aware of how unstable he really is. One minute he's a raging jihadist, and the next a poor, misunderstood nuclear genius. It takes constant monitoring to keep him semi-functional."

"You can't be with him 24 hours a day," the caller said.

"No, of course not. But I have found I can knock him out—put him into a deep sleep, even for days at a time. I have to do that to fulfill my mission."

"And speaking of missions," the caller said, "we have a slight change of plans for you and your crazy scientist."

"Tell me," Bijahn said.

And he listened for fifteen minutes.

Red Sea Coast, East of Asmara, Eritrea—January 4

Mahmood pulled a Land Rover behind a dune just as darkness fell on the Eritrean coast of the Red Sea. He checked his GPS. Yes, he was exactly where he'd been told to deliver Haji Khan, his nutty Iranian nuclear scientist. And he was almost an hour early. The pick up had been set for 10:00.

Once again it had been easy to outwit Khan. Last night he'd told his charge they would be going to the Somalian peninsula near the Gulf of Aden. He'd explained that the location, immediately south of Yemen, would soon be the staging place for his mobile laboratories and workshops—those facilities he would need to place the 5,000 pounds of Plutonium into a couple of hundred suitcase bombs. He'd even shown Khan a prototype of the suitcase, a new salesman's sample case large enough to accommodate Khan's intended content.

Then very early this morning, Mahmood had explained to Khan that the road would be rough, suggesting he take a motion sickness pill. Haji had taken the pill gratefully, knowing that most motion sickness medicines tend to make one drowsy. A nap on the way wouldn't hurt.

Of course the pill Bijahn had given him was a placebo—a simple fish oil gel capsule. The knockout drops had been slipped into Khan's small cup of thick, sweet morning coffee. Within an hour of their five a.m. departure from Addis Ababa, Khan was sleeping soundly, strapped securely in the passenger seat of the Land Rover.

Mahmood had slapped him awake when they crossed the border from Ethiopia to Somalia. His excuse for waking his charge was so the scientist could produce and show his papers. However, there was no border guard to look at any papers. Mahmood just wanted Kahn to get a groggy look at a road sign identifying the border of Somalia.

He couldn't be sure if the scientist had been conscious enough for the sign to register or not. But pointing it out to him, exchanging papers and having a phony, but brief, conversation with a nonexistent guard seemed a reasonable precaution.

Why not play it safe? Bijahn thought. *It will only take two or three minutes.*

Mahmood needed Khan to continue to sleep for another hour. Maybe a little more. He scanned the Gulf of Aden through his binoculars and saw little except the usual ship traffic. Tankers going south empty from the Suez Canal and the Mediterranean, and fully loaded tankers from the Persian Gulf headed west and then north into the Red Sea and on through the Suez with their black gold cargo to feed the oil-hungry infidels of the West.

And then, at 9:40, he saw what he was expecting. A low flying craft skimming toward him only yards above the water. It was the Republican Guard helicopter he'd been told to expect. As it drew near the coastline and hovered over a flat spot on the beach, Mahmood could see it was an air ambulance. He had been told the helicopter would pick up Haji Khan, but the thought of an air ambulance hadn't entered his mind.

Very clever, he thought. *Khan can be strapped to a gurney and kept asleep. Little chance of a rebellion.*

As he had been instructed, Mahmood blinked the Land Rover's headlights twice, just in case the helicopter's passengers hadn't been able to see it behind the dune. He heard the impact as they set the big craft down onto the beach. The engines stopped and the rotors slowly wound down.

A man and a woman, both dressed in black with Red Crescent armbands, approached the Rover.

"Are you Mahmood Bijahn?" the woman asked.

Mahmood nodded and pointed, "And this is Dr. Haji Khan, the passenger you've come to pick up."

The man said, "I'll get the gurney," and started back toward the helicopter.

"I have instructions for you, Bijahn," the woman said. "We will be taking Dr. Khan to a secret facility in the Salt Desert northeast of Tehran. We'll stop for fuel twice—at Muscat in Oman, and again in Tehran. Our orders are to keep him sedated."

"Will you have enough fuel to reach Oman?" Mahmood asked. "What's the range of your airship?"

"Our tanks are full," she said. "We just lifted off the deck of an Iranian warship not more than 20 kilometers across the Gulf."

She looked around, and then changed the subject. "If he should somehow wake up, where have you told him you were taking him?"

"I told him we were going to Somalia on the shores of the Gulf of Aden He is planning to simply inspect the site. In a few days he expects mobile machine shops and laboratories to arrive so he can build bombs. Lots of small bombs."

The woman smiled. "Oh, I think he's going to get to build bombs, all right. Big bombs."

"So you have instructions for me?" Mahmood asked.

"Yes. You are to return this vehicle to our embassy in Addis Ababa. Then catch a commercial flight to Tehran. Here are new identification and travel papers. Study the name. The papers say you are a deaf mute. So you will not have to answer many questions. How quickly do you think you can be back in Tehran?"

"If I drive back to Addis Ababa tonight, I should be able to be in Tehran by late tomorrow afternoon, *Inshallah*."

She handed him a slip of paper. "Call this number when you know your flight and arrival time. You will be met and taken at once to the Salt Desert. You are expected to continue to help control the unpredictable doctor."

The man had arrived with a gurney. They lifted Khan onto it and strapped him down. The man produced a hypodermic and injected a clear fluid into Khan's left wrist, swabbing it with alcohol-soaked cotton before and after the injection. He turned to Mahmood. "*Allahu Akbar*," my friend. Safe journey. We will meet again tomorrow."

With that, the two black uniformed figures moved Haji G. Khan,

71

Ph.D. into the helicopter. The engines spooled up, and the copter lifted off to the northeast toward a fuel stop in Oman.

Mahmood, beginning to understand what lay ahead, said, "*Inshallah*, my friend Khan."

He started the Rover, turned and began the long night's drive back to Ethiopia.

Chapter Fifteen

Uh-tteck-he~!
(Oh, my God! What should I do?)

Pyongyang

Near the Headquarters —National Defense Commission—January 3

Chang and Kwak sat inconspicuously in a park in central Pyong-yang. Each had spent a sleepless night pondering how to react to the orders of First Chairman Kim. Each realized that the other could turn, causing swift death for their counterpart. Still they were in this kettle together. And each had to trust someone.

They spoke softly.

Chang began, "Have you come to any decisions as to how we should proceed?"

Kwak answered, "I was hoping you had a good idea. So far, it seems the two of us are trapped. We have to do something to show some action . . . or both just disappear."

"You're speaking of defection?" Chang asked.

Kwak leaned in and whispered, "I believe there are several countries that would welcome us. The South for sure. The United States, too. But the problem is getting out of the country. If we decide to do that, we have little time. It's go today . . . or stay and face the music."

Chang said, "Why, suddenly, are the two of us turning rogue? We've been at Kim's service for years. Why now? Why not just go for the Plu-tonium?"

"Because if we fail, we will be executed," Kwak said. "The man is a psychopath. You know that. And right now he's got his heart set on a big batch of bomb-making heavy metal."

"So," Chang continued, "our only option is to go for the Plutonium. And get it. Otherwise we're dead men."

"Or, Kwak said, "get the hell out of Dodge."

"Dodge? What is this dodge?" Chang said.

"I don't know. But in Kim's movies of the wild West, somebody's always saying, 'Get the hell out of Dodge.'"

"What will it be, my friend? Go for it. Or get out of this dodge?" Chang asked.

Kwak pondered a moment, then said, "Meet me here again at noon today. You have your answer and I'll have mine. We'll each write our answers on a small piece of paper. If we have the same answer, then we'll go forward together."

Moscow—The Kremlin—January 2—Early Evening

President Putin spoke, "Have you caused inquiries to be made? Any feedback?"

Boris, head of the FSS, said, "These diplomats from the U.S. seem to continue to be an indecisive bunch. I personally approached their ambassador two hours ago. I did find out that they didn't know about the Plutonium."

Putin said, "Did you bring up the idea of a joint recovery effort?"

"In so many words, Mr. President, yes. Directly. I told the ambassador that the Russian Federation would welcome a joint-recovery effort among our country, the U.S., and perhaps other nuclear nations."

"And the response?" Putin asked.

"In a word, shock. The U.S. ambassador was obviously pissed that he had not been made aware of the discovery personally. He immediately called their Secretary of State, who immediately called their White House, where the presence of the Plutonium was confirmed."

"So, when will we have an answer from them?" Putin said.

Boris said, "I couldn't get a firm time commitment from the ambassador. Frankly, he seemed more distracted that the head of the FSB would have been allowed inside their embassy, regardless of the message I had to deliver. Nobody seems to be able to make a decision over there without some kind of gang-bang conference."

Putin said, "What time is it in Washington, D.C.?"

"Now?"

"Right now."

Boris checked his watch. "Three a.m., Sir. Tomorrow morning."

Putin smiled. "Boris, how would you like to give the U.S. ambassador a bad case of diarrhea?"

"Sir? What do you have in mind?"

"Go back, right now. Demand to see the ambassador. He'll see you because he's already confused. Just tell him to advise the White House that Putin will be calling the President at, let's say, noon tomorrow, their time."

Boris said, "You're cutting out the middle men?"

Putin replied, "All fifteen thousand of them. We'll see if they've got the balls to do something worthwhile—with us—for a change."

He paused, and then he said, "And, by the way, let me know what the ambassador smells like. I've heard he thinks his shit doesn't stink."

Washington, D.C.—The White House—January 3

It had taken almost two hours for the U.S. Ambassador to Russia to reach an Undersecretary of State, who called the President's Chief of Staff, who called both the National Security Advisor and the head of the CIA. The Secretary of State remained missing. The rest were converging on the Oval Office.

First to arrive was the DCI, head of the CIA, followed shortly by the NSA, National Security Advisor. The NSA asked the Chief of Staff, "What the hell's Putin up to? He's going to call the President? Why?"

"Apparently it has to do with that lump of Plutonium. I'm not sure exactly what. The Undersecretary's report to me was pretty vague. He said he had to run it by the Secretary, and she would fill in the details. So far, however, he hasn't been able to find her."

The DCI said, "Where did the word of the phone call come from?"

"Apparently from the ambassador to Russia," the Chief of Staff said.

"Then let's get his ass on the phone. Right now," the DCI said.

"Maybe we should wait for the President," the Chief of Staff said. "I'm not keen on going around protocol."

"Screw protocol!" the DCI said. "You want to be the one to tell the President we've waked him after his long flight from the West coast, and none of us knows diddly-shit about why?"

He grabbed a telephone. "Get me the U.S. Ambassador to Russia. This is the DCI . . . yes; I'm outside the Oval Office. And this is an emergency."

Before the call could be completed, the president, dressed in sport clothes, and obviously in a hurry, walked into the Oval Office and invited the gathering to come on in. Luckily for the others, the Secretary of

State appeared at that moment.

Gaming the situation, The DCI said to her, "Madam Secretary, we've really got one on our hands here, don't we?" Of course he had no idea what he was talking about, but the comment made him look informed in the eyes of the President.

His gambit almost backfired. The President looked at him and asked, "What are we talking about?"

The DCI answered, "Putin's going to be calling you in a few hours." Turning to the Secretary of State, he added, "I'll let the Secretary tell you what's happening." Thus passing the monkey to Madam Secretary while not having a clue, himself.

"Here's what I know," she began, just as a telephone rang. The Chief of Staff answered it while the others stood waiting.

"It's for you," he said to the DCI. "The ambassador to Russia in Moscow."

That bit of information stunned the Secretary of State. She said, "Hold on! Just a minute. I'll take that call."

And she did.

Meanwhile the President again said to the DCI, "Go ahead and start filling me in. We can catch the Secretary up in a moment."

This is going to sound lame, the DCI thought, *but it'll have to do.* "Mr. President, the Russian ambassador is returning my call. I expect the Secretary is getting more information. Probably best if we wait until she finishes."

The President looked to his Chief of Staff. "This meeting is looking more and more like a cluster-fuck. I want to know what the hell everybody's here for. Why are we meeting at dawn with half the brain trust of the country standing around with their thumbs up their butts?"

The Secretary of State ended her phone call. As everyone stared at her, she began an explanation. "It seems there is a fissionable chunk of heavy metal that has risen to the surface in Siberia. Thank you all very much for not informing the State Department about it. We have just been caught flat-footed by your collective and, I might add, stupid, secrecy."

She paused, staring darts at everyone but the President.

The NSA spoke sheepishly, "Yes, Madam Secretary, we're aware of the Plutonium. But what's prompted this meeting?" He turned to the

DCI. "Can you please fill us in?"

The DCI thought, *You rotten SOB*. But he said, "Since Madam Secretary has just spoken to the ambassador, perhaps we should hear from her first."

The president said, "None of you has even a bit of a clue, do you? So the ambassador learns from who knows whom that the Plutonium is there. Is that why we're all here wringing our hands and pretending we know something when we don't know shit?"

He looked to the Secretary of State. "Madam Secretary, none of the rest of these so-called intelligence professionals has a clue about what's going on. Do you?"

"Yes, Mr. President."

"Then for God's sake, speak to us."

"Here's what I know for sure," she began. "Last night, the head of the FSB approached our ambassador in Moscow about this Plutonium. Of course, the ambassador knew nothing about it . . . since nobody saw fit to inform the State Department. So he was caught completely off-guard. Besides, coming from the FSB, he felt he had to question the veracity of what he'd heard. He told the FSB chief that he would get back to him. Undoubtedly the FSB man and Putin had a good laugh at the expense of the ambassador."

She gave the NSA and DCI another withering look, then went on. "Well, it was the middle of the night here, so the ambassador naturally thought the matter could wait until this morning. She shrugged her shoulders displaying the mood of some kind of victim.

She went on, "The FSB head returned within about 90 minutes and, in effect, told the ambassador that Putin had become incensed at the 'idiotic bureaucracy,' Putin's words, of trying to work with the U.S. on a mutually-beneficial international project. Namely to secure the Plutonium. Putin said, as a result of the U.S. bureaucracy being hopelessly inefficient, that he, Putin, would just call the President at noon, our time, today. And two men, who could make a decision and 'get off the pot,' as he put it, would move forward with international cooperation."

Nobody spoke, all waiting for the President to break the silence.

POTUS, smiled, "Well, Vladimir is playing games with us, but his assessment of our ability to get anything done looks spot on this morning. As a matter of fact, I look forward to his call."

Turning to his Chief of Staff, he said, "Please be sure my simultaneous translator is available. An hour ahead of time. Just in case the Kremlin's clocks may be on daylight savings time."

He walked to the door of the Oval Office and said, "The rest of you go back to whatever intrigues you're bollixing up this morning. Madam Secretary, let's you and me have a conference call with our ambassador."

The DCI spoke up, seeming frantic, "Mr. President, it's a trick. Putin has something up his sleeve to make us look foolish. Count on it."

The president pointed to the door as if to say, "Get out of here," and then he did say, "President Putin can hardly make us look more foolish than the CIA and National Security Agency already have today. And," he added, "if you continue thinking I'm a fool and incapable of dealing with Putin one-on-one, I can find someone who better understands the role of the CIA and its DCI.

"Good day, Gentlemen."

Chapter Sixteen

Planning

Austin
Van Pelt Industries' Headquarters—Hamilton Pool Road—January 2

The six of them—Nana, Josef, Monica, Lobo, Sanjay and Grey-cloud—sit in an upscale garage apartment that stands behind a luxurious English garden where the Van Pelt mansion was before being burned to the ground by vigilantes. The fire had taken the life of Nana's younger brother, Timothy Van Pelt, known to all as *Timmy*.

Since the fire, the headquarters for the worldwide operations of Van Pelt Industries had been moved to the apartment. Nana had taken command of the company and turned it into an international juggernaut.

Sitting around the spacious kitchen's table, they each read and reread the company's contract with the Russian gas company Rosneft. Monica read the Russian original while the others read the English translation.

Monica spoke first. "Let me see the fourth page in English," she said, turning to Lobo for his copy. She quickly ran her finger down to the fourth and fifth paragraphs, read them, and then said, "Just as I suspected. The English translation loses some specifics from the original Russian. I think I've found a loophole. I wish we had a lawyer here."

Nana raised her hand and smiled. "Present."

Monica, brought up short, told Nana to look at the paragraphs in question and then proceeded to translate from the Russian version into English. When she finished, she said, "Did you catch that? Do you see the discrepancy?" Regaining her composure, she said to Nana, "You really should have a *bona fide* translator look carefully at these foreign contracts before you sign them. This time, though, the differences work to our advantage."

Now everyone looked at the paragraphs while Monica once again translated. Josef stood quickly, whacked the table with his palm, and said, "Yes! We're in."

Greycloud looked serious and said, "If Custer had understood Sioux or Cheyenne, he wouldn't have had to ask, 'Where did all these fucking Indians come from?'"

Nana said, "Hold on just a moment," and went to her office. Within a couple of minutes she returned with what looked like a four-or five-page print-out from a mainframe printer. She said, 'I've got five other copies running right now. Josef, would you go get them, please?"

She looked at the first page, and then added, "And bring a half-dozen of those highlighters. I don't care what color."

While Josef was retrieving additional copies, she said to the four looking at her in anticipation, "What I have here is a real-time list of all Van Pelt Industries' hardware—ships, trucks, drilling rigs, everything as of today. The list also shows where the equipment is at the moment, as well as what contract it's assigned to. Today."

Joseph handed copies to Lobo, Greycloud, Sanjay and Monica, also passing around highlighters.

Follow me now," Nana said, "and highlight the lines I call out as we go. Top of page two, third line, see *USS Josef*? It's an ice breaker. And it's less than 700 miles from the Plutonium."

At the word "Plutonium," Josef put his index finger to his lips and retreated to the office where he flipped a switch. Returning, he said, "White noise is on." Turning to Nana, he continued, "You've got to remember to keep that thing going every time anybody in here is talking business."

The two of them had learned from Pavlovich's eavesdropping the true meaning of *Loose lips sink ships*. And right now, the discussion was exactly about ships.

Nana nodded, returning to the list. "Highlight that ship. She went on, "About halfway down the page, find *Pavlovich's Folly*. Highlight that one, too. "*Pavlovich's Folly* is a brand-new, shallow-water drilling rig, just commissioned in November from a shipyard in Japan. It's on its shakedown cruise from where it was built in Hokkaido. Today it's in the southern part of the Sea of Okhotsk. I just had a report last week that the rig is ready. Shakedown uneventful. Josef, how long?"

Josef engaged his laptop. "Five or six days," he said. "Seven at the most."

"Go Telex both ships. Tell the *USS Josef* to proceed to the Chukchi Sea north of the Bering Strait, send its coordinates to *Pavlovich's Folly*, and stand by to link up. Tell Captain Ruggles on the new rig to proceed to the Bering Strait ASAP and watch for coordinates from the *Josef*. Sign my name to the Telexes and advise them I'll be back to them with mission assignments in a day or two. It will take that long for them to converge, right?"

Josef nodded. "At least 30 to 36 hours."

Nana continued down the list, cherry picking a helicopter from Anchorage, biohazard and radiation-protection equipment and a vertical takeoff, twin-engine aircraft from winter storage in Vladivostok.

Most of the items selected listed themselves as part of one or another of the jobs awaiting April to resume the contract work for Rosneft.

A strategy and its tactics began to emerge. Sanjay and Greycloud were first to put the pieces together. Monica and Lobo were right behind him.

"So, Greycloud said, "I see everything here but two items."

"And those two are?" Monica asked.

Greycloud said, "A land-based crane or lifting device and some kind of lead-lined container to hold the basketball. We've got to lift it up and put it in something, don't we?

"Not necessarily," Josef said. "What if we just make it disappear?"

Lobo said, "I'm listening. And, while we're talking tactics, how do we get ourselves . . . those of us who are going . . . to the site within the next week?"

"Who's going?" Nana said.

Monica answered, "I need to get back to Langley to keep an ear to the ground in Sieve City, but I want to be on site to see the action. I'll go back tonight and be ready when you are." She nodded to Nana.

"I'm in," Greycloud. "And count on Gady, too, if Craig will let her go for a few days."

"Me, too," Lobo said.

Sanjay nodded.

"Then it's a go," Josef said. "Let's get Monica back to Washington." Turning to Monica, he said, "I'll try for a direct flight."

"No need, Josef," she answered, poking at her iPhone. She flashed the phone in his direction and said, "I'm reserved. But I'll need a ride to the airport."

Nana countered, "I can send you on one of our Gulfstreams, if you prefer."

"No, but thanks. Commercial flights won't raise any eyebrows at the Company, and I'm supposed to be back in the morning. I've already texted that I'm on my way."

She spoke toward Lobo and Greycloud. "Would you two fill in Craig and Gady this evening?"

They both nodded, and Josef said, "Either Nana or I should be there. We know the hardware and manpower resources." He paused. "But I don't want more than one copy of this printout leaving this kitchen. "I'll bring mine, and I'll run the rest of the copies through our shredder."

"Can we just meet here?" Lobo asked.

"Sure," Nana said. A thought apparently struck her. "May I please be the one to call Craig? I was just remembering those five shots we shared: A military .223, one 12-gauge shotgun, and three quick pops from a nine-millimeter Glock.

"The Glock I was holding.

"Pointed at Felix Pavlovich."

She stood abruptly and left the room.

Chapter Seventeen

Sometimes Changes Are Hard.
Sometimes They're Fun.

Pyongyang

Peoples Democratic Republic of Korea—A Park Bench—January 2

Chang Sung-taek arrived at the agreed-upon meeting place a few minutes early. He still had been unable to decide how he would prefer to proceed with Kim Jun Un's orders to capture the Plutonium. He could see no way out. He projected North Korea's chances of actually getting to, and then containing and returning the prize, to be less than 10 percent.

The First Chairman greatly overestimates his country's strengths as well as his own, he thought. He's sending us on a fool's mission that will surely end, if we're lucky, with just our own deaths. If we're not so lucky, the forces of the great Russian bear will come down on our country like a fog of poison gas. But, he continued listening to the voices in his head, if we don't even try . . . or if we fail . . . we might as well just wrap chains around ourselves and leap into the Yellow Sea.

As he sat despairing, Kwak Pum Ji stepped out of his official car at the curb and walked over to him. Chang noticed that Kwak had been driving the car himself. He knew they both had official drivers for their government cars. Spies, really. Assigned to keep track of their every move and report back to the SPA, the Supreme People's Assembly. Chang, and all of those of his rank, had learned to be wary of official drivers.

"Have you come to a decision yet?" Kwak asked as he sat down on a park bench next to Chang.

"I'm thinking still," Chang admitted. "Perhaps we should both just go and pick out our coffins this afternoon. We can't stall many more hours or we'll be dead, anyway. What form of execution do you prefer, Kwak? Firing squad? Poisoning? Eating our own pistols? How do you want to go?"

Kwak simply said, "South."

Chang, at first, didn't understand. "You want to go south?" he asked. "Tell me what you mean."

Kwak answered. "Did you notice I don't have my driver with me?" Not waiting for Chang to answer, he went on, "I told him I was just running a personal errand, and I would return in a couple of hours. I gave him a small assignment: checking the odometers and maintenance schedules on the two dozen vehicles assigned to our offices. That will take him a while."

"You're speaking of defection? Am I right?" Chang said.

"Yes, Chang. I see no other way. With my credentials, I can cross the border into South Korea without too much question. I've prepared a fake warrant and signed the name of the First Chairman to it. He's sending me to Seoul to confer about the level of arms in the DMZ. At least that's what the warrant says. What flunky at the border will question me?"

"Then you have made up your mind?' Chang said. "I don't know. What do you think the other side will do to you? Won't they shoot you? Or imprison you?"

"Not likely," Kwak said. "I know too much that they would also like to know. Besides, who's kidding whom? You know they all live like kings down there. Raging economy. Great lives. And what do you and I have to look forward to here?"

"A merciful death," Chang said. "Only if we're lucky." He paused, extended his hand to Kwak and said, "I wish for you, my friend, only the very best of luck. If you make it, send me a signal, and I will follow. There's nothing for me here."

"Why don't you just go with me today?" Kwak said. "We could go together. Now."

"No," Chang said. "Better that we go separately. Send me a signal, and I'll follow shortly."

"Okay, my friend," Kwak said. "Come on, I'll drop you off at your office."

Chang climbed into the front passenger seat of Kwak's official car. At the first intersection, Kwak turned left.

"Have you forgotten where my office is?" Chang said. "We're going the wrong way."

"No, Chang, I regret that you're the one going the wrong way." With that, he pulled out a small automatic with a silencer screwed into the barrel and shot Chang three times in the left side.

Kwak spoke to his dying companion. "You thought you would rush back and report my imminent defection. And that would gain you favor with that lunatic Kim. You're off the hook, and I'm met at the border with a dozen or more machine guns."

He paused and pulled over to be sure Chang was dead. "Before they find you, I will be drinking champagne in Seoul."

With that he headed south out of Pyongyang, resolving to throw Chang's body out somewhere where it wouldn't be found for days. If ever.

Vancouver, British Columbia
Fairmont Vancouver Hotel January 3—In the Afternoon

True to his word, Four had quickly left Banff yesterday, taking the transcontinental Canadian Railway to Vancouver near the Pacific coast. He sat in the bar of the Fairmont Vancouver Hotel, one laptop open and working, the other plugged in to recharge. He noticed he was virtually alone at mid-afternoon, so he decided to get on with his three million dollar assignment,

Earlier he had learned that there are 54 patent offices in 48 countries around the world. He was only interested in one. The United States Patent Office within the Commerce Department in Washington, D.C.

Four changed his seat so his back and his screen faced an outside wall. One with no windows. He ordered another drink, and after the waiter brought him his Glenlivet, three fingers and one ice cube, he began his search. Cracking the Commerce Department computers would be easy enough. Once inside, he would move to the Patent Office, rip through whatever firewalls he found there, and download the patent filing for the entire engineering plans and equipment to produce a Fusion-Fission processor.

That would be the prize. His prize. As he worked his way into the government computers, he decided to make a small change in the scheme he had left with the three billionaires in Banff. *They may have gone back to whatever rocks they crawled out from under last week*, he thought.

Rather than send the file to their computers, he would send them a simple message.

A multi-tasker who could think and work on several different things simultaneously, Four continued with his hacking assignment as he silently composed that message:

To my esteemed single-digit colleagues,

I have the prize. And I have received the 30 pieces of silver you were to send. Thank you. Small change in plans. Before you go berserk and do something foolish, let me assure you that the change is to protect all of you. From one another. I have spent enough time with you to see clearly that any one of you would snuff out the other two given half a chance. Rest assured that I will deliver as I promised. As you have delivered as you promised.

There will be a message left for each of you at the registration desk of the Fairmont Vancouver Hotel. In each of your messages, I will tell each of you how to find one-third of the entire file you so desperately want. One caveat. The messages can be picked up in person only by the three of you . . . together. So hie yourselves en masse to Vancouver, British Columbia.

I wish you whatever success you deserve. No tricks. Everything you want will be where I have left it for you.

Goodbye.

I'll watch for you in the news. And I'll also check the obituaries.

Sincerely,
Your former best friend,

Four

Chapter Eighteen

Deluding the Delusional

Salt Desert, Northeast Iran
Top Secret Underground Laboratory—January 4

Keeping Haji Khan, the mad physicist, asleep for almost 40 hours had posed no particular problem. From his apartment in Addis Ababa all the way to the underground laboratory, he had slept soundly. But according to the dosages he was supposed to have been given, he should have started to wake up 90 minutes ago, shortly after he arrived at the Salt Desert. A nurse had checked his vital signs twice in the last hour and pronounced him "fit, but groggy."

As far as Mahmood Bijahn cared, the "fit" was good news, but the "groggy" seemed to be heading toward the perpetual. Bijahn, sitting by the scientist's bed in a darkened room, lit only by a small night light on the wall above Khan's headboard, had tried cold water, hot and sweet coffee, even a slap or two to the face.

Still, Khan kept snoring.

The head of the Republican Guard for the area stepped into the room. Though it was mostly dark, he glowed in his gold-braided uniform with three rows of shiny medals across his left breast. His insignias identified him as a colonel.

"What's the holdup?" He asked Bijahn. "Is he okay?"

"All I can think of, Sir," Bijahn said, "is perhaps those administering the sedatives may have overestimated his weight. His mass. He's not all that big underneath all that clothing. I expect he weighs no more than 55 kilos."

"I take it that you are Mahmood Bijahn?" the colonel said.

"Yes, I've been assigned to monitor Khan, to try to keep him on an even keel. He has serious mental problems, as you probably know."

The colonel said, "Join me down the hallway for a cup of tea, Mahmood."

"Am I allowed to leave Khan unattended?" Bijahn asked.

The colonel said, "I'll send a nurse to sit with him. You and I have things to talk about. Important things for the future of Iran and the Persian people. Come on."

Bijahn followed the colonel past a nurses' station where the Republican Guard official politely asked one of two nurses to sit with Khan. Bijahn detected the colonel started to use the word "prisoner," but instead corrected himself, saying "scientist" instead.

The colonel led Khan's minder to a small break room with four tables. A complete tea service rested on the table nearest the door, and the colonel sat at that table and motioned Bijahn to one of its chairs.

While the colonel checked to see that the dark tea had been properly steeped and began pouring them both a cup, Bijahn asked, "What can I do for you tonight, Colonel?" He added, apologetically, "I haven't been able to wake Haji, and I suspect he may sleep a lot longer than we planned."

"You must be tired, Bijahn," the colonel said. "I've kept up with your activities over the past 48 hours. Unless you slept on the flight from Ethiopia to Tehran, you've been going nonstop. When we finish our talk here, why don't you grab some sleep?"

Bijahn frowned. "Sir," he said, "I've been told how important it has become for Khan to be awake and fully functional by morning. If I leave him to catch some sleep myself, I can promise he won't even wake up before morning. And then it may take me several hours to re-orient him, to get his senses and awareness headed in the right direction. I've been doing this for months. He won't be ready to do anything useful tomorrow at all."

The colonel asked, "Who told you to have him ready tomorrow morning?"

"The medics who brought me here in their air ambulance from Tehran."

The colonel nodded. "Ah, yes. But let's be clear; between you and me, I'm in charge of this part of the operation. And it's just as important for you to be fully rested before you have to surround his . . . what do you call it? His aberrations?"

Colonel, I'm told by the physicians that Haji is bi-polar and that he must be continually medicated to keep him from either slipping into a deep depression or becoming insanely manic. They say it's treatable, but his condition is apparently severe. He's like a pendulum. If he swings too far to the depressive side, or too far to the manic side, it's likely that days will be lost getting him back on a straight track. I'm assuming we don't have the time for those delays to be allowed to occur."

"Bijahn, let me fill you in a bit more. Dr. Khan will be assisted by two Iranian nuclear specialists. But he will be told they are jihadist professors, and that he's in a secret facility in Somalia. Here, we're 200 feet underground. There are no windows. Television monitors in his work area will appear to pan the exterior landscape, as if it were a security camera. Birds will fly by, ships will pass, and the stationary palm trees will flutter occasionally from breezes off the sea.

Television sets inside will broadcast news and programming, all pre-recorded, of course, as if from Mogadishu.

"If no one has told you, Bijahn," the Republican Guard officer continued, "you are just as critical to the success of our work as Dr. Khan, himself."

He looked directly at a somewhat startled Mahmood Bijahn, and then finished his thought. "And why is that? Because you are the person who can, and must, keep his pendulum, as you described it, from swinging too far in either direction. And particularly to the depressive side. I'm told when he becomes depressed, he becomes obsessed with his scientific side, and then his more manic jihadist tendencies simply disappear. Is that not correct?"

"Yes, Sir, that is precisely correct, as I've reported regularly to my controller in Tehran. It's a delicate balance, but I've managed to keep him within what I like to think of as a 30-degree arc of the pendulum. If his moods swing no more than about 15 degrees either way, I can keep him fixed on a desired target."

Mahmood thought a moment, and then added, "I've worked with him for months, and I think I know how to keep him focused. I'm not sure anybody else could just walk in and be able to maintain the same balance."

The colonel, sipping his tea, reached and tapped Bijahn on the arm. "That's why, Mahmood, you're as important as he is. He's worthless to us if he goes off the rails. Nobody knows that better than you. And none of the rest of us can recognize the warning signs of an impending swing nearly as well as you.

"We need you to monitor his every waking minute. And that means you will need to rest when he's sleeping. That's another reason why you're just as important as he is. Do you have questions?"

Bijahn said, "I have one major concern and a few questions, Sir."

"Go ahead, Mahmood. Consider yourself the ultimate insider here. You're welcome to any information I have. I won't burden you with updates unless and until you want to know. So what is your concern?"

Mahmood answered, "I cannot predict where his mind will be when he wakes up. Nor can I be sure how long it will take to assess his moods and then make the necessary corrections. Once the corrections are made, I can guarantee results within minutes, literally. So what I'm saying is this: If he wakes up early in the morning as I expect, he may be ready to be productive in an hour or two. Or it may take half a day or more. So, if you will, Sir, what is the expected target timetable?"

"You can relax on that concern," the colonel said. "Let me reassure you. I personally would hope to be able to give you three or four days just to get him acclimated and comfortable with the idea that you have delivered him to a laboratory facility in Somalia. When you're ready, you can introduce the two scientists he will be told are jihadists. Bring them into the picture at whatever pace you think appropriate. In other words, you will control the timetable."

The colonel looked at his watch, "I see we've just passed midnight. So it is now January 5. If you could have him ready to begin mechanical and machine shop preparations to build, let's say, six bombs initially, within three weeks or so, that would be perfect. So take your time. We have an expedition on its way to collect the fissionable material. That collection is not going to be a swift process, as you might imagine.

"I would not expect to see any of it here before early in February at the earliest. So let's suppose he can be sharp, focused, and ready to assemble the bombs by mid-February. I have no idea how long that assembly process will take. But once we have the material here, what difference does it make? We've been working for years already. Khan holds the key.

"In case you're not aware, his deportation and the stripping of his credentials was a calculated plan to reassure the nuclear powers that we want no part of making nuclear weapons. We deported, in disgrace, the one Iranian whom we think can get us to where we want to be—as a ruse. And we sent you along later to be sure we knew where he would be when we had the materials to proceed with what we know he can do."

Bijahn said, "I suspected as much, but was told that the less I understood, the better it would be to do my job."

The colonel said, "That was then; this is now. You, my friend, are a key player in gaining for us the respect Iran and the ancient Persian empire is entitled to. Now, go get some sleep. If Khan wakens to the point he's halfway lucid, one of the nurses will fetch you. Meantime, get some rest. I'll see you for lunch tomorrow."

"If I can leave Haji," Bijahn said.

Chapter Nineteen

The Emperor Has No Clothes.
And No Sense, Either.

Pyongyang—Ryongsong Residence—January 2

The military guards surrounding Kim Jung Un's primary residence stood at a stiff parade rest, seeming to have either been painted in place or to have been suffering from far too much starch in their uniforms. They were the only people visible outside the residence. Even the guard dogs lay prone next to the closest wall, looking for all the world as if they were dead.

Inside, every member of the house staff hid. In closets. In pantries, under stairwells. An eerie silence had descended over the whole interior. Nobody dared breathe audibly.

From the basement, though, shouts emerged, getting ever louder. The sounds of heavy objects being thrown against walls and smashed into floors waxed and waned in volume like bad sound effects in an old black and white war movie.

The First Chairman had just learned that the mission he'd ordered yesterday had fallen in a ditch somewhere. Actually the somewhere was a ditch. A ditch about halfway between Pyongyang and the Democratic People's Republic of Korea's border with the South. That's where soldiers on leave from the infamous DMZ had found the bullet-riddled body of Chang Sung-taek, vice chairman of the country's National Defense Council.

To make Kim even more furious, Kwak Pum Ji, Minister of People's Security, had turned up missing. At least his office and subordinates refused to admit they knew where he might be or how to find him.

All of this information had been provided by telephone to the First Chairman. Nobody in his or her right mind dared to hand deliver bad news to Kim. More than one completely innocent bearer of bad news had been ordered executed. Forthwith.

Until Kwak could be located, Kim would not be calmed. He had ordered a mission, and one of the two he had sent forth had somehow failed, ending up dead. *What to do? What to do?* Kim thought. He would never utter those kinds of thoughts aloud. Everybody knew he was in absolute control at all times. *They damn well better know that,* he thought some more.

In truth, Kim was too young and inexperienced to know how to proceed or who to order to move forward with the obviously off-track mission. In his confusion, he shouted orders to go to Siberia to any underling he could locate, and when he couldn't find any more underlings at whom to shout, he became even more furious.

The duty officer in charge of the evening's guards made a quick exit from his normal office inside the palace to the guard house at the main entrance. Two startled guards at their posts asked him why he seemed to be in such a hurry. His only response, "Kim's pissed," provided all the explanation needed. They welcomed him inside and shared hot tea with him. He simply said, "Don't answer any calls from inside."

South of the DMZ—South Korea—At the Same Time

A South Korean military helicopter sat down softly in a field next to the highway that led to Seoul. Kwak, held in restraints in a military SUV, knew it had come for him. When he had surrendered to the Officer of the Day on the south side of the border, he had been disarmed, handcuffed and leg restraints had been placed on his ankles. The South Korean military officer had told Kwak not to speak. To say nothing. The officer's .45 automatic, held loosely in his right hand, had spoken just as loud to Kwak, The officer had reported the voluntary defection, and the now-landing helicopter had been dispatched with both a lawyer and troops to take him the rest of the way to Seoul, where what he knew would be either a long debriefing or a quick execution.

Meantime, Kwak's cell phone had been confiscated, and each time it rang, a South Korean communications officer noted the number of the caller. He did not answer any of the calls.

Kwak was somewhat gratified that the whole process had been carried out efficiently and politely. *At least, if they are going to kill me,* he thought, *it's not going to be before I get on that helicopter.* Kwak, mentally exhausted, wondered if he were thinking clearly. He didn't really believe he would be executed by the South Koreans, even after he had told them everything they wanted to know and a few more things he could make up—if he had to.

But he knew one thing for sure. Back in the People's Democratic Republic, he would soon be a dead man. Not literally, but Kim would spread the word that the defector was an imposter conjured up by the South Koreans. He would say he knew that because he, personally, the First Chairman, had executed Kwak with a bullet to the back of the head.

That lunatic will even arrange a funeral for me, he thought.

The lawyer, having come out of the helicopter to confer briefly with the Officer of the Day and the Communications Officer while Kwak was led from the SUV to the 'copter, asked, "How can we know for sure? Right now, I mean, that this guy is who he says he is?"

Holding up Kwak's phone, which he handed over to the lawyer, the Communications Officer said, "Looks like he's for real. In the past 45 minutes, he's had seven calls from the offices of People's Security. And in the last 25 minutes, he's had 15 calls originating at the Ryongsong Residence, Kim Jung-Un's private lair."

As Kwak, three military guards and the lawyer started to board the helicopter, Kwak's phone rang again. Glancing at the caller ID on the screen, the communications officer said, "That's the palace."

To everyone's amazement, the lawyer, a colonel in the South Korean Army, simply answered the phone. Not with any greeting, but rather with a terse statement: "You are speaking to a South Korean military attorney. I am just South of the DMZ, where Kwak Pum Ji has just defected and surrendered. He is in custody now, and he will not be able to speak with you."

He clicked off to the sound of a primal scream.

Back at the Ryongsong Residence

Monitors in the guard house at the entrance to the palace suddenly erupted with the sound of automatic weapons fire, accompanied by screams that were worthy of an enraged bull elephant.

"He's shooting the place up," one of the guards said.

The duty officer responded, "Grab your riot gear and the tranquilizer gun. Be sure your vests are secure and your face plates are down. Once again, we'll have to give him a sleeping dart."

He paused, and then said as if to reassure the two guards, "Don't worry, this isn't our first dance. He won't remember this in the morning."

Chapter Twenty

The Wheels of Progress Turn Slow. And Fast.

The White House—Oval Office—January 3

POTUS had banished everyone from the Oval Office except the Secretary of State, his simultaneous translator, Oksana Stotska, and his chief of staff. The four of them chatted quietly, waiting for the expected call from Vladimir Putin.

The President said to the translator, "Oksana, are you comfortable being able to pick up on Vladimir's subtleties—that is, to read between the lines to figure out what he's really up to?"

Oksana answered, "Yes, of course, Mr. President. If he's trying to slip something over on you, I'm sure I'll catch it. But," she added, "he might just have something to say you'll be interested in hearing. We'll see. How about this? If I wave my arms in the air, that will mean be cautious. He's up to something."

The Secretary of State said, "There's one more person we could use during this call. She's CIA, head of the Russian desk. She's due back from a holiday trip to Texas; the DCI would shoot me for even thinking these thoughts. But the fact is that Monica Skrabacz knows Putin as well as, or better than, anyone in government. Maybe we can run a recording of the conversation by her tomorrow . . . if you'll clear it with the DCI."

"Her name came up when this matter first surfaced," POTUS said. "I have the impression the DCI doesn't trust her and wants to keep her out of the loop."

"The DCI trusts nobody, Mr. President. I know. He's kept me and my entire staff 'out of the loop,' so to speak. And that's already put us at a disadvantage." She paused, "Do we know for sure what Putin wants to talk about?"

The chief of staff said, "No, not for sure. We've assumed it likely has something to do with this Plutonium. But he could be just letting us know that he's about to send troops into Latvia and Estonia. He's not going to be satisfied until he's reclaimed the former Soviet satellite countries. Or at least a piece of them, like Ukraine."

He paused, and then added, "Or it might be a complete surprise."

At the word "surprise," the President looked up. "Let's surprise him," he said. "Get him on the line first. We'll just exercise a little Western preemption for a change."

Austin—Van Pelt Industries Headquarters—Early Evening.—January 2

With Monica on her way back to Washington, Gady and I joined Lobo, Greycloud, Nana and Josef in the kitchen of Nana's garage apartment.

Josef had spent the time between meetings laying out a timeline that also included the various resources that Van Pelt Industries was prepared to use along the way. He spread out an enlarged copy on the table and began to follow the timeline left to right, explaining each step.

"Today is January 2," he began. "We have both the ice breaker and the shallow-water drilling rig headed for a rendezvous north of the Bering Strait. They should be together and ready to begin moving toward the target here," he pointed to January 8. "Give them eight or nine days to reach the shores off the Laptev Sea, here." He pointed to a spot immediately north of the target Plutonium.

"Meanwhile, Nana will be communicating with Rosneft and Novatek that we're conducting both an extended shake-down cruise of the new shallow-water driller and an experiment to see if it might be possible to continue exploration and drilling in Siberia year 'round."

He looked at Nana, who said, "They'll buy it. We've discussed the possibilities several times. Even speculated on an experimental run."

John Greycloud said, "Then that will put us in close proximity to the Plutonium by the week of January 13. What happens from there?"

Nana went into a detailed explanation of the plan she and Josef had concocted, ending with, "So by January 15 or so, I'll advise our contract holders that we've learned some useful things, and by January 20, at the latest, the Plutonium will no longer be there and our crews and ships will be headed back to northern Japan."

"Ingenious," I said. "You're sure it will work?"

Nana gave me a grave look. "It better work, or Van Pelt Industries is finished with the Russian Federation."

Gady couldn't resist offering an idea. "We should leave a message," she said. "Anonymously, of course. I can see the late-comers reading it now." She laughed.

I told them once again there was no way I could be gone that long, but that Gady would be able to go if I approved a short leave.

Josef surprised us all. "None of us is going to the site," he said. "Except maybe Sanjay. I talked to him this afternoon, and he's cleared his calendar. If he needs to be on site, we'll fly him to Anchorage and then on to Hokkaido. Then we'll helicopter him to the ice breaker. He could be on board by the 8th of the month, and that'll give him time to do some training for the crews about handling highly radioactive stuff . . . if he thinks that would be useful."

""What about the rest of us?" Greycloud asked.

"None of us has any particular skills that will be helpful," Josef said. "Ship's quarters are cramped, and we'd just be in the way. My choice would be that we go to our offices in Seoul where we can watch live television footage of exactly what's happening."

He saw puzzled looks, so he added, "We could do that from here. But I, for one, want to be in the vicinity so we can greet the returning ships and crack a case or two of champagne."

"You're not old enough to drink," Nana said with a wry smile.

"I *am* in Seoul," Josef shot back.

Out of curiosity, I asked, "Where else besides Seoul do you have offices?"

Nana said, "North Dakota, Anchorage, Moscow, Dubai, Glasgow and Johannesburg. These are small administrative outposts that manage the exploration and drilling work in those regions. In case something goes wrong, I don't think Moscow would be the best place to be. In fact, I'll be calling our two employees in Moscow back to the Glasgow office for the week of January 13. Just in case."

I thought a moment. "So we'll have a real-time look at progress?"

"Absolutely," Nana said.

"Then I want to go to Seoul to see the actual removal. I can take a day to get there and a day to return . . . only if the removal can be done on a Sunday. That's Sunday here, Monday there. That way, I can just take one day off and not upset Chief Garza." I thought and added, "Saturday would work, too."

Greycloud shot me a dubious look. I was almost certain he was about to tell me one of his Navajo tales about how not to upset the boss. But, instead, he just said, "Craig, I'll talk to you later. You suffer from biligaa-na-itis. But I have a cure."

I'm sure you do, I thought.

Back in the White House—January 2

At the President's request, the White House operators had placed the call to President Putin of the Russian Federation. The chief of staff put the President's phone on speaker. After Oksana explained the call to them, Kremlin operators rang directly into Putin's office.

"Da," Putin said.

"Mr. Putin," The President said. "This is the President of the United States. I understand you want to talk with me."

"How did you know that?" Putin said.

"You told our ambassador last night."

"Oh, yes, that was Boris."

"What can I do for you?"

"Well, this is certainly a surprise. You've pre-empted me. Once again," Putin said.

The President said, "You, Sir, are the master of preemption. I just wanted to see how it feels to be a half-step ahead of you for once."

Putin laughed. "So let's get down to business. We're both busy."

"What's on your mind besides world domination?" the President asked lightheartedly.

"We have a situation. I'm pretty sure you're aware of it by the way your cultural affairs officer in your embassy here is snooping around. We all know he's a spy, by the way. CIA."

The Secretary of State shrugged.

The President saw another opportunity for preemption. "You're speaking of the Plutonium in Siberia, I expect?"

This time the Secretary of State shot bolt upright and pulled a finger across her throat. *If that's not why he's wanting to talk we've just blown it, big time,* she thought.

But Putin said, "Yes. Most inconvenient. We're concerned, as I'm sure you are, that it not fall into the wrong hands."

"Though you would sell it to Iran," the President challenged.

"Please, Mr. President, Let's not get tacky. I have a better idea."

"I'm all ears, Vladimir. What do you propose?"

"So, what if your country and mine worked together to capture the Plutonium and keep it from the wrong hands. It's a bit of a nuisance to us, and I'm guessing the U.S. really doesn't want it either."

At this, both Oksana and the Secretary of State stood and waved their hands in the air wildly. The President acknowledged their waving with a sit-down point of his index finger.

"How do you propose we do this? Cooperatively, I mean," the President asked.

Putin laughed. "That's not for you and me to decide. We have 'people' for things like that. Why not let your DCI meet with Boris, my FSB minion. Let the two of them figure it out. And, oh, by the way, think about whether to include a few other countries in the mission. Sort of a worldwide show of goodwill and cooperation."

"You surprise me, Vladimir. I should have thought you'd want this to be a big secret. At least until it's completed."

"Secrecy?" Putin said. "Secrecy is a Western weapon, Mr. President. The Russian Federation has nothing to hide from the world."

At that, the President waved both hands in the air and smiled. Then he said, "I'll have the DCI contact your Boris. Let's you and I stay in touch."

Putin said, "Yes, let's talk one more time when our people have a plan ready to go. And I do agree we should keep a lid on this until it's done. Or about to be done. Maybe some press coverage of the removal, itself, wouldn't hurt either one of us. Good-bye. Mr. President. We'll talk again soon."

"Good-bye, Mr. Putin. And thank you for the call."

"You made the call."

"Right."

The President stood and held up both palms. "I know what all three of you are about to say. But can it. He may be playing games. But maybe he's not. We'll just have to see."

The Secretary of State spoke calmly. "Mr. President, I demand to be included in the entire process. The DCI alone should not be left to his own devices while State is left out in the cold, not knowing what the hell's going on."

The President excused Oksana with a "Thank you" and an unnecessary admonition not to discuss the call. He said, "We'll keep this to a small group. And we will, and I emphasize will, keep this under wraps. You and I, the DCI and the NSA—the four of us. And I will insist that any discussions with the Russians include both DCI and NSA. You don't want State in discussions at that level, do you?"

"No, not a good idea. But I want to be kept up to speed. And I mean concurrently."

"Done," the President said. He turned to his chief of staff. "Let's get DCI and NSA in here at 5:00 this afternoon."

With that, the Secretary of State rose to leave. "Thank you, Mr. President." She said.

"Any time, Madame Secretary. Any time."

Part Three

Action!

Chapter Twenty-One

When the Cat's Away

Langley, Virginia—CIA Headquarters—January 4

After arriving at Reagan National Airport in Washington, D.C. last night, Monica had taken a cab to her apartment in Alexandria and attempted to look over any emails and messages she might have received while she was on her way home. She found nothing, which simply could not possibly be right. In fact, she was not even able to get into her Company files at all. "Access Denied" popped up each time she tried even to open her Company email. She knew codes and passwords were changed periodically and with little notice. But she suspected the firewall blocking her at the moment wasn't a simple code change.

Something was up.

After sleeping restlessly, Monica had gotten up early and come into her office before 7:00 a.m. where she found no notice of code and password changes. And still no way to get into her usual files. Now she knew something was up. And she became furious.

When was the last time she'd opened her email? Yesterday morning from Austin. No problem then. *Something happened yesterday,* she thought. *I've been shut down.*

She checked her watch to be sure the IT wizards would be in, and then called downstairs. Explaining her dilemma, she waited for an explanation.

"No problem, Ms. Skrabacz," the IT tech said. "Just give me a new password and we'll have you back on line in a jiffy." Her call had clearly been expected, and the response was just as clearly rehearsed.

"Let's go with *Monica4prez,*" she said. "Now get me going."

"We'll have you back up right away. Try again in about 15 minutes," the tech said.

Monica, still furious, said, "Oh, no, I'll hold on. You do your magic, tell me when, and I'll check it out before I hang up."

"If you say so," the tech said. "Hold on, then."

This guy is not a trained field agent, Monica thought. That canned answer was a little too pat. "Are you still there?" she said into what sounded like a dead line.

"Yes, Ma'am. I won't hang up on you."

"You better not. I know where you are, and I'd just as soon come down there and separate you from your balls as sit here too long."

"Yes, Ma'am. I'm working on it."

Following a two-minute pause, the IT tech said, "Okay, try it now."

"You stay on the line," Monica ordered as she went to work on her keyboard. And there it was. Both files opened right up. But there was nothing prior to Christmas Eve on either her email or her master files.

"You listen to me, and you listen good," she said to the IT. "I can get into my emails and my files, but all the historical files have been removed. Where the hell are they?"

The IT stuttered, and Monica heard him shuffling papers, scrambling as if looking for something on his work desk. *A script, maybe?* she thought.

"Oh, yes, I'd forgotten," the tech said. "It's just a matter of periodic purging. We did that at year end. All your files are still around. In storage, sort of," he said.

"Then how do I get to them?" Monica said.

"You, yourself, don't. But if you will tell me specifically what you want from your old files, I'll be glad to retrieve it and forward it to you."

Monica counted to ten. "Okay, find me an email message from me to the head of IT the day before Thanksgiving in which I tell the whole bunch of you assholes to go fuck yourselves!" She slammed down the phone.

Immediately she grabbed her directory and punched in the number for the CIA secure phone in the basement of the U.S. embassy in Moscow. Normally she would remember that number, but in her frustrated state, she didn't want to end up talking to the embassy switchboard with a misdial. She knew Moscow was eight hours ahead and it would be 4:00 p.m. there. But she also knew the time of day didn't matter. That phone, in the soundproof kiosk in the basement at the embassy, would be answered at any hour, any day.

As expected, a Marine noncom answered after the first ring using the standard answer he had been told to use this week. "You have reached the zookeeper. How may I direct your call?"

"This is Monica Skrabacz on the Russian Desk at Langley. I need to speak at once to the cultural affairs officer."

"Yes, Ma'am. I'll connect you," the Marine said.

"No, no," Monica said. "I need you to get him to take my call right there, in the booth where you're sitting. This call involves national security."

"Yes, Ma'am. Stand by, please."

Monica, and everybody in the embassy, knew that the Russians worked diligently to eavesdrop on any and all conversations within its walls, spoken or by phone. That's precisely what the booth is the basement was for. There could be absolutely no interception of anything said inside it.

Instead of the usual elevator music one might hear on hold, Monica heard the expected random electronic tones and blips. They had something to do with the security of the line. She didn't know what, and she didn't care. The line met its intended purpose. That was enough information.

"Carrot Top, this is Peppermint Stick. How can I help you?" The voice on the line used both Monica's and his most recent field code names. He, in fact, remained Peppermint Stick, though Monica's code had been changed to Bear Desk, a direct reference to her new position inside Company headquarters.

"Hello, Roland," she said. "What have you heard from the Kremlin? Anything about a special kind of surprise in Siberia?"

"You mean the Plutonium?" he asked. "As far as the embassy is concerned, I know the ambassador finally heard about it late last night . . . from the Secretary of State herself. But he was already pissed, because the DCI and NSA had failed to include State in their little game. And get this. The DCI called me personally a few hours ago and filled me in. At least I know what's up to a certain extent. But you obviously haven't heard the latest."

"What's that, Roland?"

"Putin and POTUS talked on the phone yesterday. One on one, if you can believe that. Something's cooking between the Company and the FSB, and the NSA and State are involved. But nobody, and I mean nobody, knows what the hell's going on. Do you?"

"Not yet," Monica said. "Let me ask you a question. Were your codes and access parameters changed a few days ago?"

"No. Why do you ask?"

"Just to confirm something, Roland," Monica said.

"What's that?"

"That a bunch of political appointees and petty bureaucrats are attempting to deal with the Plutonium on their own—without anybody who can find his ass with both hands and a mirror on board."

She paused. "I've been cut out of the loop, Roland. Put in for leave and come back here. You and I have some parties to crash."

"God help us all," Roland said.

And Monica knew he meant it

Chapter Twenty-Two

The Invisible Man

Martim Vaz Islands—Where Nobody Cares What Time it is—January 5

Four sailors shoved off on a 52-foot launch of the Brazilian Navy from a short pier on the rocky coast of a tiny island in the South Atlantic: Trinidade and Martim Vaz, an archipelago barely north of the Tropic of Capricorn and 750 miles east of the Brazilian port of Vitória.

In the scheme of world geography, Trinidade and Martim Vaz are tiny. With a land mass of four square miles, it's the home of 32 human inhabitants, all Brazilian sailors, lots of birds, and more volcanic rocks and up-thrusts than the Brazilian sailors stationed there care to count.

The three enlisted men aboard knew only that they had been ordered to Vitória to pick up a passenger in two or three days. So they were curious. The helmsman, after setting the twin diesel throttles at 90 percent power and charting a course almost due west, asked the officer in charge, "Lieutenant, why are we going today? Our normal monthly run for supplies and equipment was just last week. What's up?"

The Lieutenant, realizing that this run had not been labeled "secret," said, "We have a passenger to pick up on Tuesday the 7th. Right now I don't know much. But he apparently is some kind of computer wizard the Marinha do Brasil has hired on a contract to give us access to advanced communication hardware and software. He's supposed to be with us for about six months . . . or however long it takes to bring us up to snuff. You know we're a decade behind the rest of the world. So I'm looking forward to getting him aboard."

The helmsman gave the officer an incredulous look. He said, "Does this guy have a clue about where we're going to take him? The 32 of us are there because the Marinha put us there. You know it's not an assignment anybody except a genuine masochist would look forward to. What's the guy's story?"

"He may be a masochist, Chief, but we know he's a geek. I was told that in his contract he asked not to be returned to the mainland until his work here is finished, except in case of a medical emergency."

"Well," the helmsman said, "Martim Vaz will make him as crazy as the rest of us."

"It would make a great prison. Or just a place to get away from the world and hole up for a while," the Lieutenant said.

Fairmont Riviera Maya—Quintana Roo
Where Nobody Else Cares What Time it is—January 5

Four, registered as Señor Cuatro, sat in a cabaña, sipping a cold drink and watching turquoise waves roll into the white sand beach on the eastern Mexican coast south of Cancún. Tomorrow he would visit the Mayan pyramids in the jungle behind him.

Why not have a little fun along the way? he rationalized. *After all, in two days you'll be heading to one of the most remote and inaccessible places on the earth.*

Four had spent some time researching places to hide out for a while. Places to hide long enough for both the authorities and the billionaires to stop searching. And for him to change his identity forever and to find a paradise where he could do as he damned well pleased with their three million dollars. What could be better than Brazil, with no easily accomplished extradition treaties? But he knew that would be the first place he might be suspected of going. So he devised yet another human firewall— his contract with the Brazilian Navy that would send him to Trinidade and Martim Vaz for at least six months.

The pay was lousy, but with his money from the billionaires safely deposited in the Caymans and Switzerland, he didn't need money. At the island where he would be working, there was no place to spend any money, anyway. Free food and shelter from the navy. And nothing to do but what he loved best—hacking and building software that would defy anybody else from hacking. He knew he was king, and he wanted to stay that way.

"The navy will love me," he thought. He knew well that the billionaires would not.

Love him, that is.

He'd found the tracking device they had slipped into the case he carried one of his laptops in—the canvas cover with the handle. Thinking that action the worst kind of clumsiness, he'd shipped the cover, stuffed with tissue paper, to a fictitious person and address in Oslo, Norway. Either somebody would receive a surprise package, or that package would sit in a dead storage bin for years. In either Oslo or the U.S. And, if he was lucky, the inept billionaires might send somebody to Scandinavia looking for him.

If he had even more luck, they would run into unfriendly trolls of the forest instead.

Real trolls. Not Facebook contrarians.

Sure, he'd screwed with them. Just a little. As promised, he'd delivered the complete blueprints for the fusion-fission process. With one minor exception. He'd sent it in three pieces. And he'd held back one critical operation. Their scientists would spot the problem within a week or two, and eventually they would be able to fill in the blanks. Any capable physicist would be able to do that.

He sat now watching the waves, and the tourists splashing in them, pondering why he had really held back just a bit. At first he thought maybe he would get back to them in a week or so, and when they demanded the missing piece, he'd collect another million or two. But he knew that wasn't his real reason for messing with them.

No, he just didn't like the bastards. It was immense fun to mess with them. To say, "You rich sons-of-bitches can't have everything you want just handed to you. Your money might make you more money, but I, Señor Cuatro, formerly a poor and wanted hacker, can fuck with you. Slow you down."

In his heart, he hoped the patent's real developers would be able to beat the billionaires at their own game, leaving them having spent a measurable piece of their fortunes, ending up too late to the fair.

More importantly, he would have them using up a larger measurable portion of their lives, and that would serve the bastards right.

After the pyramids on January 6, he would fly from Cancún to Mexico City, then on to Rio and a shuttle flight from there north to Vitória where he would meet his new companions for a two-day ride to Martim Vaz. And to the no-challenge project that would keep him anonymous and safe until mid-summer. By then, he would have found his more permanent residence, and he would move on.

Meanwhile, his millions were growing steadily.

Robinson Crusoe has nothing on Señor Cuatro! He thought.

Chapter Twenty-Three

Iranian Irony

Underground Laboratory—Salt Desert, Iran—January 6

Haji Khan woke after three days, thinking he was in Somalia. And thinking he'd slept overnight when, in fact, the sedation had kept him asleep for 74 hours.

Looped video screens depicting a Somalian seashore masqueraded as windows in his room and in the main laboratory confirmed the fake location for a man still dazed from massive doses of sleep-inducing drugs.

When Khan woke up at 6:30 a.m., Mahmood Bijahn came immediately to his bedside to be sure the charade went just as planned.

"Good morning, Haji," Bijahn said. "You've slept all night. I've brought you into the Al-Shabaab machine shop as I promised I would. After we've had some breakfast, I'll show you the lab. It's perfect. You're going to love it. And, best of all, the assistants you asked for are here, too, and waiting for your instructions. We can go ahead with all the preparations while Al-Shabaab retrieves the Plutonium you'll need to finish the bombs."

Khan rubbed his eyes, sat up and said, "I have to pee."

At the Same Time—Niavarin Palace—Tehran, Islamic Republic of Iran

The head of the country's Republican Guard joined President Rouhani in Grand Ayatollah Ali Khamenei's office where the three sipped strong tea and nibbled on Nan Gerodooee cookies and Morala-yeh Beh Jam.

The Supreme Leader asked, "Have the two of you come up with a plan yet?"

Rouhani looked to the Republican Guard's leader, who said, "Yes. The lunatic scientist Khan now resides in the Salt Desert Laboratories, although he believes he is in Somalia. Mahmood Bijahn and my people there will continue to make him think he's in mobile machine shops and nuclear laboratories. Bijahn will get him started with a team of our best scientists and machinists to produce everything we will need for five or six bombs, initially, while we await the transport of the Plutonium."

"Will he not recognize these scientists?" Khamenei asked. "Who will he be led to think they are?"

This time Rouhani answered. "A nip there, and a tuck here and there, and the application of some stage makeup will conceal the scientists' former looks. He will believe they're Al Qaeda, and that the laboratory and machine shop have been supplied by Al-Shabaab operatives from Somalia."

"Very clever," the Grand Ayatollah said. "And what of the effort to retrieve the Plutonium? Where do we stand on that?"

The Republican Guard general said, "As far as Khan is concerned, he has been told that the Plutonium is being retrieved by an Al-Shabaab ship heading from the Bering Strait to the Siberian shore where the prize lays waiting."

He paused, and then went on, "Of course, there is no Al-Shabaab ship. In the Arctic, or anywhere else—except with the pirates in the Gulf of Aden. I have arranged for a small convoy of only five vehicles to retrieve the prize by land. They are, in fact, in southern Kazakhstan as we speak, awaiting my orders to proceed by night through Tomsk in the Russian Federation and on across the Siberian plains."

"Tell me about this convoy," the Grand Ayatollah said. "What's it composed of? And how long will it take it to get there and return?"

President Rouhani said, "It is disguised as a mobile drilling crew of the Russian gas producer Novatek. The drilling rig is one vehicle. The other four are a personnel carrier, a mobile kitchen, a fuel and food supply truck, and a covered six-ton flatbed containing a lead lined container. That container is made to look like the concrete blocks normally used to stabilize the outriggers of the drilling rig when it's in operation. The flatbed also contains sleeping cots and a kerosene stove to provide warmth during the short days while the crew sleeps. All in all, a compact and efficient group."

The general picked up the narrative. "There are nine men traveling with the convoy. Each wears an authentic Novatek uniform, and each carries a very real-looking Russian passport and papers."

He looked at the President and Supreme Leader and concluded, "Their chances of success are extremely good. Nobody will question a Novatek crew. Novatek has become a 500-pound gorilla in Russia. Politically invincible; and an economic powerhouse."

"How long?" the Supreme Leader said again.

"Today, they are just more than 3,000 kilometers from the Plutonium. Some of their route will have to be across country—where there are no roads. We project they can be at the destination in about 18-20 days. The return will be more than 4,500 kilometers all the way to the Salt Desert. That will require another 25-28 days."

He toted up his answer, looked at a calendar, and said, "The prize should be safely in place in the desert by the week of February 16. Figure late February at the latest."

"One more question," Khamenei said. "How will they be provided with fuel and supplies along the way? Can one truck carry enough?"

The general started to answer, but President Rouhani interrupted. "You should not be burdened by such details. All has been arranged, so please spend time asking Allah for their success rather than being preoccupied with detail. The Guard is experienced and capable."

The Grand Ayatollah nodded. "Inshallah."

Back at the Salt Desert Laboratory—Later in the Morning

The regional Republican Guard colonel spoke quietly with Mahmood Bijahn while Khan surveyed the instrumentation clusters in the laboratory.

"How is he responding so far?"

"He's still a bit groggy, Colonel," Mahmood said. "But just look at him. He's like a kid in the proverbial candy store. He found the machine shop 'extraordinary,' and he is literally drooling at what's here in the lab."

The colonel said, "Any sign that he's suspicious?"

"None, Sir. Remember, it's been more than two years since he's had access to anything more than rudimentary tools. Certainly he has seen nothing like these facilities in a long time. And that helps keep him in his scientific genius mode," Mahmood answered.

"But don't we want him to be at least somewhat the jihadist?" the colonel said.

Mahmood said, "If he swings too far from the vessel of Mohammed, I'll show him the sample cases intended for the dirty bombs he thinks he's going to be making. I also have a list of targets for those bombs. A bogus list to be sure, but it will whip his brain into vengeance mode in a heartbeat."

The colonel continued, "I know it's early, but what big problems do you foresee in getting him to fashion more than suitcase bombs? I mean the five or six big nuclear devices we have in mind?"

Mahmood Bjahn drew in a deep breath and then spoke quietly and directly to the colonel. "You should begin soon to understand that it will be necessary—mandatory even—to allow him to build a few suitcase bombs. Maybe even a dozen or so. That will have to come before he's confronted with the need to concentrate on the real weapons we expect of him. If we don't do that, he may swing from manic to depressed, back and forth, very rapidly. We could lose control of him. I could lose control of him."

"What do we want with suitcase bombs?" the colonel asked, frowning. "Iran has no use for terrorists of any kind, including Al Qaeda and Khan's imaginary Al-Shabaab Somalians. Building suitcase bombs is contrary to everything in the Persian culture . . . and in our government's position on terrorists. Even our individual moral characters."

"Of course, Colonel," Bijahn said. "Think of the small dirty bombs as just another mood stabilizer for Dr. Khan. As he finishes each, we will take them further into the mountain, remove the fissionable materials and destroy the rest of each. You have my word. None of those weapons will ever leave the Salt Desert. Or even see the light of day."

The colonel said, "And I can assure the Grand Ayatollah and Rouhani that these miniature disasters will be disarmed and destroyed here? No question of even any word of them leaking outside these facilities?"

Bijahn put one hand on the colonel's shoulder and whispered, "It would be best not to burden Ali Khamenei and Rouhani with even a hint of the suitcase bombs. They are merely placebos for a brilliant, but very troubled, mind. We don't need them thinking about non-issues, do we?"

The colonel nodded, smiled and said, "Go tend to your loony charge, Bijahn. And keep up the good work.

"Allahu Akbar."

Chapter Twenty-Four

Korean Kerfuffle

Workers gathered in the hallways of the offices of the People's Security headquarters. An atmosphere of unease had settled over the entire facility as rumors flew at breakneck speed from one to another to another. It seems that word had come in on their missing leader, Kwak Pum Ji.

Kwak's second in command, fearing some kind of uprising, immediately called for a general assembly of the 70 or so who worked regularly in the building. Hallways cleared as the workers streamed expectantly into a small auditorium, finding seats in scattered folding chairs. When the room had been filled and the doors locked, Kwak's second in command spoke to the gathering.

"I have received a Telex, claiming to be from the offices of the president of the Republic of Korea, Madam Park Guen-hye. In the past hour I have determined that the Telex did, in fact, originate at Madam Park's offices. Rather than attempt to explain it and its meanings and the future it portends, I shall simply read it. At this point, we cannot speculate on anything other than the message's content, itself."

With that, he read the Telex slowly:

This message is to inform your government and your offices that your former leader, Kwak Pum Ji, has illegally entered The Republic of Korea through the Demilitarized Zone that separates our two countries. Mr. Kwak surrendered voluntarily. He has requested political asylum, and he has also requested that he not be deported to the Democratic People's Republic of Korea, claiming such a deportation would result in his execution.

For the present, pending discussions with your government, Mr. Kwak will remain in the custody of our country.

He has asked that we relay to his friends, associates and

*co-workers that he is well and that his decision to come to our
country has been completely voluntary.*

Signed: Park Geun-hye
President, The Republic of Korea

An uproar erupted, and the second-in-command held up both palms, asking for quiet. He said, "All we know for sure is that the message came from President Park's offices in Seoul. We don't know if the contents are true . . . or fabricated. We also know Mr. Kwak has been missing since early yesterday. As his second in command, I will temporarily assume leadership of this office until we can verify or disprove President Park's message."

He went on, "Meantime, you have been told of a top secret matter. It is not to be discussed among yourselves, nor is it to be spoken of outside these walls until such time as the content of the message has been verified.

"Or denied."

Looking somber and pointing an index finger at the assembled workers, he said, "Penalty for spreading any unverified information, I need not remind you, is death by firing squad."

He let that soak in for a moment and then added, "Do not waste the rest of your life on this matter."

The door was unlocked, and the workers began to file silently from the room. Nobody spoke, but the second in command thought, *Now many people know what only I knew a half-hour ago. I can deny that I've had any part in leaking the information. I've made the workers vulnerable. And who can determine which of them is guilty of repeating what I have said are unconfirmed rumors?*

With that, he went back to his office to think about who he could send to pass the Telex on to the First Chairman of the Supreme People's Assembly, Kim Jung-Un. *The person I send,* he thought, *will surely not return.*

Within the hour, however, the messenger had indeed returned. Returned with a message from Kim, himself. The messenger reported, "We are to gather a big crowd before Residence No. 55 two hours from now. The First Chairman wishes to speak on a serious subject involving the national security of our country. I have been told to enlist the aid of the vice chairman of the National Defense Commission. But Chang

Sung-taek, too, has disappeared. What shall I do?" he asked the second in command.

"Go back to your work," the new, acting head of People's Security said. "I will contact my counterpart at the National Defense Commission, and together we will see that a huge crowd is in place for Kim."

Residence No. 55—Two Hours Later

Being accustomed to unpredictable summonses, a huge crowd had, indeed, appeared before the Ryongsong Residence. There was little anticipation among them. This would likely be yet another harangue about something none of them could do anything about, anyway. They would be warned to toe the line as good, faithful and patriotic followers of the First Chairman. The "or else" most likely would remain unspoken. Each one in the crowd knew he or she must summon up some rabid enthusiasm. Photos would be taken, and those not displaying joy at the sight of the First Chairman would be sought out and likely sent to retraining—wherever that might be.

In unison they raised their arms into the air and cheered when Kim Jung-Un appeared on the permanent speaker's platform at the front of the palace. Guards carrying Russian-made Kalashnikov automatic weapons ringed the crowd and mingled within it.

Kim raised his arms, not in recognition of the greeting, but rather to quiet the crowd. The silence came instantly. These people knew the drill. And they intended to follow it perfectly.

Kim stepped up to a microphone and began to speak: "It is with a sad and heavy heart that I must inform you, and all of the people of the Democratic People's Republic of Korea, of the need to make some high-level changes in our government. Sadly, the People's government has experienced the evil of treason in the past 24 hours. My former good friend and servant of the people, Kwak Pum Ji, Minister of People's Security, a man whom I have relied on for counsel and advice, has murdered the Vice Chairman of the National Defense Commission, Chang Sung-taek, yet another trusted friend and advisor."

Kim sipped from a glass, looked back at the crowd, and continued. "We don't yet know why this has happened, but you may be sure I will find out. And then it will be my sad duty to execute Mr. Kwak. I will do that, myself. Because he was my friend. I will ask no one else to carry out this very personal punishment. Kwak is being held in Residence No.

55, behind me. I will inquire about his reasons for this heinous act until he confesses. Then I will do my duty to mete out the punishment he deserves.

"Please remember with me the fine servant of the people, Chang Sung-taek. I shall miss him and his wise counsel."

Kim started to back away from the microphone, though not a person in the crowd moved. They knew he had a habit of testing their attention. And he expected all to stand in place until he had retreated into the residence.

As he backed away on the podium, an aide leaned in and whispered to him. Immediately Kim returned to the microphone. "One more thing," he said. "We have many enemies who will rejoice at these troubles within our governing body. Untruthful claims will be made, both by our unworthy neighbors in the South and by the whole cadre of Western imperialists. To attempt to create problems within our country, they will, as they usually do, issue contradictory lies. I urge you, our people to dismiss those lies. I have today given you the truth.

"Believe it, and defend it," he concluded.

Kim left the platform and retreated into the Ryongsong Residence, satisfied he had defused the South Korean claims, at least in North Korea. He thought, *My people will believe me and not that Western lap-dog, Madam Park. They have no choice, do they?* he rhetorically asked nobody in particular.

For Kim Jung-Un, every triumph deserved a reward. He picked up a phone and said, "Rack up *Shane*. I will be down in five minutes."

Chapter Twenty-Five

And the Rich Shall Inherit . . . A Surprise

The Fairmont Hotel—Vancouver, B.C.—January 12

As Four had instructed, the three billionaires came to Vancouver to the Fairmont Hotel to each pick up his individual package. What they found was not exactly what they had expected. It seems that Four had divided up the patent details and given each of the three of them different pieces. Was it all there? They had no way to know, so they immediately called in their two top scientists—a nuclear physicist and an engineer whom they expected to take the blueprints and notes and produce a working process to reduce nuclear waste to harmless dirt.

Each of the billionaires had received a CD and a printout of that disk's content. Immediately assuming the contents of the three packages to be sequential, they set about to find the right order. but even with the help of their physicist and engineer, that effort proved fruitless. It soon became apparent that Four had divided the patents into multiple parts, and he had then downloaded the parts in some kind of random order, giving each of the billionaires approximately one-third of the parts, but in no apparent order.

One, most qualified as a nuclear physicist, became frustrated. "That little shit! He's made this unnecessarily difficult. We need to make him pay for that. Where does that tracker say he is with his computer cover?"

Two answered, "That tracker was a stupid idea from the get-go. We lost contact with it almost immediately. He probably found it and sent it someplace crazy . . . like Norway. Or Australia."

Three had words of caution. "Forget him for now. First we need to be sure we have everything, and none of us can unscramble the puzzle. Put the physicist and engineer to work on the three packages. I personally think Four has done what he said he would do. Just for spite, because he thinks we're a bunch of assholes, he's scrambled up the patents and notes.

119

So, first things first. Do we have it all? That's all that counts right now."

While the billionaires' discussion became more heated and took on the appearance of an argument, the engineer leaned over to the physicist and said, "These guys are going to end up killing each other. I see bloodshed coming. Soon."

The physicist said, "No doubt. Let's stay out of the middle of it. I don't have a dog in this fight."

In exasperation, Three turned to the technical team. "Take all this shit, go back to your rooms and see if you can put it together in the right order."

Glad to be dismissed, the two technical advisors bundled up the three packages and their CDs and left the now feuding billionaires to fight it out.

One said, "Where are they staying?"

Three said, "I put them in a suite upstairs so they could work together."

"A suite?" One said. "I hope you're paying for it. Maybe we should move them to a cheaper hotel."

Two said, "Spoken like a true, rich asshole. Keep them close."

Brazilian Naval Base—Martim Vaz—January 12

After overcoming a bad case of sea sickness on the ride from Vitória to the islands, Four had settled in. His room was Motel 6 quality, which meant he didn't get a chocolate mint on his pillow each night. Or perfumed soap. He quickly learned he even had to make his own bed and do his own laundry. The trade off for a few extra chores came as the solitude he knew would keep him outside the reach of authorities. And the billionaires.

Following two days of orientation and get-acquainted time, Four had begun work in earnest yesterday. First he had to understand the communication systems currently in place. And that required some effort because the technology was so old that it pre-dated his experience. He'd never seen much of the kinds of software that ran the naval base's systems. Within hours, he had come to a conclusion.

Four told the Brazilian Naval commander, "There's not much I can do with what you have here. I think the best approach is to simply start from scratch and create application software packages one at a time."

"How long will that take?" the commander asked.

'Less time than trying to patch things together. Once I have all the programs developed, I'll pull them together into an integrated system. And then we'll take a day or two to just cut over to the new system. We'll need to be sure the base's diesel generators can maintain a steady voltage output, too."

"Meantime we keep using what we have?" the commander said.

"Right," Four said. "You will be down for a day or two during the final installation, but I'll give you plenty of advance notice so that you can advise Vitória you'll be off the network temporarily—a week or two in advance."

Four knew the job wouldn't be nearly as difficult as he'd intimated to the commander. Mainly, he would just have to modify some cutting-edge software he'd already developed to meet the peculiar and specialized needs of a remote naval base. And then install it on new, state-of-the-art hardware. Hardware he would specify within a month or two.

Nor would the project really take him six months to complete. He'd have to stretch it out for two reasons: first the Marinha do Brasil would pay him for at least six months; and, too, he would need that much time to locate a few options for his final place of residence—the place he would settle in to watch the world go by.

He thought he'd completed his assessment of the communication systems now in place on Martim Vaz, and his thoughts turned back to the billionaires. *I wonder how pissed they were when they got what I had promised them? I did what they asked. I gave them everything but one little item, and they can figure that out . . . once they put the pieces of the puzzle back in order.*

He thought of a comedian he'd seen regularly on television when he was a child. Flip Wilson was his name, he remembered. Wilson became famous for, among the characters he created, one sentence he worked into his routines: "The Devil made me do it!"

Had the Devil made Four scramble the patents into a puzzle? He was sure the answer was "no." But whatever had driven him to screw with the billionaires crept back into his thoughts as his work day came to a close. He would check in on the billionaires to see how they were progressing. No, he had to admit he didn't give a rat's ass how they were progressing. But he couldn't help himself. He just had to tweak them once more.

Maybe the Devil was at work here, after all.

Just to rattle their cages and reinforce to them that all their money couldn't compare to his technical abilities, he sat down to send them an email. An email they could never trace back to him, although they would know he'd sent it. In fact, he would sign his number to it.

> *Dear Single Digits,*
>
> *I thank you for the consulting stipend you provided during our get-acquainted time together. And I thank you for the payment I have received for the services I have provided to you. Services that you will soon come to admit nobody else could have provided. By now I trust you have discovered that all the material you requested has been provided. You have, no doubt, seen also that it is presented as a bit of a simple puzzle for you to piece together.*
>
> *I want you to know why I decided to present it to you in pieces. First, the act of piecing it together will either bring the three of you closer together. Or it will result in bloodshed among you. Either way, I don't particularly care, but the result will make a good case study in the clashing of three super-rich egos, no?*
>
> *Just so there's no confusion, the other reason I chose to present the material in pieces is simply because . . . I don't like you. In fact, you are all three disgusting to me. Let's be clear about that, okay?*
>
> *As a reminder, you will never find me, so don't bother looking. FYI, your crude little tracking device is in Oslo, Norway. I am not in Oslo, Norway.*
>
> *Having done my part in your program, I will continue to monitor the global news . . . and the obituaries.*
>
> *Cordially,*
>
> *Four*

Chapter Twenty-Six

Truth and Consequences

Langley, Virginia—CIA Headquarters—January 12

Monica sat at her desk and listened as Roland, her replacement as cultural affairs attaché in the U.S. embassy in Moscow, recounted for her the sequence of events leading up to the phone call between POTUS and Putin. As she had suggested, he had made his way quickly to Washington so the two of them could get a handle on what was happening between the two countries vis a vis the Plutonium.

Roland began, "This guy Boris, who is head of the FSB, broke the news to the ambassador that the Plutonium existed. You can bet the ambassador was plenty pissed when he found out the DCI and NSA—and maybe the President—already knew about it, and had known about it for some time. But nobody at State had been clued in. So Boris put the question to the ambassador, 'Would the U.S. care to cooperate in grabbing the Plutonium with the Russians?'"

He paused as Monica rolled her eyes in disbelief. Then he went on, "Well, the ambassador had to ask for time to make some contacts here in Washington. But within hours, before he'd even made any calls, Boris was back, complaining about the fucked-up American bureaucracy. He said Putin had told him if the ambassador didn't have a definitive answer on this second trip, to just tell him that Putin was tired of waiting and weary of dealing with bureaucrats, so he—Putin—would just call POTUS direct."

"Putin did," Monica said. "But I can't get any information about that phone call or what the two of them decided to do. The pipeline is shut down completely, and I'm pretty sure I've been declared *persona non grata*. Nobody around here will even speak to me about the fact it's snowing outside, let alone anything about Russia. And, as you know, Russia is my responsibility. None of my analysts even speak to me these days."

She leaned back in her chair and then asked, "Roland, do you know anything about what happened on that phone call? Or anything that's happened since?"

"This may not be important," Roland said, "but I think it might. Just before I checked out of the embassy two days ago, the ambassador received a phone call from the Secretary of State. Apparently she's now been included in the loop. You can imagine her anger at State being kept in the dark so long. Well, anyway, it seems Madam Secretary told the ambassador to prepare to have a meeting in the embassy on January 14. The players will be the DCI and the NSA. But the ambassador is not invited."

'Did the Secretary of State say who else would be there?"Monica asked.

"According to what I heard, maybe just a Russian or two," Roland said.

Monica looked amused. "And just how did you come by this information? About the meeting and the phone call from the Secretary?"

"May I remind you," Roland said, "that I'm a spy? I have my methods."

Monica laughed. "It's good that you're here, Roland. Let's go upstairs and see if the DCI might be around. I know it's Saturday, and I know he's averse to work, but maybe we can catch him. As his two highest-ranking Russian experts, we are at least due some answers concerning his meeting in Moscow. At the very least, he owes us the courtesy of an audience."

Roland added, "And I know the coffee up there is better than this warm brown water we get down here."

They headed for the elevator. Monica got out her "Top Floor" pass, the key-card required to open the elevator doors on the top floor. *At least they haven't taken that away from me yet,* she thought.

As they stepped into the elevator, Monica said to Roland, "Don't be taken aback if I get testy with the DCI. I've been around here a long time, and I consider myself immune. He knows there's nobody more up to speed on Putin and the Russians than me. So I'm not taking any crap off of him. He has no idea what field work is really all about."

Roland gave her a curious look, and then nodded.

Office of the Director of Central Intelligence (DCI)—Moments later

As luck would have it, the DCI was, in fact, in his office. As Monica and Roland approached, the DCI's secretary was heard to shout, "No, dammit!" and she burst through his office door rearranging the top of her blouse. Red faced, she recovered quickly and said, "Monica, what can I do for you?"

"I take it the DCI is in," Monica said.

Giving her answer no thought, the secretary said, "The asshole's in there, but don't go in alone." Then she noticed Roland and asked, "Who's your friend?"

Monica introduced Roland as a visitor from the Moscow embassy. "You want to announce us?" she asked.

The secretary, having regained her composure, said, "Not if you expect to see him. Best you just go straight in and head for his desk before he realizes you're there." She winked at Monica and returned to her desk.

Monica said to her, "I like your style," as she opened the DCI's door and rushed in, followed by Roland.

Without looking up, the DCI, sitting at his desk, said, "Marie, I want to apologize." Then he saw his visitors were not Marie and erupted, "How the hell did you get in here?"

Monica, not to be outdone, said, "We just popped up through the floor. It's the newest thing in spy stuff. Called 'Eclectic Generation.' Seems we stepped into a booth downstairs, dialed up your office, were transformed into energy and, voila, here we are, our mass restored."

"Always the wise-ass, huh, Monica?" the DCI said. "Now, tell me why you're here. And, if you have any sense of decorum left, introduce the startled-looking gentleman with you."

Monica smiled. "If I were you, Sir, I don't think I would refer to decorum this morning." *Gotcha*, she congratulated herself. Then she continued. "This startled-looking gentleman, as you called him, is the cultural attaché in the Moscow embassy. He goes by the name of Peppermint Stick. I could tell you his real name, but then I'd have to kill you."

She paused. "Do you want that name?"

The DCI said, "You're our man in Moscow?"

Roland said, "One of them."

Turning to Monica, the DCI said, "Okay, you've gotten in your licks.

Now what do the two of you want?"

"As head of the Russian desk and, I might add, the only person around here who knows diddly-shit about Putin and the Russians, I want to know who you and the NSA are meeting with in Moscow on the 14th, and why you're meeting with them? That's not too hard, is it?"

The DCI simply said, "Need to know."

"Bullshit," Monica said. "I'd really enjoy telling a closed-door Congressional oversight committee that their DCI and their NSA are walking into a meeting with the Russians totally unprepared, and the Company's one true Russian expert is being lied to."

"I haven't lied," the DCI said. "I just have no comment at this time."

Monica decided to go for the jugular. "That Plutonium is going to fall into the hands of Al Qaeda, Al-Shebaab, the North Koreans, the Iranians, or God-knows-who-else while you dick around, honoring protocol and wasting time. Let me guess. The FBI wants in on the game so they can claim heroics. Homeland Security sees Siberia as just another part of our homeland. The Coast Guard claims it's on a coast, and the Army wants to do some white-weather training."

She paused while the DCI just stared at her. Then she said, "Are you going to just screw around forever while 200 or more dirty suitcase bombs fall into the hands of jihadists? You need to get over yourself."

The DCI stood, red in the face. "Let me remind you I spent 20 years in Special Ops. I'm not a beginner."

"You're not a finisher, either," Monica shot back. "Special Ops. That means you had difficult assignments under stressful conditions. But," she said, pausing, "you always had somebody higher up giving you orders. Telling you exactly what to do and likely how to do it. You have not the slightest idea what intelligence gathering out there in the real world is all about."

The DCI started to say something, but Monica interrupted. "I'm not through. Don't tell me about your heroics. I've spent 15 years for the Company putting my life on the line every fucking day. In shitholes you can't even imagine. You're not any hot-shot hero to me."

The DCI said, "Are you finished?"

"Not until you answer the questions I asked. Why are you and NSA going to Moscow? Who are you meeting with? And why? Three simple questions that I, as head of the Russian Desk, have every right, and need, to know the answer to."

Recognizing that Monica was, indeed, an extremely valuable resource, and seeing no benefit to continuing to argue credentials with her, the DCI said, "Look, Monica, I'll tell you what I can. But only in general terms. The meeting is about retrieving and defusing the Plutonium. A joint effort between the U.S. and the Russian Federation. The problem is well in hand. Go back to your routine and forget about it. We'll take care of it. That's all I can say."

"Who's put the quietus on me?" Monica said. "And don't tell me it's you. You don't have the cojones."

The DCI said, "Do you want my job, Monica? Is that what you want?"

"If I had your job, there would never have been WMDs in Iraq. And the bullshit about Uranium sales to Saddam Husain from Nigeria would never have been a topic for discussion. Saddam would have been taken out with a single $4 bullet, and 5,000 American young people wouldn't be dead today. Not to mention tens of thousands maimed. This place suffers from people like you. Political appointees who are 'Yes' men, afraid to not follow protocol. Scared to stand up to dumb-ass Congressmen. And beholden to the President so much you're afraid to tell him 'no.' Is that about right?"

The DCI sat down. "I'm going to end this meeting with two thoughts, Monica. I suggest you listen and react accordingly. First, I want to apologize to Peppermint Stick, here, for this unseemly scene. I'm truly sorry, Sir. Second, I'm forced to tell you why you're out of the loop, Monica. At least for the moment."

He folded his hands on his desk, looked around the room, and said, "Here it is. POTUS demanded that this whole issue be kept among me, NSA and State. State, even, is not to be involved in meetings with the Russians. I asked the President if I could include you—because you are, as you say, a valuable resource. His answer was not just 'No.' But he told me to lock you up if I had to keep you from being involved.

"Now you know," the DCI said. "Are you happy?"

Monica stared stone faced. "So the President, who knows little or nothing about me, and nothing at all about intelligence gathering in Russia, is now running the CIA. Pretty soon, he's going to figure out he doesn't need you."

She paused. "You're not in charge here. The President has whacked off your balls . . . if you had any to begin with."

She turned, took Roland by the elbow and made for the door just as Marie, the secretary stepped in. Monica said, loudly enough for the DCI to hear, "Marie, I'm going to send Legal Affairs and HR up here to take a deposition from you."

She paused, then added, "And don't worry. You're safe, The DCI has no balls."

As she pushed 'Down,' she said to Roland, "We're not through yet. I have no respect for, and I pay no attention to, weak men. And that son-of-a-bitch is as weak as they come."

On the elevator, Monica pushed "B" for the parking garage. "Let's take a drive . . . away from the cameras and microphones. I have some ideas to bounce off you."

Chapter Twenty-Seven

Needles North

Austin—Headquarters of Van Pelt Industries
Early Evening—January 12

This group is on a roll. As promised, the Van Pelt Industries' new shallow-water drilling rig has met up with their ice breaker north of the Bering Straits, and both are making their way, hugging the coastline, toward the Laptev Sea, 75^0 north latitude. Josef tells me that today they are approaching the New Siberian Islands that separate the Laptev on the west from the East Siberian Sea to the east.

Josef is speaking to the group. "Global warming may be on our side today. The ice breaker reports that their job of clearing a path for the driller is a bit easier than they had expected. Apparently the thickness of the ice is less than usual."

Lobo asked, "Where does that put them, time wise, from the prize."

Nana answered. "Two days, maybe three. It all depends on the condition of the ice and how easily they can pass through it."

Dr. Pradeet said, "So where does that leave us? In terms of departure for Seoul, I mean? I have a full-time job, so I'll need to make arrangements to be away for a few days. I'll also need to know about when we can be expected to return. University bureaucracy, you understand. It's the curse of nuclear physicists as pedagogues everywhere."

I jumped in. "Today's Sunday. So let's say they arrive at the location on Wednesday the 15th. How long will they need to be ready to retrieve the Plutonium?"

Josef grabbed is satellite phone and said, "I'll be right back." He turned to me, "You'd like a weekend recovery . . . if we can do that. Right?"

"Right," I said, "but I don't want the timing to be dictated by me. We need to get it and go. If it works out to be the weekend, fine."

With that, Josef left to go outside to make a call. I looked puzzled, so Greycloud said, "Satellite phones won't work inside buildings or cars.

You have to have a clear shot to the open sky."

I learn something new every day.

Just as Josef left, the office's landline phone rang. Nana picked it up. "It's Monica," she said. "I'll put her on speaker."

"Hello. Hello!" Monica, as usual, impatient.

"We're here," Nana said. "The whole team. What's going on with you?"

"I'm packing for a flight to Moscow. It seems I still have some value around the Company—even if the President suggested to the DCI that I should be locked up."

"That sounds like a story we need to hear, Monica. This is Greycloud."

Monica answered, "It's a short story, John. Here's the sanitized version. When I got back to Langley, it was clear I'd been frozen out. Nobody would look at me or talk to me. After a couple of days, I'd had enough of the bullshit. So I went, with my replacement in the Moscow embassy, to see the DCI. Caught him molesting his secretary, but that's another story."

Sanjay said, "I want to hear that story first." That provoked a laugh or two.

Monica went on. "I explained to him how the cow ate the cabbage. At first he weaseled. And weaseled some more. Finally he admitted the President had put the subject on a four-person basis. I was not one of those persons. So I asked the DCI if he or the President was running the CIA, reminding him he'd just surrendered his need-to-be."

Gady asked, "How do you get by with haranguing your bosses? Craig wouldn't like it if I tried that."

I thought, *You don't have Monica's death wish, Gady.*

"Fact is, Gady," Monica said, "I've got bigger balls than any boss I've ever had. I know more about what they need to know than . . . " she stopped. "Let me rephrase that. I am the expert they need because they mostly don't know shit. How's that?"

Josef had come back inside and given me a thumbs up. He said, "Monica, it's your little brother. Why are you going to Moscow?"

"Last night," she said, "I was invited by the DCI to join him and the NSA on a private flight that leaves in the morning from Andrews Air Force Base. Seems the two of them have a meeting in the embassy with some unspecified Russians on Tuesday. And I guess they finally realized that, together, they'll come up a brick shy of a Russian load."

I said, "So eat humble pie, and bring Monica back into the loop, huh?"

Monica laughed. "There'll be no humble pie. Arrogant assholes never admit mistakes. They'll come up with some incredible rationalization for bringing me along. Just one more thing they'll be keeping from POTUS."

Lobo asked, "Is the meeting about the Plutonium? Do the Russians know about it?"

Monica laughed. "They not only know about it, but Putin and POTUS have already spoken by phone about it. That's what brought on this little confab on Tuesday."

"Should we back off and let the two superpowers deal with it, then?" Gady asked.

"Good God, no!" Monica said. "Let me tell you how this is going to progress. The meeting Tuesday will be about arranging another meeting to actually talk seriously. But before that second meeting happens, there'll be a few more meetings: one to decide where and when the next meeting will be; and one to decide the size and shape of the table for the meeting. Then, of course, they'll have to meet again to decide who sits on which side of the table—north, east, west, and south. And that meeting will conclude with the need for a round table. One with a lazy-Susan type device with place cards on it—that can be spun by someone neutral, like the Swiss, to determine who sits where. By now it will be the end of March, and the meeting intended to be the second will be at least the sixth."

She paused, and then said, "Left to the U.S. and Russia, it will be mid-July before a plan is developed, and then they'll decide it's too cold to act until next spring." The she added, "And there're not two super powers at the table. Only Russia's growling bears and POTUS's ball-less wonders."

Hearing no laughter, Monica went on. "You think I'm kidding? I've been down this road too many times. Mark your calendars now. The big-two powers will converge on the site to find it empty. And they'll wonder why. They'll actually believe nobody or no country could move faster than themselves."

"They'll find my note," Gady said, adding, "I'm leaving a note in a bottle for the late comers."

"What will it say?" Monica asked.

Gady said, "You couldn't win a three-legged race with four legs under you."

"You can do better than that," Monica laughed.

Josef said, "That's good news, as ridiculous as it sounds. Let me tell you where we are. I'll begin by telling you that we're less than two weeks from recovering the Plutonium ourselves. With a little luck, we might just be able to grab it next weekend. How much detail do you want to hear?"

"Nothing else," Monica said. "Not before the meeting Tuesday in Moscow. When it's over I'll call you from the secure phone in the embassy basement. It'll probably be somewhere around mid-day. I'll be nine hours ahead of you. Or eight. Daylight savings always screws me up on time zones. Just stand by."

Nana said, "Call on the headquarters' land line. Let it ring twice and then call on my satellite phone. I'll step outside. After Pavlovich's eavesdropping, I still don't trust real confidentiality in this office."

"Nana," Monica said, "you killed Pavlovich. Get over it!"

Sanjay Pradeet stood and looked around the room. This secret wasn't one meant to be shared with him. Or shared with anyone outside the former Pavlovich-chase group, which included all present except the nuclear scientist.

Realizing Sanjay's surprise, Lobo went to his side. Sanjay backed up, reached behind his back and said, menacingly, "I'm armed. Stand back!" With that he pulled a snub-nosed pistol from his belt and fired at Nana . . . a stream of water. She flinched as the rest of us joined Sanjay in a good laugh.

This guy, I thought, *is the class clown.* And I know from long experience that every successful group needs a class clown, the one person in every group who gives perspective and keeps the keel even.

Chapter Twenty-Eight

Ursus Arcto v. Raptor

Moscow—U.S. Embassy—January 14

Arriving in Moscow late Monday evening for the Tuesday meeting, Monica had made the rounds of her former associates in the embassy and taken wagers as to whether the Russians would be asked to leave at gunpoint, or the DCI and NSA would flee from the embassy in fear. She dubbed the game, Bears vs. Eagles, and gave odds on the eagles folding first.

Yesterday's 10-hour flight was aboard a chartered plane owned and operated by one of the CIA-controlled airlines known to insiders as "Spook-Air." Of course, this particular Gulfstream carried the ID of the U.S. State Department. But let the Secretary of State try to use it and, shazam, it would disappear.

The DCI and NSA had grilled Monica during the flight as if she were a terrorist. They intended to sop up the entirety of her 15 years of field experience in a few hours. *Typical of the hopelessly unknowing,* she thought. She also knew that if anyone were to count the planes operated by the various "Spook" carriers around the globe, the total would be larger than any legally-operating air carrier in the world.

Spook Air is a big business, run out of Langley, mostly to do dastardly deeds.

Monica was not surprised when she was invited not to attend the meeting. Rather she was ordered to stand by in an adjacent room where she could neither see nor hear what was going on in the meeting. She was told she might be needed to clarify a point or two. How about understanding how the Russians are screwing you? She thought. *I can speak their language. I spoke it as my first language before I ever learned English.* Though born in Philadelphia to an American mother and Felix Pavlovich, her Russian father, Monica's then family moved back to St.

133

Petersburg when she was still an infant.

Monica knew, of course, that her stand-by exclusion from the meeting had nothing to do with knowledge or qualifications. If either of those qualities were actually needed, DCI and NSA would be back in Washington.

The Russian contingent included just one man—Boris, the head of the FSB. He spoke first. "Since I'm sure neither of you has learned to speak Russian, I shall speak English for your benefit. And I see that, as usual, it takes two Americans to do the job of one Russian. Not surprising. How many additional Americans have you brought? I know how you operate. As for me, I represent Vladimir Putin. Just our President and me,"

Seeing he was going to be allowed to continue his monologue, Boris said, "Who, in your country, knows about the Plutonium? In Russia, it is just me and Mr. Putin. Only two of us."

Already on edge, the DCI said, "There are the two of us, our Secretary of State, and the President. Of course, you've already unceremoniously involved our ambassador to your country."

Boris snickered, "Because in your secret foolishness, you thought your State Department didn't need to be aware. President Putin and I got a big laugh out of getting one up on your ambassador. That is correct English, no? 'One up?'"

The NSA nodded. "You have invited us to this meeting on the premise that our two countries might cooperate in containing and disposing of the Plutonium. If you're finished with your little insults, perhaps we could get on with that discussion?"

Boris laughed. "You see, my Amerikanski friend, you have no sense of humor. Putin and I find your ways funny, and it would be to your advantage to take note of that. We know from years of experience that you are disposed to think of Russians as stupid and Russia as backward. You've had a whole corps of your people here who have tried to contradict that notion. Why? Because they came to know Russia and its people. These visitors to our nation have told you over and over again that you underestimate us."

Boris paused, smiled a big smile and said, "Of course when you go to your Congress at budget time, you try to paint Russia as the 500 pound gorilla, no? I believe you might call us a 'mean motor scooter.' Just to worry your Congress enough that they give you money. Money you certainly don't need to use against Russia. But that's the way it works, no? The American system?"

The DCI spoke, "Boris, are we going to discuss the Plutonium? Or are you going to continue your anecdotal analysis of the U.S.? Because if we don't get to the Plutonium soon, my associate and I are going to simply leave the room and return to Washington."

Boris laughed. A hearty laugh. "I see you have learned nothing of our culture. You are in our country. Here we don't just sit down and get right to business. That's considered very impolite. No, we first must have some of what you call 'small talk,' then a few cold vodkas. Then, before you know it, we do get down to business."

He paused, "You are the host of this meeting. In your embassy. So where is the cold vodka?"

The NSA grabbed a phone to call for some cold vodka. The DCI tried to stop him, but the NSA said, "Don't be a fool. I'll get him some vodka. A shot or two might not hurt you, either."

Within seconds, Monica came into the room with a silver tray containing an ice bucket, a bottle of Stolichnaya and three frozen glasses. Without saying a word, she opened the vodka, poured three fingers into each glass, and passed the glasses around. Then, to the amazement of DCI and NSA, she held the bottle up, said, *"zap Zhen -shushed,"*[1] took a big pull from the bottle, and then walked calmly from the room. As she left she said, "There is an old Russian proverb: *Only problem drinkers don't toast before drinking.*"

Boris burst into laughter. "There, you see. There is an American who knows how to behave in Russia. Of course, I recognize her. Alice was her name while she was here as cultural affairs attaché. But, of course, she was CIA. We all knew that, but we did miss her when she left. Yes, Alice was a good old girl. Is that proper American English?"

Again he laughed.

`The DCI, remaining oblivious to what he was being told, said, "Now can we please get down to business? May we talk about a joint effort to remove the Plutonium?"

Boris simply shook his head and looked sad—a hangdog look. One he'd obviously practiced and perfected as Russia's top spy. "Okay," he said,

1. "To women."

"here's how this is going to go down. Russia will make all the plans and preparations to retrieve the Plutonium. We will supply all the manpower and equipment. You are to do nothing until you hear from us. We will share this opportunity for a highly-visible cooperative effort between two great powers. I, Boris, will let you know what the next step on your part will need to be. You just stand by."

DCI interrupted, "We cannot agree to what you've just said. It is not a cooperative effort. Russia is controlling everything. We have no real part in the recovery operation."

"Ah, no, so," Boris said, "your part is to show up and be on hand for the cameras and reporters. Mother Russia is giving you credit—equal billing, I think you would say. But we don't trust you enough to make you truly an equal partner."

"And why is that, Boris? Why the lack of trust?"

"In our country we have elections, just like you do. But when the elections are over, those who are elected actually do something. They get things accomplished. We do not have fifty layers of petty bureaucrats who must meet incessantly before we can take a shit. Your country is hamstrung, tripping all over its own dick."

"You have more apparatchiks than we have bureaucrats, Boris. This talk is nonsense."

"No, my naïve friend. It is true we have many layers of apparatchiks, but there is a difference."

"And what is that difference, Boris? I don't see it," the DCI said.

"Of course you don't. Because you're bound by some archaic notion that an apparatchik might be worth as much as a leader. In Russia, and mark this well, because you simply don't get it. In Russia, the apparatchiks have no voice in decisions. They are in place to do the will of the elected leaders. To be sure, they are useful, and we benefit greatly from their presence."

He paused as if seeking another way to make his point. Then he continued, "In this case, as an example, President Putin and I will handle the Russian end of things. Engineers and physicists will do our bidding. When we tell them. They're happy with their jobs and positions in our society. Troops will show up when and where we say. Heavy equipment and lead-lined suits will appear when they are needed.

"And guess what?" he continued. "Not one soul will have had to make a decision on anything. Not one meeting will have been held. Not one study ordered done. Hardly even a discussion. Two people. One set of decisions. Quick. Simple. Expeditious."

NSA asked, "Is it really that simple, Boris?"

"I know you can't imagine it, you Americans. Burdened with the idea that input must be received, studies must be conducted, and the proletariat must be consulted on every little issue. You're handcuffed. What we are offering you is equal billing to perform a simple task. If . . . if you will stay the hell out of the way and not get your bureaucratic shorts in a twist. It's that simple, gentlemen.

"Equal billing, a huge photo op, a chance to show the world you're not the greedy imperialists we all know you are.

"And all you have to do is *sit . . . on . . . your . . . bureaucratic . . . asses . . . and . . . smile . . . for . . . the . . . cameras."*

He spoke as if spitting out each word with exuberance.

The tone and content of Boris's offer clearly irritated the DCI, although he showed little of it in his facial reaction. The NSA, though, truly was pissed.

The NSA said, "Thank you, Boris. Not just for the offer, but also for the lessons in Russian efficiency. I'm sure I've learned something today."

"But what is your answer?" Boris said.

The DCI said, "We will consult with our President, and we will respond after that discussion."

Boris stood, DCI pressed a button, and a fully-armed Marine guard entered to escort Boris off the premises.

As he left the building, everyone could hear him laughing loudly. Nobody had to be told that the score of Monica's game was Ursus Arcto-1, Raptor-0.

Chapter Twenty-Nine

Never the Twain Shall Meet

Seoul, South Korea—Cheongwadae Residence—January 14

Kwak Pum Ji, former Minister of People's Security in the North, had been moved in secret from the National Assembly Building to the official residence of the South Korean President, Park Geun-hye.

President Park had readily agreed to the relocation, saying, "I want to spend some time talking with this defector, myself. It's possible we may be able to make good use of his knowledge."

For his part, Kwak had been singing like a crazed canary. His rationale for telling all was simple: *These are also my people; they lead prosperous lives, never in fear of being murdered by a madman with power. I owe nothing to Kim or the North any longer. Kim would kill me because he loves killing. What have I got to lose? Maybe I can earn my way here with the knowledge I bring with me.*

And so, on this day, guarded by three armed members of the KNPA, Korean National Police Agency, Kwak waited for his first meeting with Madam Park. Oddly, he had no fear. Government leaders had struck terror in him his entire life. But he could see things were different in the South. Even the President was a woman. Unthinkable in his former country.

As Madam Park entered the room, the KNPA officers came to attention. "Relax," she said to them. "I wish to speak with Mr. Kwak alone." Seeing the concern in the officers' eyes, she added, "I have a button in my pocket." She held up a small black object the size of a cigarette package. The name *Samsung* was plainly etched on its face. There were two buttons below the name—one green and one red.

Madam Park said to the officers, "If I push this red button, I shall be needing some assistance."

The officer obviously in charge said, "How will we know when you push that button, Madam President?"

She smiled, looked at Kwak, and said, "The entire alarm system for this residence will sound. If you miss that, you must be comatose." Again she smiled at the officers and nodded toward the door. They filed out quietly.

"Now, Mr. Kwak, we have known of you for many years, of course. But your country is, as I'm sure you will agree, somewhat secretive. So we know who you have been and what your responsibilities have been. You are, or were, a dedicated Communist, sworn to both serve and protect Kim Jung-Un and the people of North Korea. In that order, I might add. So, Mr. Kwak, tell me who you are today. And why you decided to join the real world."

Kwak said, "Are we being recorded?"

"Yes, of course. And videotaped. The officers can see us on video monitors, but they cannot hear what we're saying. For the moment, our conversation will be just between you and me."

"And later," Kwak said, "will you send recordings to Kim?"

The President stared at Kwak. "No. We have no reason to involve Kim in your situation." She paused. "I can appreciate, to some degree, your paranoia. It will not go away easily. If we decide you may remain in our country, I will personally see that you receive counseling to help you adjust."

"You're speaking of retraining?" Kwak said.

"We do not recognize any value from the Communist programs of retraining, Mr. Kwak. To us, they are merely another form of punishment for minor offenses. I understand that major offenses usually result in death by firing squad in the North."

Kwak nodded.

She went on, "You will come to learn we are humane here. We believe in justice, but not in vengeance. One day you will come to know the difference between these two concepts. But I suppose they are one and the same to you right now."

Kwak summoned some courage. This lady, after all, didn't seem threatening. Maybe she was bullshitting him, but he had little to lose by asking more questions. He said, "What will happen to me? I have a great store of information that you and your associates might find useful." He paused, and then said, "And I am willing to tell your people everything I know. Facts, data, whatever you wish."

The President said, "I suspect that's true, Mr. Kwak. And I expect we will take you up on your offer. But before we can get to that point, there are some problems with your defection."

"What problems?" Kwak said.

"What crimes did you commit in connection with your defection?" Madam Park asked.

Kwak considered the question, and then he answered."I think only three: I broke my allegiance to a clinically insane leader and a bad government. That's the big one. Second, I had to kill an associate to prevent him from reporting me before I could get across the border. And finally, I stole my official government car. I brought it with me through the Demilitarized Zone."

The President said, "Our troops at the DMZ have returned your vehicle to the North. As far as your oath to the government of Kim Jung-Un, that oath has no meaning here in the real Korea. The murder is another matter. It may be that Kim will seek to extradite you on that charge, and that's a problem that will have to be dealt with."

Kwak leaned across the table and said, as if in confidence, "Madam President, there will be no extradition papers filed. I can already see that I can be useful to you. No, Kim will claim to have me in custody, and—most likely—claim that he has already killed me. Or had me killed. But I think it will be a claim of personal killing."

"He's already made that claim, and you have had a funeral in disgrace," the President said.

"Then everybody in the North will believe I am dead. If Kim says so, nobody dares to even think otherwise. So why, I ask, did you mention extradition?"

Madam Park said, "Your Kim is unpredictable, to say the least. A request for extradition need never surface in the North. He may choose to play games. But he's not a very good player."

The President's Samsung S-6 chirped. She looked at the message and said, "I must go now, Mr. Kwak. You will be interrogated by our KNPA officers for a few days. Be honest with them. They won't hurt you in any way. We're looking for the information you've said you have. Then I will personally visit with you about a matter that might just interest you. But we'll see."

With that, the President left the room, and the three officers returned to escort Kwak to his temporary quarters in the basement of the presidential residence.

Pyongyang, North Korea—Ryongsong Residence—January 14

The household staff cringed and hid, if they could find a safe place to hide.

Kim Jung-Un was in one of his moods. He was in the below-ground target range firing magazine after magazine until one after another AK-47s locked up because their barrels turned red hot. His targets? Full-size paper images of Kwak Pum Ji. If he couldn't actually shoot the defector, as he'd said he had done, then he would blast the effigies with thousands of rounds. Obliterate them.

To make matters worse, he had sent for the two men he'd chosen as replacements for the murdered Chang Sung-taek and the defector Kwak Pum-Ji. That Plutonium was just sitting there, and Kim had visions of dozens of nuclear bombs—just waiting to be built.

The two men hesitantly entered the firing range, watching silently as Kim tossed aside one over-heated AK-47 after another. Neither man really wanted to be here where Kim had automatic weapons by the dozens at his disposal. But they had been honored—had received the highest honor—by being selected to such important positions within the government of the Democratic People's Republic of Korea. Both wanted to get on with their new responsibilities.

Kim, however, had something else in mind.

Replacing his current automatic rifle in a rack and removing his ear protectors, Kim motioned the two to sit with him at a small table near the range's bar and refreshment center. Typical of the First Chairman, he got right down to business. Small talk was for ignorant peasants. And Russian apparatchiks.

"Gentlemen," he said. "I have your first assignment. It's the job that Kwak and Chang failed to do, although I can hardly fault Chang since Kwak murdered him and dumped him in a ditch on his way to defection."

He paused, and then decided to go on with his tale. "Of course, Kwak was intercepted and I, myself, had the satisfaction of ending his diseased life. Right here in this range." He pointed to the latest riddled effigy of Kwak. "See that target? That's where I made Kwak stand. Then I shot him

141

in the knees. Then the shoulders. I made him suffer for what he tried to do to his leader and his country. Finally, heeding his whimpers, I shot him in the heart. Then the head. We are rid of the traitor Kwak. Forever."

Kim went to what appeared to be a rifle carrying case, zipped it open and pulled out the same satellite shot he'd discussed with Kwak and Chang. He pointed to the dark egg white with the soft orange glowing yolk—a yolk tiny in comparison to the size of the white.

"He said, "This is your assignment. You will have a warrant from me to assure you have all the human and material resources you need to retrieve that small orange object and bring it back to our scientists. A simple assignment. Aided by the full force and power of the First Chairman's warrant. I want you to go get it. For the future security of our nation."

The two newcomers looked at the photo. One of them summoned up some courage and said, "What is it?"

"It is enough pure Plutonium for us to be able to build dozens, maybe hundreds, of nuclear weapons," Kim said.

"Where is it?" the second newcomer said.

Kim answered, "In the remote far northern edge of the Siberian Plains, right on the shore of the Laptev Sea. North of the Arctic Circle."

The first newcomer, not yet accustomed to personal interface with Kim, said, "How can we get it?"

Kim's eyes bugged. His face turned beet red. He stood and slammed his palms on the table top and screamed, "If I wanted to do your job, I wouldn't have chosen you for it. You figure it out. Don't bother me with petty details. Just get your asses out there and bring that Plutonium back!"

He then calmed as fast as he'd exploded.

Smiling at the two, he said, "I have confidence you will know how to retrieve this most precious treasure. And when you bring it back, I shall personally see that you are both rewarded beyond your wildest dreams. Get it for me."

The two newbies assured Kim they wouldn't fail, and they left as quickly as they could find their way back to the front door of Residence No. 55.

Once clear of the grounds, they sat on a park bench. One said, "This is a suicide mission. You know that."

The other said, "Let's give it a go. We have nothing to lose but our lives. And we've sworn those lives to the glory of the First Leader and the people of his country."

The first speaker rolled his eyes, shook his head, and looked to the South.

Chapter Thirty

Playground for a Mad Scientist

Iran's Salt Desert—Underground Laboratory—January 14

After more than a week in the underground laboratory, Mahmood Bijahn had, so far, been able to keep Dr. Haji Khan busy and mostly placated. To end the mad scientist's demand to accompany the expedition to recover the Plutonium, Mahmood had told Khan that the nonexistent Al-Shabaab ship had already recovered the prize, but that bringing it back by water would take several weeks.

On hearing that timetable, Khan had thrown a fit. "It must be here by Mohammed's birthday or I will never be able to fabricate enough little bombs for the big bang to take place on the first night of Ramadan. That timing is critical."

Thinking quickly, Mahmood had faked a phone call and then reported that the ship, rather than sailing with the Plutonium all the way to the Gulf of Aden, would dock at Shanghai on January 28. There the Plutonium would be transferred to an air carrier that would arrive in Mogadishu on the 30th.

"You will have your heavy metal no later than the end of the first week of February," Mahmood had said, to pacify his charge. He knew, of course, that the prize would likely not arrive quite that soon, but he would address the delay if, and when, it happened. *An easy fix,* he thought, *can be accomplished by simply altering the calendars in the lab facilities.*

At Mahmood's suggestion, Haji busied himself working with two experienced machinists. He taught them to build the shells and high-tolerance metal inner workings for suitcase bombs. It took them three days to machine and assemble one set, which Haji proudly slipped into one of the sample cases Mahmood had bought for him.

"We will be able to work more quickly after my assistants have made

144

three or four," Haji said. "The tolerances are very fine, but the machinists are capable. And we have the finest air-bearing machine tools I have ever worked with."

Khan cornered Mahmood at lunch in the lab's canteen and demanded to know how Al-Shabaab had been able to secure such high-grade metals and the state-of-the-art machine tools. Thinking quickly, Mahmood had said it was Al-Shabaab that supplied the mobile labs, but Al Qaeda had come up with the metals and machine tools. Haji bought it, as a matter of fact, even though none of it would make any sense had the scientist not been constantly drugged.

Thanks to the wonders of modern tranquilizers and mood stabilizers, Mahmood thought.

Mahmood's plan, still officially unknown to the Grand Ayatollah and President Rouhani, would have Haji continuing to prepare the casements and inner workings for up to 20 suitcase bombs. He would then be allowed to arm three or four of them, each of which would be defused immediately. The Plutonium in each would be returned to the stockpile from which Haji, the machinists, and two hand-picked Iranian nuclear scientists would be working.

It was agreed that everyone would be party to the deception. Except, of course, Haji himself.

Late in the day, while Haji was hard at work in the machine-tool area, Mahmood caught up to the colonel from the Republican Guard. "I'm seeing the need for some additional assistance," Mahmood said.

"I've been told to provide whatever you need," the colonel replied. "What do you need?"

"Soon I need to sit down with a psychiatrist. Or maybe two of them. The day is going to come when my monitoring and lying and drugging alone will not be strong enough to cause Haji to abandon his suitcase bombs and work on the five or six big nuclear devices we want to create."

Thinking further explanation might be necessary, Mahmood continued. "You are aware that Dr. Khan's diagnosis is severe bi-polarism. He swings like a pendulum from manic to depressive. So far, I've been able, with those lies and drugs, to keep him on a more or less even keel. But the minute he learns that he's to stop making suitcase bombs and begin building more powerful, bigger bombs, that pendulum is likely to do a one-eighty. And who knows where it will end up. He'll likely be dangerous not only to himself, but also to everyone else working here."

The colonel said, "It seems to me that you have the situation in hand."

"Oh, no," Mahmood said. "I am neither a psychologist nor a psychiatrist. What they do is way beyond my understanding. That's why I need to spend some time with them to try to better understand how to deal with an unpredictable madman."

"I thought the idea was for the doctor to continue to make suitcase bombs until he had produced 20 or 25—maybe into June," the colonel said. "So what's your rush to meet with these healers of the mind?"

"Colonel," Mahmood said, "these healers of the mind study their craft for what? Ten years? Twelve years? I have less than six months to at least get up to speed on what they recommend. What I can expect Haji to do. How I can expect him to react.

"Haji's the genius. I'm not. In fact, I would be more comfortable if we could bring a psychiatrist on board right away. We could disguise him or her as some kind of analyst. Maybe to help refine our target list for the suitcase bombs. The bombs that will never really be."

Niavarin Palace Complex—Later That Evening

President Hassan Rouhani stood in an otherwise deserted hallway in the palace complex speaking quietly with the head of the Republican Guard. Rouhani asked, "Where is our Novatek caravan today?"

"I just heard from them," the Republican Guard general said. They've reached Astana in the north of Kazakhstan. Maybe a hundred kilometers from the border with the Russian Federation. They're hoping to reach Tomsk in two more days. But then the going gets harder. It will be colder and colder the farther north they go. What roads are there are primitive and, frankly, dangerous this time of year. And of course there are no improved roads for the last 350-400 kilometers to the site. My captain advises me they will be fortunate to cover 25 kilometers a day over that last stretch."

The general shrugged, "Mr. President, they'll be slogging, relying on GPS to keep their heading right. I'll know more next week, but the ETA we talked about last week may turn out to be optimistic."

Rouhani said, "We do what we can do to the best of our abilities. Inshallah."

Then he changed the subject, as presidents are wont to do. And allowed to do. "Do you know any eminent psychiatrists? Or psychologists?"

The general looked concerned. "Are you having problems, Mr. President?"

Rouhani chuckled. "No, at least not that I'm aware of. But Mahmood Bijahn, our minder of the mad nuclear scientist, has requested that a psychiatrist or a psychologist be posted to the laboratories in the Salt Desert. It seems he is concerned about the future mood swings of Dr. Khan."

"That's understandable. The guy's a certified nut case," the general said. "I don't envy Bijahn's job. My colonel up there tells me Mahmood is walking a tightrope every day. Doing a sleight of hand, slipping in a drug here and there, making up whatever lies will work at the moment. So far, I'm told, he's got Khan fairly focused, although certainly not rational."

Rouhani said, "Well, yes, but it seems to be to our advantage that Khan's only semi-rational. Or even irrational. I hear that makes feeding him whatever lies seem appropriate somewhat easier. But, back to my question. What about psychiatrists or psychologists? Ones we can trust. Doctors who are loyal to Islam and anxious to see the great Persian Empire returned to its former glory and rightful place among nations? Who do you know?"

"Offhand, Mr. President, I hesitate to give you names. You've just described a set of characteristics not easily found within the medical profession. Those practitioners tend to be personally independent. They dedicate themselves to their work. But I'll see what I can find out and give you some recommendations tomorrow or the next day. Will that be soon enough?"

"Sure. The need is not urgent, General," Rouhani said. "I've had a thought. Look into very young doctors. First they will be better trained, though less experienced. But the likelihood of finding a true Islamic might be greater among this group. What do you think?"

"Mr. President," the general said, "We will certainly look among that group. But I also want to see if we can find doctors known to have been firebrands in the late 1970s. Perhaps some of them were instrumental in the effort to depose the Shah."

"Good thinking, General. That group, by the way, would be my generation. Yours, too, I suspect. Check them out and keep me posted."

The general looked at his watch, and then said, "We're going to be late for dinner."

Rouhani responded, "I won't be eating for a while. I'm off to bring the Grand Ayatollah up to date."

"Allahu Akbar, Mr. President."

"Inshallah," General.

Chapter Thirty-One
All's Well That Ends Quickly

Vancouver, British Columbia—January 14

Volume 68 + Number 0114   Tuesday, January 14

The BC Daily Recorder-Journal

Bodies of Two Foreign Visitors Found in Local Hotel Massacre
By Nigel Crump and Olivia Simpson-Weatherbie

Vancouver, British Columbia—January 14—The mutilated bodies of two foreign males were found in a suite in the posh Fairmont Hotel Vancouver last night according to local authorities.

Vancouver Police spokesperson Evelyn Rottingham released the following statement to The Daily Recorder--Journal:

"A night-shift concierge for the hotel's floors of suites discovered the dismembered bodies of two men who are believed, at this time, to have been registered to the suite in which their bodies were found. A third man listed as a guest in the same three-bedroom suite has not been located. Authorities would very much like to find this third registered guest."

Asked by our reporters for identifications of the three men, Ms. Rottingham said, "Hotel management has released the passports used when the three guests registered. As is their habit with foreign visitors, hotels keep passports in their safes and release them, on request, during the guests' stay and on departure, of course."

She went on, "I am at liberty at this time to tell you that the passports of the two deceased guests were apparently issued by the governments of South Africa and Myanmar. The passport of the third person had been picked up by that guest last evening. Copies of the third guest's passport showed it to have been issued by the government of Yemen, and it showed an address in what is called The Empty Quarter, a portion of Yemen adjacent to the Saudi Arabian border. The Empty Quarter is sparsely inhabited, a barren desert, and most of its residents are Bedouin tribes."

When asked for specific names, the officer said, "Initial RCMP analysis strongly suggests all three passports are likely fakes. Copies of their three visas also appear to be counterfeit. So the names we have at the moment for the two victims and the missing third guest are of little or no value in attempting to identify either the bodies or the third guest."

Pressed by reporters, Officer Rottingham did add one peculiar note. "The names, as I said, are of little value, but there was a peculiarity in them. Each had a number for a middle name. The two slain men, an Asian with a Myanmar passport, and a Caucasian carrying the South African passport, listed middle names as 'Two' and 'Three,' respectively. Oddly," she continued, "the third guest, the one carrying the Yemini passport, carried

a middle name of 'One.' He is believed to be of Arab descent.

"For now," she continued, we're simply identifying them as One, Two, and Three."

Asked for details of the slayings, spokesperson Rottingham deferred to local RCMP Commander Emerson Windsor. Commander Windsor seemed hesitant, but in light of the pressing need to find One, the missing third guest, he said, "Both the victim's throats were cut and their heads were both completely severed. In addition, their genitals were removed and left stuffed in their mouths."

He paused to let that graphic description sink in, and then he went on.

"The wounds and methods of mutilation and dismemberment are consistent with what authorities in the Middle East have described as routine in assassinations by Muslim radicals. The most likely weapon used, also, is common to the Arab countries in the Middle East. He showed a rendering of what he called a jambiya, a

The Jambiya, shown above, is typically carried by virtually every male in Yemen, particularly by Bedouin tribesmen in The Empty Quarter, a barren desert in Northwest Yemen that is home to many Bedouin tribes.

semi-circular blade with a handle on one end--and with a sharp inner blade sufficient to encircle half the circumference of a cantaloupe . . . or a human neck.

Officer Rottingham stepped back to the podium. "So you can see why we have so much interest in finding the missing third guest. If he is, in fact, from Yemen—or that general area--we know that the vast majority of males in the region routinely carry a jambiya. In the open—open carry." She smiled.

"Along with AK-47s, jambiyas are as common as scarves, or even shoes. We've also learned that Bedouins, in particular, believe a jambiya must not be removed from the holster, or sheath, in which it is carried . . . unless it is to be used for purposes of killing something—or someone."

The Vancouver RCMP barracks has released the following description of the missing guest, based on hotel video surveillance and descriptions from hotel personnel who observed the three guests during their three-day stay:

• Arab male
• 5'11" to 6 feet tall; black hair; dark, probably black eyes
•Prominent (hooked) nose; strong chin; dark complexion; clean shaven
• Educated and well spoken; likely dressed formally—in custom-made suits

Local police and the RCMP caution anyone seeing a person fitting this description to make no attempt to approach him. "Please call either our offices or the RCMP at once," Officer Rottingham said.

RCMP forensics teams have begun working to attempt to determine the identities of the two slain men. Meanwhile the government in Ottawa is contacting officials in Myanmar, South Africa and Yemen to ask them to check their passport records. Copies of the apparently forged passports and definitely forged visas will be transmitted to the three governments for their inspection and conclusions.

Both Officer Rottingham and Commander Windsor described the investigation as "in the early stages."

Trinidade and Martim Vaz Islands—Brazilian Naval Base—January 15

Each morning before beginning work on the new communication systems at the remote naval base, Four made a habit of scanning world headlines . . . with particular emphasis on American and British newswires, the BBC, USA Today, and The New York Times' international edition. He felt certain that what he expected to see would eventually turn up.

Today he hit pay dirt: *"Two Foreigners Mutilated in Vancouver; Third Hotel Guest Suspected."*

Four laughed so hard he found himself slapping his thighs as tears poured down his face. The laughter became so loud that the base commander looked into his quarters and asked, "Are you okay, Senhor?"

Four turned to his guest and, through his attempts to curb his feeling of hilarity, said, "Everything's great. My ship has come in, and I've found the pot of gold at the end of the rainbow."

Then he laughed even harder.

The visitor, somewhat confused, gave him a thumbs up and withdrew down the hallway.

Four spun to his laptop. *The first thing I'll do, he thought, will be to send that email to the International Patent Office, the Institute for Fusion Studies at The University of Texas at Austin, and, the piece de resistance—to good old Vladimir Putin, himself.*

Taking extra care to be sure the message would bounce around the internet through servers in at least six different countries, Four pulled up the draft, and with a feeling of heroics, gleefully hit "Send."

"Game on!" he said aloud, as he began to prepare yet another email that, like the first, would be completely untraceable.

> *To: RCMP Barracks, Vancouver, British Columbia, Canada*
> *From: Senhor Cuatro, the friend you need today*
> *Subject: Just Being a Good Citizen*
> *Hello, Mounties:*
>
> *The man you seek in the double slaying-mutilation in the Fairmont Hotel in Vancouver is as follows:*
> *Name: Ali bin-Salam, a.k.a. One*
> *Occupation: Rich son-of-a-bitch*
> *Education: Ph.D. in nuclear physics from Massachusetts Institute of Technology; undergraduate degree in physics from Stanford University*
> *Hometown: Sana'a, Yemen*
> *Fastest way to find him: Call the U.S. embassy in Sana'a. Don't even try the Yemen government. They're a bunch of incompetent, sleazy ass-wipes.*
>
>

Your friend,
> **Senhor Cuatro**
>
>
> *P.S.—Don't bother to try to track back to find me. Or, if you just must, you will hit a wall Reykjavik, Iceland. I'm not there. But*

count on finding the clues to the whereabouts of One at his home base, above.

P.P.S. – There's no question he killed the other two, but you may play hell getting to him in Yemen. Good luck.

Once again, Four created a circuitous and irretrievable pathway. Then he hit "Send."

Satisfied with the first two emails, Four thought, Just one more--for today—anyway.

To: One, a.k.a. Ali bin-Salam
From: Your old buddy, Four
Subject: A Dozen Virgin Attaboys—And Paradise is Closer Than You Think

Hello, One, you goat-fucking piece of Bedouin shit.

I knew you'd be the one, One. Evil just oozed from you like smoke from the fires of Hell. And, speaking of Hell, you might begin getting prepared for your visit—permanent residence—there. Attached you will find two emails I have sent today, just a few moments ago. You will see, One, that you're in deep caca.

It was nice doing business with you, One. But it was no pleasure being around you. You stink like an infidel whore's breath after she's given blow-jobs to a dozen camels.

So, adios, adieu, arrivederci, aloha, and shalom.

Sorry about the virgins. Rot in Hell.

as-salaam 'alaykum.

Four

Four sent the message and left to go to work, humming *Whistle While You Work*.

Part Four

The Race is On!

Chapter Thirty-Two

Bon Voyage

Austin—Headquarters of Van Pelt Industries—January 16

Gady and I were last to arrive at the early evening meeting. Gady had needed to interrogate a suspected arsonist, and I wanted to watch her from behind our one-way mirror—just in case I might have a pointer or two for her for future use.

At the Hamilton Pool Road headquarters of Van Pelt Industries, the kitchen-office buzzed with anticipation. Josef and Nana had made John, Lobo, and Sanjay wait for our arrival before giving them the daily update. We sat down with fresh Colombian coffee that Josef had received from an exporter in anticipation of Josef's upcoming role as liaison for the Commerce Department for South America--in Buenos Aires. Lobo remarked that it was the best cup of coffee he'd ever tasted. I wouldn't disagree with that.

Josef looked to Nana, and she began her update, clearly excited.

"Our ice breaker has proceeded seven kilometers west of the Plutonium site. The shallow-water drilling rig is at anchor near the shoreline directly at the site. As part of my cover story to Rosneft, the ice breaker has sent ashore two Sno-Cats, one with a bulldozer blade and the second with a hydraulic hammer—the kind we sometimes use for underground soundings."

John said, "What's your cover story?"

"I'll get to that," Nana said. "Let me get all our equipment in position. Then the story will make more sense to you." She continued. "There are three crew members with each Sno-Cat. They have proceeded four kilometers inland and set up what will appear to be a drilling rig site. All six of them are busy moving snow and ice, pounding the permafrost and driving stainless- steel rods into the ice at intervals that will appear to be early preparations for installing a serious drilling rig. To be sure they're seen, each of the rods has an LED flasher on top."

She showed us a photo of what the rods look like, with and without the LED flasher, explaining that the flashers often are attached on remote sites to mark the rods at night.

"Meanwhile, while the drilling rig appears to be completely station-ary, which it is, we've begun an almost horizontal drilling operation from the shoreline to the Plutonium. I say 'almost horizontal' because we're drilling at an upward angle of about six degrees. The drill will end up about two feet beneath the Plutonium."

She sketched a cross section on a poster board tacked to the wall.

"Worst case," she went on, "we'll cause the Plutonium to simply fall back into the crevice it created while popping up. Best case, we'll grab it and pull it back through the two-foot diameter tunnel the drill's creating as we speak. The early drilling was through rock and dirt, but we've bro-ken into the permafrost and expect to be moving more rapidly soon. I should add that most of the drilling happens at night so there's no activi-ty apparent on the drilling rig's decks. But the Sno-Cat crews are merrily making themselves busy during daylight . . . for all the world to see."

Gady asked, "What happens when the Plutonium disappears off the satellite feeds?"

Josef answered, "Glad you asked. Our crews are very inventive. For-tunately, they had a clear-glass mixing bowl in one of their kitchens. A bowl almost exactly the diameter of the Plutonium. It's been sanded until the outside is translucent. And then fitted with a lithium-ion battery and a small orange LED lamp scavenged from one of our instrument panels. Look again at the satellite photo here." He unrolled it on the table. "You can see a dull orange glow coming off the Plutonium. We'll just replace the Plutonium with this jerry-rigged decoy and—voilá--the Plutonium's back on the screens."

Sanjay looked worried. "How long will this transition from Plutoni-um to decoy take? Won't everybody watching see the glow disappear? And then reappear?"

Nana answered. "We've timed pulling the drill back to the ship sever-al times. Keep in mind that it's not to the Plutonium yet. But the drilling engineers think the elapsed time will be no more than 10 to 12 minutes."

Sanjay said, "And everybody watching will go ape-shit. Right?"

"Probably," Nana said. "Whoever is watching at that moment, if anybody, will just sit and stare for a couple of minutes. Then they'll scramble to get on their phones to the next supervisory level up the food chain. Phones will ring. Alarms may even go off. But by the time anybody with enough clout to actually act gets to the scene, bingo—the Plutonium's right back there, orange as you please."

"That's a risk," Sanjay said.

Josef shot back, "Not nearly the risk of having this stuff fall into the wrong hands."

Sanjay nodded.

The phone rang. Josef said, "Monica's on the line. I've already filled her in." He put the phone on speaker.

"Is everybody there?" Monica asked.

"All here," Josef said. "Are you going to tell us about the meeting in Moscow?"

"Right," Monica said. "Well, it was just as I expected. Boris has always been a bully. True to form, he successfully emasculated both the DCI and the NSA. Of course, they wouldn't let me into the meeting. I would have enjoyed grabbing Boris by his bulbous nose and then twisting it until something popped. He brought a plan, which is no plan at all. Typical Putin. They propose to recover the Plutonium while the U.S. stands in the cold and watches. And our guys let him get away with that bluff. And it is a bluff. I wish I could see them tomorrow morning when they report in person to the President. He's going to shit a meat-axe."

"We're moving here, Monica. If they ever do anything at all, it'll be too late," Greycloud said. "Just as you predicted."

Monica answered, "Predictions based on years of observation are too easy, John. Anybody who's been around Washington more than six months could have made that prediction. And they'd have been spot on."

She paused, and then said, "Do you guys need anything from me?"

Nana said, "Keep your eyes on the satellite Sunday. I'll call you from Seoul Saturday night and give you an approximate time for the big switch. You may even want to report the short anomaly."

"You know how to reach me," Monica said. "Never on my CIA line, as you should all know. I don't even call my mechanic on that line."

Monica signed off.

I had to ask, "You said you would fill us in on the tale you spun to Rosneft. I think I could almost figure it out, but maybe you should go ahead. Details will trip you up every time. At least in the detective business."

I turned to Gady and Lobo. "Right?" I said.

They both nodded.

Greycloud added, "Try being a Shaman. I've memorized both the words and the stagecraft for a half-dozen long and complicated sings. And if I forget a phrase or slightly miss-shape a sand drawing, there's going to be somebody at the ceremony who will not only call it to my attention publicly, but also demand a total reenactment. Even if I stumble on the sixth day of a seven-day sing."

Ready to get on with business, Sanjay said, "Tell us the cover story, Nana."

She began, "Rosneft has been told that we've monitored earthquake patterns in the Arctic Ocean area and Northern Siberia. Based on the analyses of our geologists, we believe there's a sure-fire big gas field in the area where we've got our Sno-Cats pretending to be doing some preliminary exploratory work. I've told them that if our soundings look promising, we'll do some shallow drilling with the idea of looking at core samples down to maybe 500 meters or so. The purpose of our activities this week is to get our hands on those core samples for our geologists to further examine."

She looked around the room. "Rosneft is cool with that."

Sanjay said, "Can the shallow-water drilling rig operate on land?"

"No," she smiled, "but they don't know that. The ship's our own unique design—the first of its kind. There's no way for them to figure out that it's for shallow water only. If they even pay that much attention."

"One more question," I said. "You mentioned Sunday on the phone to Monica. Is that the recovery day?"

Josef answered, "Yes. As of right now, at least. Here's the plan: All of us but you and Gady will leave tonight from Austin-Bergstrom International in one of our Gulfstreams. Headed for Seoul. We'll make a fuel stop in Anchorage tomorrow morning, and we'll be in Seoul tomorrow evening. As for you and Gady, the plane will immediately return to Austin, where you and a new crew will depart Saturday early afternoon. Be at the Signature Aviation Services FBO—Fixed Base Operator--by 1:00 p.m. unless you hear from Nana or me in the meantime. That will get you to our offices in Seoul by early Sunday morning—just in time for the big show."

He looked at me. "Will that work for you?"

Gady answered, "We're in."

I added, "As long as I can be back here by Monday night."

Josef said, "No problem for our aircraft. How about the two of you? Can you sleep on an airplane?"

"We're in," I said.

Chapter Thirty-Three

Ring Around the Cabinet

White House—Oval Office—January 17

The President's chief of staff had squeezed in what the Secretary of Commerce had described, redundantly, as an "urgent emergency," for a short, early morning meeting in the Oval Office. The Commerce Secretary had been warned that POTUS had an 8:30 meeting with the DCI, NSA and the Secretary of State. "So be organized, and keep it quick," he'd been told.

"What's up?" the President said, as Commerce came into the office. POTUS found any true emergency in Commerce to be highly unlikely.

The Secretary of Commerce, an African-American from Texas and a former mayor of Dallas, got straight to the point. "Mr. President, our International Patent Office has been hacked, and the plans and patents for an incredible breakthrough process seem to have been stolen."

Before he could elaborate, POTUS asked, "Who are the patent holders? Have they been notified?"

"Actually, they read about it on Reuters and notified Commerce. We've verified the story. The patent holder is The University of Texas at Austin's Institute for Fusion Studies."

POTUS groaned. "Does this involve Plutonium?" he asked, careful to avoid specifics.

Commerce answered, "Well, it certainly involves all kinds of radioactive materials. Specifically, the patents are for a process to reduce unwanted radioactive waste to harmless dirt. The spokesperson at UT told me the process has been known to be feasible for almost 50 years, but their Institute had perfected the details. They're ready to build the apparatus needed to do the job."

POTUS looked at his watch. He leaned back in his chair and said, "Let's you and me have a cup of the morning's freshest coffee. The folks

161

coming over here in 20 minutes are going to be interested to hear the details. Hold them for the next meeting."

He picked up a phone and said. I'll take that coffee right now. Bring an extra cup."

Seoul, South Korea—Offices of Nana's Company
Evening—January 17

Having slept most of the way on the flight from Anchorage to Seoul, members of Monica's advance team paid attention as Josef set up tele-conferencing links to both Monica's home in Virginia and the ice-break-er just offshore from Siberia on the Laptev Sea.

When everyone was on-line, he began an explanation. "You can see Captain Tamaki on the ice breaker and Monica in Virginia," he noted as he turned on two monitors. "Monica, can you see and hear us?" Captain Tamaki?"

The captain nodded, and Monica said, "Good job, Josef. You're in Seoul?"

"Yes, we're in Seoul. Captain, tell us how things are going for you and your crew."

"All goes well, Mr. Reynosa. I have here with me Captain Ruggles of the drilling ship."

Tamaki stood aside, and Captain Ruggles entered the frame. Tamaki said, "Captain Ruggles has a report on the actual drilling. I haven't heard it yet, so we can all be brought up to date together."

Ruggles, still center in the frame, said, "The crew you have given me, Ms. Reynosa, is top-notch. Every day they have impressed me more—not just with their abilities, but also with the knowledge of our business as they put it to work. They seem to have an ingenious solution every time we run into a little problem."

Monica, tiring of the obvious brown-nosing, said, "So, Captain, tell us where you are and what you expect to accomplish in the next 48 hours."

Ruggles smiled. "Laying it on a little too thick, was I, Ms. Skrabacz? Right, in 48 hours, we will either have the target on board and be head-ing back to Hokkaido, or—worst case—it will have sunk back into its hidey-hole. That much I can guarantee. As far as details are concerned, our drill bit is within two meters of the target. We're doing some jiggling. Vibrating the permafrost to see if that has any affect on the target. So far, it hasn't."

He took a sip from a large, steaming mug and continued. "Naturally, we're moving slowly, cautiously." He turned in the direction of Tamaki and asked, "Captain, have you tested the permafrost at this location yet?"

Tamaki, off camera, answered, "Solid as a rock, Captain. If it were rock, I would compare it to limestone. Stable, yet porous, and easy to drill through."

Monica, ever impatient and lacking an understanding of geological formations, interrupted. "So, when will you make the capture?"

Nana broke in. "For God's sake, Monica. Let the Captain tell us at his own pace. I can afford the satellite time."

Ruggles said, "Thank you, Ma'am. Here are the details. We intend to inch along and be directly under the target by your Sunday. That is, at about mid-day when it's Sunday the 19th in the western hemisphere. Then we'll wait for it to be early evening here. It gets dark about 3:30 in the afternoon this time of year. I will give each of you two hours' notice. At a time which we'll communicate on your Sunday, we'll make the switch. You can all see it happen, just like we're seeing one another right now."

Sanjay broke in. "This is Sanjay Pradeet, the nuclear physicist crazy enough to have joined this escapade. Two questions: First, are you absolutely sure you have taken every precaution to protect your crews? And second, what kind of a container do you have for the plutonium? And, oh, one more. What happens if the mass actually drops beyond your reach?"

Ruggles said, "I'll let our on-board geologist answer. Here's Dr. Adam Ion."

A tall and bearded man moved into the frame. "Hello," he said. "And yes, that's I-o-n as in the particle. Perhaps I was destined to be a scientist. To answer your questions, one: yes, we have well-tested protective gear for the crew, and we will be using it, although only two of us plan to get anywhere near the mass, itself."

He paused, "What was the second question?"

"The container," Sanjay said.

"Right," Ion said. "We have a hollow, two-foot cube of solid lead, with six-inch-thick walls and a lid. It sits inside a five-foot cube of solid concrete—six inch walls, too, and also with a lid." He smiled, "If any

163

gamma rays can get out of that, we've just invented a hurricane proof backyard barbecue."

Ion looked up as if trying to recall something. "Ah, yes," he said. "Plan B. If we lose the mass to Mother Earth once again, I'll simply add some isotope material to the decoy to give it a tiny amount of almost harmless radioactivity. Then we can all watch on Ms. Skrabacz's satellites as the first pretender to arrive gets a few Roentgens and a big surprise."

Lobo asked Josef, "Will we have time to get Craig and Gady here for the big show? And then back to Austin by Monday night?"

Josef answered, "Shouldn't be a problem. The Gulfstream that brought us here has a new crew, and they're already halfway back to Anchorage. They'll pick our detectives up mid-day Saturday—tomorrow—there. If there are any problems with the aircraft, our other Gulfstream is in Fargo, North Dakota. It can be back to Austin in three hours."

Nana spoke to the two monitors. "Pardon us for our shop talk. We have two old friends coming aboard here for the switch." She looked around the room. "Any more questions here?" Seeing none, she spoke to the monitors, "Monica? Captains and Dr. Ion, do any of you have further questions?"

"We're good," Captain Tamaki said, adding, "If anything interesting happens before your Sunday, we'll Telex you so you can go outside for a sat-phone call. Meantime, Ms. Reynosa, we never had these kinds of challenges when we worked for your father. Where is he, by the way?"

"He's incognito," Nana said. "Forget him. You'll never hear from him again." She paused, "But thanks for asking."

As Josef shut down the links, Greycloud announced, "If you can spare me for a few hours in the morning, I'm going to have tea with an old friend."

Sanjay asked, "You have friends in Seoul?"

"A few," Greycloud said. "But this one is special. Madam Park and I go way back. When she was an underling—an important underling—I did several jobs for her. She's quite a lady."

Back at the White House—30 Minutes Later

The President had moved the 9:00 meeting to the Cabinet Room, leaving one of his two administrative assistants outside the Oval Office. During the interval while he and Commerce had enjoyed a cup of coffee, POTUS had filled Commerce in briefly on the business of the Plutonium, asking him to hold the details of the theft from the patent office until the next meeting.

POTUS, after everyone had been coffeed, pastried, and had taken seats, began the meeting. "I have included the Secretary of Commerce in this meeting because he's brought to my attention an illegal act that I'm sure has some bearing on our on-going kerfuffle."

Turning to Commerce, he said, "Please start from the beginning, and then fill us in on everything you know for sure. No conjecture, please. Just what you know that we need to know."

Commerce told the assembled group about the hacking and about the patents and plans that apparently had been downloaded. Then he continued. "I received a call last evening from a representative of the Institute for Fusion Studies at The University of Texas at Austin. It seems one of his associates, a Brit, had found on the Reuters newswire a strange story about the theft from the Patent Office files of plans and procedures for turning nuclear waste into harmless dirt."

DCI went to interrupt, but POTUS held up both palms and said, "Let him finish."

Commerce passed around a FAX of the Reuters news story. "As you will see, he said, "the hacker, who remains anonymous and will likely never be identified, has blown the whistle on two of the decapitated billionaires found in the Fairmont Vancouver Hotel. And he or she claimed that the third was most certainly their killer. The hacker further identifies the three men as one from South Africa, one from Myanmar, and the third, the supposed killer, from the Empty Quarter of Yemen."

Expecting that someone might not have a grip on their geography, State said, "The Empty Quarter is a barren desert along Yemen's common border with Saudi Arabia. Its population is more than 90 percent Bedouin . . . and there aren't that many of them."

"Thank you, Madam Secretary," POTUS said. Turning to Commerce, he said, "Go on."

"According to the RCMP and Interpol, these three seemingly-unconnected billionaires plotted to steal the patent files and procedures to be first to the market with the process. This hacker, who identified him- or herself as 'Senhor Cuatro,' named all three and provided a backgrounder on each, including their plot. And, get this, he notified our offices, The University of Texas, and President Putin of the plot."

"When did you receive that message? From this Senhor Cuatro?" POTUS asked."

"Apparently it came in some time yesterday," Commerce said. "Thinking it was some kind of hoax—since we've all been assured there's no way to get into our files—one of our techs set about to try to track it back to its source. Remember, the files weren't removed. They're still right in place."

POTUS asked, "Any luck identifying the source?"

"None," Commerce said. "We apparently hit a dead end in Greenland. Or Iceland. Somewhere in the North Atlantic."

DCI blurted, "Why don't you know where?"

Commerce responded, "Is that really important? Why did CIA claim there were WMDs in Iraq?"

"That's enough!" POTUS said. He directed his comment to the DCI, a man already three-fourths of the way to extreme paranoia. He then said, "You said 'senhor,' right?" Commerce nodded. POTUS went on, "That's a Portuguese word, isn't it? Same as señor in Spanish? Did your techs look into Portugal and Brazil?"

Commerce said, There are a dozen or more countries where Portuguese is the dominant language. I was told all of them had been scoured, but the dead-end always came back to Iceland." Turning to the DCI, Commerce said, "It was Iceland."

"All right," POTUS said, "let's add these three players to the cast of what's becoming dozens, and then let's proceed with the original business of this meeting."

He looked at Commerce, "You're on the team now. You might as well stay to hear the rest."

NSA spoke up. "We met with Boris, head of the FSS, at our embassy in Moscow. He presented Putin's plan. It was not acceptable. It had Russia doing everything. No real role for the U.S. Apparently they want us to just stand by and wait for them to summon us to the goal line. Then, in their magnanimity, they'll announce a major cooperative effort to keep the Plutonium out of the hands of terrorists."

He paused, and then added, "That's the nut of it, anyway."

POTUS turned to the DCI. "What was your response to Putin's proposal?"

The Secretary of State interrupted. "Did you just say the head of the

166

FSB was invited into our embassy? Whose cockamamie idea was that?"

Shedding any responsibility, the DCI said, "I suppose it was your ambassador's."

POTUS said, "I don't give a shit if Putin, himself, dances on the ambassador's desk. I want to know what was your response?" He looked daggers at the NSA and DCI. That required some rapid head movement since they sat at opposite sides of the big table.

Seeing DCI withering , slumping in his chair, and trying to look invisible, NSA said, "We told him it was insulting. We rejected it forcefully."

POTUS was livid. His face turned beet color and he shouted, "Did either of you nimrods even think to get on the fucking phone and ask me what I thought about it?"

Hearing no response, POTUS said, "You represent the only superpower left in the world. And you don't have a stinking clue how to deal with the Russian Federation? After 30 years of a cold war between us? Seems like the only two in this room, besides me, with any decision-making ability are State and Commerce. And Commerce's not home free yet on that count."

DCI started to stand as if to leave.

"Sit down!" POTUS said. "This meeting's over when I say it's over."

Grabbing a phone at his elbow, he spoke to his chief of staff. "Clear the decks, Roger. I want the entire cabinet in this room at 5:00 this afternoon. Tell them it's a 'Come to Jesus' meeting, and they damned well all better bring a piece of the cross with them."

"Now, then," he said to those in the room., "You be here, too. But keep this in mind. It will be my meeting. If I want to hear from any other person, I will personally direct that person to take the floor. Are we clear on that?"

The question was, of course, rhetorical. Nobody dared to speak.

POTUS ended the meeting. "This job I have is tough. To do it well, I need each of you, and thousands of more government employees to keep just a few simple things in mind. At 5:00 today, I'll enumerate those simple things. Once again. And I will expect every person in that room to not only take them to heart personally, but also to rigidly enforce them among all who report to them.

"That's all. Please go back to serving the people of this great country."

As his visitors left the room, POTUS once again picked up the phone.

"Roger, see if you can get me President Putin on the phone."

He listened for a moment and then said, "It's what time in Moscow?" Listening briefly again, he said, ""Okay, line up my simultaneous translator, Oksana Stotska, for 2:00 this afternoon. We'll call at 2:30.

"And Roger, let the Secretary of State know about the call so she can alert the ambassador. And tell her she's welcome to sit in . . . if she wants to."

Chapter Thirty-Four

Fools' Errands and Other Intrigues

Port of Nampo—North Korea—January 18

Kwak and Chang's replacements, both having higher levels of testosterone and lower levels of angst than their predecessors, had determined their only viable course would be to follow through with Kim Jung-Un's demands and pursue the Plutonium.

So, warrant from Kim in hand, they enlisted the services of two vessels of the Korean People's Army Naval Force—KPN. For their mission to the Arctic Ocean and the Laptev Sea, they selected a helicopter-carrying light frigate as their base of operations and a PT small torpedo boat, in case they needed to get away from the Siberian coast rapidly.

The two had spoken with the commander of the frigate about the need for an ice breaker. He had assured them the KPN had one on station in the Bering Sea. "We can rendezvous with her in the North Pacific, south of the Bering Strait. But first, we have to clear the East China Sea."

The new Minister of People's Security asked, "Would it not be faster to skip the East China Sea and go directly through the Sea of Japan?"

The commander answered, "Yes. Faster and more direct. But that route would take us right between Vladivostok and Hokkaido. And those are two places we really don't want to be seen . . . unless you don't mind drawing attention to our mission from both Russia and Japan. The Japanese, in particular, can be quick-triggered, and an international incident won't serve your purposes."

They quickly agreed.

"How long to the target?" the new vice chairman of the National Defense Commission asked.

"Ten days," the commander said. "If we're lucky and the ice breaker can keep us moving at a reasonable pace." He then asked, "Why do you want to drag along the PT torpedo boat? What use will it be to the mission?"

"You don't think we'll need it?" the new Minister of People's Security said.

"I can't imagine how," the commander said. "Unless you plan to start a war."

"Then cancel it. We need to get moving. Our target may be stationary, but we don't know who else is heading for it," the Minister of People's Security said.

Because the Port of Nampo sits on the western side of North Korea, on the Yellow Sea, they knew it would be necessary to sail several hundred miles to the Southeast, opposite the direction of their target, before they could turn north toward the Bering Strait.

The Frigate, outfitted with both helicopter and a long-arm crane, weighed anchor at noon on Saturday, January 18. In the estimation of the commander, if they were lucky they would reach their intended destination on Monday, January 27.

Seoul, South Korea—Official Residence of President Park
Morning—January 18

Madam Park and John Greycloud spent a pleasant hour sipping tea and reminiscing about their joint efforts in the past. She brought him up to date on the defection of Kwak Pum Ji and asked his opinion, which she had come to value over the years. "What would you do with him?" she asked. "If you were me, I mean?"

John said, "Obviously I would think you'll want to drain him of all the information he can provide about Kim and his unstable cohorts in the North. That could take a while. How cooperative do you think he'll be? And how much of what he unloads do you think will be credible and not just fantasy?"

"We're working on that," Madam Park said. "So far, Kwak seems to be willing to tell us anything and everything. We, of course, have enough of our own intelligence to be able to spot big lies. As you Americans say, 'The devil is in the details.' We have ways of checking most of what he says, but the real juicy stuff? I don't know yet how much we can rely on his veracity."

John said, "One thing's for sure. He doesn't want to be sent back to the North. That should give you some pretty hefty leverage, I think."

"John," the President said, "he's been willing to spend 10 to 12 hours a day downloading to our interrogators. So far, he hasn't shown any sign of hesitation. He's answered every question promptly, and he seems to be as informed and knowledgeable as one could expect of a highly-placed government official, even in a country where everything—and I mean everything—is secret."

Greycloud asked, "Do you know exactly why he decided to defect? What's he told you about that? Not that getting out of the cross-hairs of Kim isn't reason enough."

"John, the reason he's given us is credible. It seems that Kim ordered Kwak and the vice chairman of the National Defense Commission—Chang Sung-taek--to put together an expedition of some sort and enter northern Siberia to retrieve a large mass of what appears to be relatively pure Plutonium that popped to the surface of the permafrost near the shores of the Laptev Sea."

Greycloud tried not to react, but Madam Park saw him wince.

She continued, "The Plutonium is there. We've verified that. And you can just imagine why Kim wants it. To Kim, it's just another couple of hundred nuclear bombs. The North's delivery systems are suspect, but there's no doubt they have a few nukes. And they obviously know how to build more."

She paused. Looked directly at John, and said, "I saw your reaction when I mentioned the Plutonium. You Navajos may have the reputation for being stoic, but you flinched. Let me guess. That Plutonium is at least the major reason you're here in Asia. Am I right?"

Greycloud smiled. "I've never been able to pull the wool over your eyes. You caught me. Yes, I'm here in Seoul with some associates because of the Plutonium."

Knowing he could trust Madam Park with the darkest of secrets, he continued. "You see, we intend to retrieve that Plutonium before it falls into the wrong hands. That's our plan, and so far, we're right on track to grab it tomorrow and replace it with a clever decoy."

"Ah, hah," the President said, showing little surprise. "That would have meant that Kwak and Chang couldn't have succeeded in their assignment for Kim."

"And he would have shot them," Greycloud said. "What happened to Chang? He didn't defect too, did he?"

Madam Park said, "No. Distrust is so rampant in the North that

171

Kwak knew Chang would blow the whistle on him. So he shot Chang and dumped his body on a roadside on his way to the DMZ and the border. As you may have heard, Kim has boasted that he, personally, has executed Kwak."

"More lies from the evil muppet," John said. "Where do you have this Kwak now?"

"Interesting you should ask, John," the President said. "He's downstairs in a special apartment for special visitors. Our security people come here to interrogate him every day."

She thought a minute, and then said, "Would you like to meet him? In the last few days he's come up with an idea of how our country could put him to use. Secretly and quietly, of course. It might be of interest to other countries as well. I'm not sure we're ready to go along with his idea. Certainly we'll never be ready to be associated publicly with the idea. But maybe you'd like to listen to him describe it himself? Do you want to listen to him? He speaks English."

"I'll bet he doesn't speak Navajo," John said. "What are your reservations about his plan . . . before I listen to him? No pun intended."

"I personally have three concerns," the President said. "It will be costly. It will take a long time to develop. And no democratic country in the world will want to be tied to it in any way."

"Sounds like something the CIA might cook up," John said. "If you want my thoughts on it, bring him on up."

Madam Park speed-dialed a number on her phone and said, "I have a very trustworthy old friend upstairs in the library who would like to meet Mr. Kwak. Please bring him on upstairs."

She asked John, "Will you have time to stay for lunch?"

"Probably not. I really need to get back to my associates downtown. But, if you're serving kimchi, I definitely won't have time."

Madam Park laughed. "You don't like that stuff?"

"No more than you would like my grandmother's goat enchiladas."

Momentarily, two officials brought Kwak Pum Ji into the library and, seeing John Greycloud with her, immediately left him with the President.

When introductions had been completed, Kwak became very animated. "Are you really an Indian medicine man? Like the Indians in Alan Ladd's movies?"

John had been through this before. Explaining his role to *biligaanas*

172

had become second nature to him, but answering a Korean might be more of a challenge.

"Mr. Kwak," John said, "my people are the Navajos. Many years ago, we lived nearby—in what is now Mongolia and Manchuria. We crossed the land bridge that once joined this continent with the Western hemisphere. The many clans of my people now live in the Southwest United States, mostly in New Mexico and Arizona. We have never been Indians. I don't take scalps, don't wear war paint or feathers, and I sure don't scream from horseback. Let's just say I'm descended from Asian ex-patriots."

President Park enjoyed this explanation, but she didn't want Kwak's fascination with Kim's old movies to disrupt the reason she'd had him brought upstairs. She said to the defector. "Mr. Greycloud is interested in hearing your idea. Will you explain it to him?"

With that, Kwak's eyes lit up. He had been pushing his idea for several days. But until this moment, nobody had shown the slightest interest. The chance to tell this mysterious medicine man from America what he had in mind was, for him, the sign of a potential breakthrough.

So Kwak spent the next 15 minutes detailing a plan that he had obviously thought through carefully. Having had the experience of briefing Kim Jung-Un, he had learned to be succinct, precise and straight to the point.

John Greycloud was taken aback with Kwak's opening statement: "The world will be a much safer place when it is rid of Kim Jung-Un and the Communist oppressors running the Democratic People's Republic of Korea. It's neither democratic, nor is it a republic. Korea should be united once again under a real democratic-republic form of government."

Whoa!

Chapter Thirty-Five

Blinded—By Snow and Power

Russian Federation—50 Kilometers Northeast of Tomsk—January 18

The Iranian convoy, disguised as Novatek Gas crews, had crossed the Ob River at Tomsk and set their course for 12 degrees by their GPS. Of course they wanted to stay on roads as far into Siberia as possible. But in the blinding, drifting snow, they often lost sight of what might be a road. Sooner or later, they knew they would have to strike out across country, and they were not looking forward to that.

As they crept to the northeast, each day's light became shorter. The big V-shaped plow on the front of their first vehicle wasn't working as well as they had expected. A flat blade would have been preferable in these conditions. A flatter surface would be better than banks of snow piled too high to see over on either side of their path. But they had a job to do, and they were determined to do it.

Job one had become not freezing. They dared not turn off their diesel engines. They knew that at 20 degrees below zero, Centigrade, a diesel likely would never start again. They had only one engine block warmer, and it had to be used with a portable generator only during refueling of each vehicle—when the engine had to be shut down.

The commander of the expedition thought more often each day, *Who came up with this bat-shit-crazy idea, anyway?* Knowing the orders had come from the Niavarin complex in Tehran, he kept that thought to himself, even when he wanted to scream it into the incessant wind and blowing snow.

At the rate they had progressed, each member of the party suspected a little more strongly each day that they would not have enough fuel to make it all the way back to Tehran. If they ever got to the shores of the Laptev Sea, anyway. To be sure, they had satellite phones and numbers to call in Tehran to get more fuel and food. But the powers that be might just be reluctant to send an air-drop into Russian air space . . . unless the expedition had the Plutonium on board. Otherwise, if they didn't make it back to the Kazakhstan border with the prize, they might just become dispensable.

Or disposable.

The leader was somewhat encouraged by the lack of difference between night and day. He decided that since they could see no better in daylight than at night, they might as well make their drive continuous—day and night. Meals could be prepared while they kept driving; and sleep, in shifts, also would not require stopping.

So on they pushed, ever more slowly, dreading the coming lack of any kind of road. And the need to strike out across country, depending on their GPS to keep them moving toward the prize.

Iran—Salt Desert Laboratories—January 18

Mahmood Bijahn faced his first real crisis in the desert with his charge, the unpredictable Dr. Khan. Bijahn had been awakened this morning and told that Khan had been found naked in the laboratory, curled in a fetal position, drooling and mewling incoherently.

When he reached the lab, Bijahn had to admit, at least to himself, that he had not seen this particular behavior before. *This is exactly why I need the counsel of a psychiatrist or psychologist,* he thought.

"How long has he been like this?" Bijahn asked the technician who had found Khan.

"I don't know," the technician said. "I came in, as I do every morning about this time, to turn on the lights and see to the instrumentation. The door was unlocked when I got here. It's supposed to be locked at night—until I open it up myself."

"How did Khan get in then?" Mahmood asked.

"I don't know that, either," the technician said. "Only the colonel and I are supposed to have keys to this room. Yet Dr. Khan had to have had a key. I locked the doors myself at 2130 last night."

The two of them rolled Khan over to see if there might be a key underneath him or in one of his hands. They found him completely stiff. Unbending and unbendable. Like rigor mortis had overtaken him and progressed to its maximum effect.

And they found no key.

Mahmood said, "Would you please go to find me some help? I've got to get him back to his room and in his bed. He's going to be useless for a day or two."

"What will you do?" the technician said.

"What I always have to do," Mahmood answered. "I'll knock him out and make him sleep for 24 hours. We'll just have to see who he is and how he's behaving when he wakes up tomorrow.

"And while you're finding me some help, track down the colonel. He's going to have to get me some qualified professional help up here. Or I'm going to declare this whole scheme a disaster."

As the technician left, Mahmood regretted that last statement. He thought, *As important as I am to keeping Haji focused, I'm in no position to be issuing ultimatums. But dammit, I asked for a professional several days ago.*

Niavarin Palace Complex—At the Same Time

President Rouhani walked into his office to find his hotline phone to the Republican Guard ringing.

"Rouhani here. Allahu Akbar."

"Mr. President, it's the general. I have found your psychiatrist."

"Tell me," Rouhani said.

"He's of our generation as you suggested he might be. Trained in America. M.D. degree from Johns Hopkins in Baltimore and certified in psychiatry from Harvard Medical School."

"So he's qualified," Rouhani said. "But tell me his motivation. Why is he right for this assignment?"

"During the revolution to rid our country of that vermin, the Shah, our doctor worked night and day caring for both physical and mental cases. In the revolution, he was a firebrand. And, I'm pleased to report, he has retained his dislike for the Western countries that propped up the Shah for so many years. He is Muslim, but not any fan of Al Qaeda or ISIS or any terrorist, for that matter. Do you want to meet him?"

Rouhani recoiled. "Absolutely not. You keep this project strictly the business of the Republican Guard. Do not involve either Ali Khamenei or me. Is that understood?"

"Perfectly, Mr. President. So you will know, I took the liberty of informing my colonel at the Salt Desert laboratory about this find late last night. He was pleased. He said he's concerned that Mahmood Bijahn is stressed to the point that he may not be able to control Dr. Khan."

"Excellent, General," President Rouhani said. "How soon can you get the good doctor up to speed and to the desert?"

"I'll take him myself. We'll leave within the hour. Inshallah"

Salt Desert Laboratory—An Hour Later

After getting Khan into bed and to sleep for at least another day, Mahmood took the time to calm himself down, as well. He headed to the canteen to find himself some coffee and a pastry or two. As he sat contemplating whether to take, for himself, one of the mood stabilizers intended for Khan, the colonel joined him.

"I have good news," the colonel said. "We have a well-qualified and loyal psychiatrist on the way, and he's dedicated to our cause."

"When will he be here?" Bijahn said.

"Before noon today. The general himself is bringing him."

The colonel saw a pill bottle on the table beside Mahmood's coffee. "What are those for?" he asked.

"They're mood stabilizers," Mahmood said. "I use them when the need for only a slight correction in Khan's mind is needed." He paused, and then added, "But I was contemplating taking one or two of them myself. Have you heard about our early morning adventures with Dr. Khan?"

"Yes, I was told he'll be out of commission for at least a day. Was it bad? In your experience, I mean?" the colonel said.

Bijahn said, "The worst yet. I've been wracking my brain to try to remember anything from yesterday that might have caused him to go completely off the rails."

"But nothing comes to mind?" the colonel said.

"Not yet, Colonel. But if it's all right with you, I think I should get an hour or two of rest before the doctor gets here. In a way, it's good that Haji won't need looking after this afternoon. Maybe I can use the time to fill in the psychiatrist. I wonder, though, if he'll believe me? Or will he just think I'm exaggerating?"

"If there is any question, count on me to back you up, Mahmood," the colonel said. "Remember, though, this doctor has been practicing for almost 40 years. He's seen worse, I imagine."

"I hope so," Mahmood said. "I certainly never have. Not worse than this morning for sure."

The colonel stood to leave. He pointed to the pill bottle. "Don't take those until you see the doctor. He may have a better idea for you."

Chapter Thirty-Six

Where Have All the Searchers Gone?

Trinidade and Martim Vaz Islands—Brazilian Naval Base
Sunday, January 19

Normally Four, aka Senhor Cuatro, would be taking Sunday off—a day to rest. But Four had become bored with the creation and installation of the communication systems for the Marinha do Brasil. Oh, he would finish the job. After all, he'd signed a contract and given his word. And the work was so easy for him that it had turned into an almost mindless task.

But Four had decided he could finish the six-month's assignment in as few as 90 days. So he began working seven days a week, 8-10 hours a day. He wanted personal permanence. Soon.

With his single-digits former partners either dead or on the run, the only excitement left in his life involved the pursuit of a permanent home and lifestyle. He'd resolved to spend two hours each evening trolling the internet looking for just the right place—a place secluded, requiring neither cooling nor heating year-round, nothing to wear fancier than shorts and a T-shirt, and access to a beach.

Four loved the ocean, one of the reasons that had brought him to this outpost in the South Atlantic.

It hadn't taken many hours for Four to narrow down his search. He had four prospective sites on a short list so far—New Caledonia, Auckland Island, Mauritius, and French Polynesia. And he was becoming anxious to go see each of them. Comparing the tasks ahead of him with a calendar, Four targeted April 15 as the day he would finish the creation and installation of the island's communications system.

April 15. Would he file his U.S. Federal Income Tax return for last year? Probably not. *I'll just send in a death certificate signed by a Brazilian doctor,* he thought. The fact that he didn't know, or ever want to know, a Brazilian doctor was of no consequence to Four. He could create the documents, himself. Who, at the IRS, would check the authenticity? Nobody.

Socotra Island—Gulf of Aden—South of Yemen

One, aka Ali bin-Salam, had been warned that the U.S. embassy in Sana'a, his home country's capital, had been making inquiries as to his current whereabouts. Traveling incognito, he had reached the island of Socotra off the south coast of Yemen by first flying into Djibouti. Then he had hired a boat to bring him overnight to Socotra. The boat's crew were likely Somalian pirates, but One paid them handsomely. And he still carried his jambiya, a weapon even pirates respected.

I should have killed that little hacker, One thought. *If I had been more careful I would be sitting on trillions today. Instead, I'm a wanted—no a hunted—man, even in my own country.*

Ali bin-Salam had a plan to return to the Empty Quarter. He would travel by night by boat into the Red Sea. His Bedouin tribe would pick him up and protect him—keep his presence secret. His family ranked among the most respected and powerful of the Bedouins. And Bedouins are clannish, putting family above all else. Especially above officials of the corrupt and incompetent government of Yemen. If the Bedouins despised any group more than the country's current rulers, it would be Al Qaeda. Only terrorists ranked in contempt slightly higher than the hated government officials in Sana'a.

One knew he would have to change his identity. Still, he expected to have to remain in the Empty Quarter for years before venturing anywhere besides Saudi Arabia. The Saudi ruling family had unwritten agreements to cooperate with Bedouins, and One's family had close ties to several Saudi princes.

Still he would wear no more of his Savile Row suits for a while. Only the traditional robes and headgear of the desert.

And his dreams of trillions from reducing spent nuclear fuel to dirt? They had vanished. Pfft!

Central Siberian Plateau—Approaching the Yenisey River

In near-whiteout conditions, the Iranian convoy had managed to move less than 120 kilometers in the past two days, guided by GPS in what might as well have been total darkness. They knew they should be approaching the Yanisey River from its southwest. They also knew there were places where the river should be frozen all the way across. Frozen to a thickness sufficient that they would be able to simply drive their vehicles to the other side, one at a time.

But in these near-blind conditions, the convoy's commander knew he had to test the thickness of the ice before trying to cross. Testing the ice's thickness meant sending a three-man crew out onto the ice with drills. They would have to be lashed together with rope and tied to the lead vehicle. Otherwise the howling wind might just push them down the frozen river to a sure death.

His problem now was being sure they were actually drilling on the river. Drilling on the snow- and ice-covered banks would prove nothing, and it would be misleading. That meant the drill would have to go all the way through the ice into whatever water below still had not frozen.

If the river had a sufficiently-thick ice layer, he thought they could just turn to the north-northwest and drive along the river. In 300-350 kilometers they would be fairly close to the target's latitude. Then they could strike out to the east across land to the target that lay to the north-east. The frozen river's bed offered a longer, but faster route than across country.

To compound his enigma, Tehran kept calling for position reports. And not seeming to be satisfied at the progress the convoy was making. He thought about just lying to them, but he knew that would eventually bite him in the ass. And he couldn't be sure some kind of satellite transmitter hadn't been hidden on one or more of the trucks. If it had, they would know where the vehicles were anyway.

He thought, *This is turning into a fucking nightmare. I hope those assholes in Tehran know what the hell they're doing. Because I sure don't know what they're doing.* "Go get this heavy radioactive ball. It's right there. Bring it on back. No problem. Piece of cake!"

Bullshit!

Tehran—Niavarin Palace Complex—Office of The Supreme Leader

The Grand Ayatollah Ali Khamenei had summoned President Rouhani and the general to his suite of offices. Without chit-chat, he asked, "Where are they? Mark them on this map."

He unrolled a large map of Siberia and pointed, "Show me."

The general carefully stuck a pin at 58 degrees north latitude and 90 degrees west longitude. Right in the middle of the West Siberian Plain.

"Now show me where the Plutonium is. How far are they from

it?" the Grand Ayatollah said.

The second pin entered the map at 74 degrees north and 105 degrees east. The general said, "They're still about sixteen to eighteen hundred kilometers from the Plutonium, and most of that will have to be across empty land, without roads."

"How long?" President Rouhani said.

Again the general did some mental calculations. "During the white-out they've experienced the last 24 hours, they've only been able to advance at a rate of three to four kilometers per hour . . . very, very slowly. However, if the weather clears, I'm told they can expect to move at a rate of maybe 20-25 kilometers per hour."

He thought a second, and then said, "Best guess is four to five days."

President Rouhani asked, "Is there anything we can do? Or provide? To help them move along faster?"

The General glanced at Ali Khamenei and said, "Ask for Allah's help."

Ali Khamenei answered, "Inshallah."

Iran—Salt Desert Laboratories

Haji Khan, Ph.D. had awakened after his bizarre behavior of the day before. Immediately, Mahmood Bijahn knew he was not going to be able to function. Bijahn and the newly-arrived psychiatrist conferred, and the psychiatrist decided to spend some time with the physicist to try to determine the severity of his current mood swing.

Bijahn and the colonel met for coffee while the doctor examined Khan. Bijahn said, "I spent most of yesterday afternoon filling the psychiatrist in about my observations and what I've done in the past to try to keep Khan on the straight and narrow."

"Did the doctor see him yesterday?" the colonel asked.

"No," Mahmood said, "Khan was zonked out. Totally unconscious. I had to do that to him to even get him relaxed from his curled-up position. I explained to the doctor what I had given Khan, and he said we'd wait until this morning."

He paused and shook his head. "Only this morning Haji most resembled some kind of zombie. He was awake, but not alert. His movements were all slow motion. He tried to speak, but obviously was not able to say anything coherent. I've never seen him like this before. This is different."

The colonel said, "We have time. Maybe the doctor can figure out how to get him back to normal."

Mahmood laughed. "Colonel, there is no such thing as normal. Not for Khan."

The White House—An Unusual Sunday Session

Yesterday, the Secretaries of Education, Interior and Home Land Security had been too far from Washington to make a 5:00 p.m. cabinet meeting. So the chief of staff had called an unusual Sunday afternoon session, telling the traveling Secretaries to "Get back to Washington."

POTUS began the proceedings by giving his own briefing of the situation with Putin and the Plutonium. This required some backtracking since most of the cabinet knew nothing about the appearance of the heavy metal to begin with.

POTUS concluded by saying, "I've brought you all into the fold. Roger has locked the door, and we are not going to leave this room until we have come to a unanimous decision on this matter. And you will all sit quietly and listen to me convey that decision by phone to Vladimir Putin. He's been told to expect my call this evening—early Monday morning for him. He's further been told that the United States will have a decision, and that I will report it to him personally."

He paused. "Any questions?"

Nobody spoke. They all stared down at the table in front of them.

As the President fully expected, the group lapsed into a discussion in which virtually every cabinet minister began to hold out for whatever he or she thought might benefit their piece of the government pie. The President let that go on for about 15 minutes. And then he called a halt to it.

He said, "We can't come to a decision with each of you protecting your patch or feathering your own nest. This is not about a piece of the Executive; it's about the security of our country . . . and of the world. So stop thinking micro, and start thinking macro."

Justice asked, "Have you informed Congress of this matter?"

POTUS said, "That will be State's job after I talk to Putin today. Maybe sometime next week. Meantime, we don't need any partisan bullshit or dopey opinions from some of the camera-loving nitwits."

The discussion went on for an hour. No decision or unanimous strategy appeared on the horizon. Thoughtful and productive exchanges soon returned to petty bickering.

Finally, POTUS said, "Roger, get Putin on the line, and get the Vice President in here. I'll need Oksana. She's waiting in the Oval Office."

He turned to the Cabinet members and simply said, "You are about to see and hear our unanimous decision."

He looked slowly at the faces around the room, and then he added. "I want it absolutely silent in here. Putin doesn't need to know we have a throng of people here who can't figure out how to cooperate long enough to bake a cake."

South Korea—Cheong we die Residence of Madam Park

Madam Park had invited the ambassadors from the U.S., Japan, China and Great Britain to what they believed to be an informal get together—a Korean barbecue. She had given this event considerable thought and had decided to just play it by ear. She would guide the conversation. And if the appropriate chance arose, she would go directly into the potential topic for the day: the plan that Kwak Pum Ji had been selling for the past week. If the time didn't seem right for the group, she would ask the ambassador from the United States to stay a few minutes for "an important talk."

One way or another, she intended to get a feel from South Korea's biggest ally—a reaction to the crazy idea Kwak had proposed.

Or was it so crazy?

East China Sea—Between Shanghai and the Island of Kyushu
Aboard the KPN Light Frigate

As the frigate, on its way to a rendezvous with another NKP vessel—an ice breaker, passed from the Yellow Sea into the East China Sea, they picked up a Japanese naval ship following them. It was a guided missile destroyer, smaller and faster than their frigate. And the destroyer obviously intended to follow them to see where they might be going. Japan took a dim view of NKP ships sailing beyond the Yellow Sea.

The new Minister of People's Security asked the frigate's commander, "What do we do if she keeps on following us?"

The commander answered, "I'm not concerned if that's all she does. But if we pick up a half-dozen patrol boats and a few helicopters on radar, then we have problems. Big problems."

"So what do we do, then?" the minister asked.

"We can either go back to Nampo, or we can tell them we're going to the Arctic on a training mission—and see what happens."

"What do you think will happen?"

The commander answered, "I don't have a clue."

Chapter Thirty-Seven

Excitement and Anticipation

Ted Stevens Anchorage International Airport—January 18

What we'd expected to be a seven-hour flight to Anchorage turned out to be closer to nine hours. We'd run into stiff headwinds coming out of Austin; our crew decided to make a precautionary fuel stop in Portland. So here we are in Anchorage in the middle of the night in January.

When I say it's cold here, I mean meat-locker cold. To a Texan, this cold is unimaginable. Our steward insisted on showing us a trick. Since we had to leave the plane anyway to clear passport control before leaving the U.S., we watched his demonstration on the tarmac. He had brought a cup of hot coffee from the plane. To make his trick even more spectacular, he'd heated the coffee in the microwave until it boiled. Once down the stairs he said those often-dangerous words, "Watch this!"

With that, he shot the cup up from knee level to his shoulder so that the scalding coffee flew upward out of the cup. And simply vanished. Vaporized. He explained that the change in temperature from more than 200 degrees Fahrenheit to the air's minus 20 degrees simply turned the hot liquid into gas vapor, passing so quickly through the solid state that ice didn't really even form.

"That was spectacular," I said to him. "How long can we stand here before we, too, become gas vapor?" He laughed, but I was serious. Gady, from Southern Arizona, jumped up and down and rotated her arms in a futile effort to retain some body heat.

Fortunately, both Gady and I had been able to sleep on the leg from Portland to Anchorage. And we had another six or seven hours to sleep until we reached Seoul. Since we hadn't heard from either Nana or Josef, I assumed the grab-and-go would still be on—but not before we got to the Van Pelt offices to watch.

As we pulled onto the runway to depart for Seoul, Gady said, "You know, don't you, that we could have watched from Nana's kitchen in Austin? That would have required just an additional hook-up."

No, I thought, *not being a tech nerd or even as electronically savvy as most five-year-olds, I actually had never thought that our location could be almost meaningless in the world of today.* Not giving away my ignorance, I said, "But a champagne celebration is more fun with a group, don't you think?"

She smiled. "You never thought of that, did you?"

I replied, "Go to sleep."

Seoul, South Korea—Van Pelt Industries' Offices—January 19

The overnight flight from Anchorage to Seoul must have been uneventful. I had gone to sleep right after lift-off and didn't stir until our wheels hit the runway at Inchon International Airport. I'm not sure what I expected Seoul to be like, but what I saw on the ride from the hotel to the downtown offices of Van Pelt Industries surprised me.

The Seoul I saw was a beautiful city, with wide streets and parks as clean as Disney World. On a typical morning, little children, seemingly alone, walked the streets and played in the parks, apparently without fear. I asked our flight attendant about that, and he said Seoul is a very safe city. "Small grade-school children often ride the subways alone. Not so in New York, huh?"

Not so much in Austin these days, either, I thought.

We arrived mid-morning at the Van Pelt offices. I don't want to mislead you. When I say "offices," I'm referring to a two-room suite in a low-rise complex. Maybe a total of 1,200 square feet. Since there are only two full-time staff, I suppose offices that size might be more than adequate. One of the rooms appeared to be an office with two desks, two computers and multiple phones and file cabinets.

The second room most resembled a miniature NASA flight control center. Two walls contained maps—big maps—of the entire Eastern hemisphere, from the North Sea to Indonesia, including the Pacific Rim. Pins of several colors marked what must have been production sites, exploration sites and contract-pending sites. A third wall was crammed with monitors and an impressive array of instrumentation. Of course, I had no idea what any of it was for, but I could at least see a lot of computing power at three work stations in the center of the room.

I couldn't help but wonder how some of these electronic gimcracks and gewgaws might help us in the detective business to catch bad guys. On a small scale, you understand. Like Austin. Or thinking big, maybe Travis County.

The four of those who'd left a couple of days earlier than Gady and me welcomed us at the front door and invited us to join them in coffee and a giant platter of Korean pastries. Greycloud seemed to know all about the goodies. He gave Gady and me a quick rundown of three of them which he most highly recommended—Gyeongju, Kultarae and his most favorite, Hotteot. "Try one of each," he encouraged us. "Just don't try to spell their names."

Now I've heard that Koreans, and Asians in general, eat some pretty weird stuff. But John was right. None of these was slimy or slippery, and none had apparently crawled from under a rock or up on a beach somewhere. I had missed breakfast on the flight. Gady hadn't. She'd told the attendant to let me sleep. I think she wanted to eat both our meals. Proof of that became clear when she just picked at the pastries. I ate two of each and considered going back for thirds. But I found them as rich as butter and cream could make them. So I had a second cup of coffee, instead.

Gady asked, "When does the show begin?"

Josef looked at a clock on the wall. "We got the two-hour countdown signal from the *U.S.S. Pavlovich's Folly* about a half hour before you arrived. So I would say 80 or 90 minutes.

I noticed that Sanjay had disappeared. "Where's our nuclear physicist?" I asked.

Lobo said, "He's up on the roof." Then he waited patiently for Gady or me to ask the obvious.

So I did. "Why is he on the roof?"

Greycloud said with a wink, "We think it's an Indian thing, peculiar to ex-patriot nuclear physicists. I'm speaking, of course, of the kinds of Indians who are really Indian. From India"

I could tell everyone here was in a celebratory mood—as if they knew the plan would go off without a single hitch.

I looked at Nana and shrugged.

She explained, "Sanjay is on a satellite phone to the Josef, our ice-breaker. He's working with our geologist to be sure the crews are properly protected when they pull the Plutonium on board—until they get it in its cage."

"Cage?" Gady said.

Nana said, "That's what Sanjay calls it—the cage."

I wondered if that might be a technical term of some sort.

Before I had a chance to ask another embarrassing question, Sanjay came in the door, shed his coat and gloves and said to Josef, "Can you fire up the video connection a little early? Your geologist has something he wants me to see."

As Josef and Sanjay went into the second room so Sanjay could look at whatever he needed to see, Monica called on one of the landlines.

"How's everything going there?" she asked.

Nana assured her that everything was on schedule and told her to stand by her computer screen starting in about 60 minutes. "We're counting down right now to about 75 minutes for the grab," she said. "The ships' crews and all our on-site people are very confident."

Monica said, "Well, wait until you hear what's happening at the big White House in Sieve City."

"Tell us," Greycloud said.

Monica said, "It seems that POTUS has gone ballistic. He's apparently finally realizing how screwed up his bureaucracy is. And it took Vladimir Putin to call it to his attention. I spent half the night with the DCI and NSA downloading as much as I had time for about Russia, Russians, and Putin, in particular. DCI and NSA are two frightened puppies. It seems the two of them have managed to screw up so badly that they're afraid that POTUS is considering replacing them. The DCI told me that POTUS got so exasperated yesterday that he called a cabinet meeting to remind all of them that their jobs are to serve the interests of the entire country. Not just their little fiefdoms. So far, State seems to be the only one not on thin ice. Because of some bad judgment by the DCI and NSA, she got to the party late, but apparently has managed to at least pull some kinks out of the pipeline."

"What's he going to do?" Lobo said. "The President? He can't fire the entire cabinet."

Monica laughed, "He can if he wants to. He's making the point I've been trying to make since Moses was in a basket. Our bureaucrats are obsessed with their territories and saving their own asses. Too few of them have the courage or smarts to make a decision or, God forbid, to act unilaterally. This group-think has become debilitating."

"What about the deal with Russia?" I asked.

"Who knows?" Monica said. "One thing's for sure . . . the President is going to call Putin with the entire cabinet listening in. He's going to show them how to get off their asses and make a decision. Starting with that phone call, it's the POTUS-Putin show. The cogs of the big machines will begin spinning."

"So who's going to win?" Gady said.

Monica said, "See, that's the problem. Why does one side always have to win? I don't know what Putin's trying to prove with his cooperative offer, but we've fucked up the response. Now the two top guys, both of whom have better things to be doing, have to show their underlings—and the world, I suppose--that it doesn't take a cast of hundreds, and dozens of studies, and months and months to get something accomplished. As Nike says, 'Just do it.'"

Nana said, "How is this brouhaha going to affect you?"

Monica said, "Until the next know-it-all, testosterone-driven nimrod comes along, I'm golden. But lessons are never learned well nor remembered long inside the Beltway. Give this show of executive strength a few months, and it, too, will be forgotten, And we'll be back to the CYA Serenade."

Josef and Sanjay came back into the front room. Josef announced, "They're ready. Showtime in 15 minutes. I'm cranking up the big screens. Grab your popcorn and take your seats, ladies and gentlemen. The magic of free-enterprise efficiency is about to take center stage."

Chapter Thirty-Eight

Double Dribble

74° North, 105° East—January 19

Captain Tamaki's crew from the ice-breaker *USS Josef* had suspended their work last night and brought all their equipment back aboard their ship. Just as they did every night. Also as they did each night, they had left in place the stainless-steel posts that appeared to mark the boundaries of a potential drilling site. And, as always, they had left the night lights. Turned on, of course.

One thing had happened differently. After returning to the *Josef* last night, Captain Tamaki had weighed anchor and returned the seven kilometers to the east to lay-by aside the shallow-drilling rig, *USS Pavlovich's Folly*. Crew members moved back and forth at will between the two ships using a quickly-rigged overhead wire like a one-person monorail.

In the drilling rig's pilot house, Captains Tamaki and Ruggles spoke with their on-board geologist and a drilling engineer. "When will you be ready?" Tamaki said. Ruggles looked expectantly to the engineer.

The geologist turned to the engineer, who nodded. "We're ready," the engineer said. "It's best we get this done within the next two hours while the seas under the ice are as placid as they are now."

The geologist added, "The timing is also good for the remaining daylight. Not that nightfall will interfere with satellite images, but making our way back to the east in darkness will help us all to think we're being clandestine." He smiled. "It's a mind trick. Our rational side knows we're really not hiding. But our fantasy side still feels more comfortable."

Tamaki asked Ruggles, "Then are you ready for me to give the call?" He meant, of course, the call to the company's offices in Seoul where Josef waited to put the video connections together—the ship to Seoul, and Seoul to Monica's computer in Virginia.

Ruggles said, "Let's do it!"

189

With that, the geologist and engineer returned to the drilling-rig's control room to get ready to *double dribble*, their name for the switch-out.

Seoul—Van Pelt Industries Offices

The expected Telex arrived, and Josef and Sanjay climbed back to the roof to receive what they expected to be a satellite phone call from Captain Tamaki . . . in five minutes.

That's about the time that Gady and I arrived.

Nana then assigned each of us specific things to concentrate on during the exchange of the Plutonium for the mixing bowl. My job would be to take a stopwatch Josef had handed me and time the lapse between the disappearance of the Plutonium's orange glow until the return of the decoy's light. Not too complicated.

Josef had two cameras aboard *Pavlovich's Folly*. One from the top of the wheelhouse would transmit an image of the glowing Plutonium. That's the one I'm supposed to watch and time. The second would show the transfer, on board the ship, of the Plutonium from the end of the drill shaft to its lead cage—and the loading of the mixing bowl decoy and its insertion into the underwater shaft from which it would be pushed back to the surface opening some 12 meters from the shoreline.

Sanjay and Josef returned from their call. Josef said, "Five minutes from . . . NOW!" as he looked at his watch while Sanjay set a digital countdown clock on the wall to 300. It began to flash immediately as the seconds counted down.

Two 50-inch Samsung monitors flicked on, one showing the Plutonium and the other showing the drill shaft inside the ship and under the waterline. Sanjay explained that the drill would come through a sally port equipped with a scupper so no sea water could spill into the ship. "All very neat and tidy," he said, pointing out the glowing mixing bowl in the lower corner of the screen. "There's our decoy."

Two crew members moved either side of the drill shaft opening, revealing the concrete-encased new home for the radioactive metal. Both looked like giant snowmen in thick white suits with visored-hoods over their heads.

Sanjay said, "Those two are the geologist and a trained assistant. They'll be the only two on this particular deck until the Plutonium is secured in its container. The engineer is on a higher deck controlling the drill. He can monitor the prize via a fiber-optic camera strung along the drill shaft."

"All set?" Josef said. "Mark . . . 60 seconds. Monica, can you see? Which camera do you want to watch?"

I can see the long shot of the basketball. That's fine if you're recording both cameras so I can watch the inside transfer later."

John Greycloud decided to do the final ten-second countdown in his native Navajo. "Just for the hell of it," he said. "But watch my fingers. I'll put one up for each number until I run out. Then you'll know we're to zero."

A card with 20 seconds printed on it flashed in front of the interior camera, followed by Sanjay's "Fifteen."

Greycloud said, "Eleven," followed by a hurried set of guttural sounds. It seems Navajo is a bit longer than English when it's spoken. When his last finger went up, the orange glow from the permafrost's surface simply disappeared. As if it had fallen into and been swallowed up by the earth.

A voice from the ship said, "Successful capture!"

Monica shouted, "Yes!" as the rest of us held our breath. I had started the stopwatch at Greycloud's last finger's appearance. The room was so silent that I could hear the watch's analog dial ticking as its big hand rotated slowly.

Finally Sanjay broke the silence. "For those watching the inside camera, I'll narrate. Pulling the drill shaft with the captured Plutonium back into the ship should take about four minutes. It has to be done slowly so as not to lose the grip at the end. Then, once inside, the transfer of the Plutonium to its enclosure will take another three minutes. Remember, it's heavy, but the geologist will be using a powerful hoist. While he is sealing both the lead and the concrete lids, his assistant will load the lighted mixing bowl and give the engineer upstairs the thumbs-up to begin re-inserting the drill shaft."

He stopped, stared at the clock on the wall, and then said, "Getting the decoy back into place should take about another four minutes. Again, we don't want to drop it along the way."

Lobo said, "Then, start to finish, we're talking something around 11 minutes until I can shout, *'Eureka?'* Nine more to go."

We all sat as if frozen in place, staring at one or the other of the monitors. I don't know about the others, but I peeped from one to the other.

There was nothing to see on the long outside shot. And that, of course, might cause a big problem if the decoy took too long to appear."

Gady, assigned by Nana to rewrite her message in a bottle—a joke assignment—asked Monica, "Any word on the cabinet meeting yet?"

Monica responded. "Nothing to report yet. Except I got a text about 45 minutes ago from the DCI. He wants to see me in his office in a couple of hours. I'm assuming for me to give him another Russian lesson—not language. Culture, Putin's personality. Why Boris is an asshole, but the best asshole the FSB has."

She paused as we all watched the clock. "I'll get back to you later today."

Suddenly the Plutonium was in full view and being fitted with a steel mesh harness that, without question, would follow it into its new home. With almost no delay, it began to rise, and an overhead boom swung it out of the camera's view.

The geologist shouted, "Target resting," as we saw the mixing bowl appear. It looked surprisingly like what I could remember of the Plutonium I'd just seen for maybe 10 seconds. And then the mixing bowl moved through an opening and was gone.

Sanjay said, "Capture complete and at home at four minutes, fifty seconds. Decoy away at five minutes fifteen seconds. We're ahead of schedule, folks."

A cheer went up from aboard the drilling rig.

But our room remained silent. And transfixed.

Decontamination had begun in the ship where it had been exposed to the radiation. There wasn't much to see there, so Josef shut down that camera and switched both big monitors to what was now an empty hole in the ground.

I watched as my stopwatch ticked past seven, eight, nine minutes. Everybody else watched a big clock on the wall. My job was the stopwatch. So, by God, I wasn't going to look away from it now for a nanosecond.

Just as the stopwatch clicked past nine minutes and thirty seconds, a shout went up in what had been a room as silent as a sarcophagus. I clicked the stopwatch, looked up to see the orange glow back on the ground, and announced, "Nine minutes, forty-one seconds."

Another cheer went up.

Monica said, "Congratulations. You did it. And, by the way, I had a text about a minute ago about the missing glow. I told the satellite monitor to check with the NSA. 'See if they can see the light.' That'll take them a few hours of discussion.'"

Nana had popped a bottle of cold Dom Perignon and begun to fill little plastic flutes when Gady asked a question. "What have you decided to do with the Plutonium now that we have it on board?"

We all suddenly realized that, while there had been some discussion about that, all our energies had been devoted to the plan to just get our hands on it in the first place. Perhaps it had been so important to get it away from potentially harmful—scary, even—users, that we still had no definitive answer. *I asked myself, What do you do with 5,000 pounds of radioactive stuff that nobody except those up to no good wants?*

With both screens now blank, Greycloud broke the silence. "When are you scheduling the plane to take us back home?"

Josef said, "Going east using the polar route, the crew would prefer to leave early this evening." Looking around the room, he asked, "Does anybody have a problem with that?"

Greycloud said, "I have an idea. But I need maybe three hours to go see a friend across town. Can you give me that much time? If I can help provide an answer to the question?"

Sanjay and Nana both said, "Yes." Josef texted his flight crew to give them a later departure time.

Nana added, "We'll meet the crew in Hokkaido in nine or ten days." It was another random statement in what by now had become a gathering of randomness.

Greycloud said, "I'll be back," and started for the door.

Josef interrupted, "Take the Hundai SUV. Keys are on the wall in the outer office."

Nana and Josef went up to the roof to call and congratulate the crews and their captains.

The gravity of Gady's question, or at least its answer, had begun to sink in to the rest of us. Sanjay thought out loud, "I wonder who John's going to see. And what that meeting might have to do with disposition of 4,800 pounds of Plutonium?"

Sanjay was sticking to his prediction that the ball of energy didn't weigh a full 5,000 pounds.

Chapter Thirty-Nine

Mopping Up

In the Air—Enroute From Seoul to Portland—January 20

John Greycloud had called the Van Pelt Industries' offices within 90 minutes of having left last night to meet with a "friend." He'd told the group that he needed several more days in Seoul to discuss a matter of extreme importance with officials of South Korea . . . and maybe "two or three other countries." He said, "I'm working on a deal to dispose of the Plutonium quietly and permanently." And he'd declined to add any further comments.

"Just go on home," he'd said. "If I have anything to report right away, I'll give you a call in the plane. If not, expect to hear from me in a day or so. And, whatever you do, do not tell anyone where I am or what I'm trying to do. It's not that I don't trust every one of you. But the people I'm dealing with don't know who you are or exactly what you've been doing. They have insisted on complete secrecy."

He paused, and then went on, "And given what we're trying to do—and why we're trying to do it—they're entitled to that secrecy. For sure, I cannot discuss specifics until I'm back in Austin. And what I have to say then, whether my negotiations here work or not, will be from me to all of you. In person, and in private. I'm just asking you to trust me for now and to sit tight."

When the corporate Gulfstream was about halfway to Portland, its only refueling stop, Monica called on the plane's satellite phone. She asked to be put on speaker and to be sure the three-person crew would not be able to hear what she had to say. With the steward secured with the two pilots in the cockpit, she began.

"It seems at least one person in Sieve City understands the hazards of bureaucracy and indecision. The DCI has related to me that POTUS spoke by phone with Putin, and a serious plan is in place to secure the

Plutonium by the end of the month—on the 30th or 31st of January. Apparently State came on board immediately. But true to form, the DCI and NSA wanted to argue, to urge caution.

Monica continued, "Get this: POTUS gave them each one minute to either submit their resignations or to accept the plan he and Putin had agreed to, reminding them it took him less than 10 minutes to solve a problem they've been screwing around with since Christmas Eve.

"I'm told he said something like, 'You two have had almost a month to do something, and nothing's happened. I spent 10 minutes on the phone with Vladimir, and the whole matter's settled.'"

She paused, and then said, "Does that prove my point about bureaucratic indecisiveness? I asked the DCI that, and his response was that maybe I should apply for his job—since he didn't expect to be around Langley much longer."

Sanjay asked, "Tell us about the deal. And what's going to happen when they find the Plutonium is a mixing bowl?"

Monica laughed. "First," she said, "I expect the DCI will be packing his office in about a half-hour. Then all hell's going to break loose in Moscow and Washington. They already know about the billionaires' failed attempt, and apparently Madam Park of South Korea informed our ambassador yesterday that Kim Jung-Un is also hot to get the basketball. They don't know who else might be after it."

"Neither do we," Lobo said. "But we know for damn sure whoever it might be isn't going to succeed."

Sanjay said, "It seems to me that we have less than two weeks to have the Plutonium turn up in safe hands." He paused a moment, then added, "But we don't have a real plan for that yet. Monica, what are your thoughts?"

"Right now, Lobo," Monica said, "I'm thinking about the feasibility of trying to go directly to the President or, at least, the Secretary of State, and just telling one of them where they can find the Plutonium."

Nana started to protest. Monica interrupted, "No, I don't mean on one of your ships, Nana, but some place where it could be dropped off before I tell them the location."

Josef said, "I wasn't raised in this country, so I'm not clear on how something like that might work. But I can tell you that in Argentina, you would end up the subject of an intense investigation . . . and be lucky if

195

they didn't drop you out of an airplane from 40,000 feet over the Atlantic."

Knowing Greycloud better than any of us, Gady spoke up, "Monica, John Greycloud isn't with us. He asked to be left in Seoul for a few days to work on a plan to be sure the Plutonium ends up in safe hands. That's all we know at the moment, but I know him. If there's a miracle out there anywhere, my Little Father will find it. I strongly suggest we all just resolve to sit on the status quo--for a few days, anyway--to see what he comes up with. And keep our mouths shut."

She looked around the cabin to see if anybody wanted to disagree with her, and then said, "Will you go along with that, Monica?"

Monica said, "That's very interesting. I hope he knows what he's doing. And sure, a few days won't hurt.'"

I thought of a question that I wanted answered. "Monica, Craig here. What does the POTUS-Putin plan call for in terms of securing the site between now and the end of the month? The fact that we could go in there in plain view and grab the prize tells me the security right now's not worth a fiddler's damn. I'm not particularly worried about Kim Jung-Un since Greycloud told us his first two adventurers ended up as a defector and a corpse. But we don't know who else is on the hunt."

The stupidity of the question hit me before Monica had time to say, "Craig, you're being anal again. There's nothing there for anybody to find. Unless that mixing bowl is made of top-secret materials."

Everybody laughed. I deserved that. Time for me to go to the back of the plane, lie down, and sleep until we get to Portland.

Josef said, "Sit tight, Monica. If we hear anything, we'll call you. You do the same." He ended the call and invited the attendant back into the more comfortable environs of the luxurious cabin.

Then the phone rang again. Without prompting, the much-traveled flight attendant stood and headed back for the cockpit.

"It's Greycloud," Josef said. And he put the phone back on speaker.

John spoke, "I'll make this short and sweet. We have a deal, I think. Only everybody involved doesn't know about it yet. I need five days, until Friday, to say with certainty it's a green-light go. But the ambassadors of Japan, China and the president of South Korea have reached a handshake deal. That's where I've been—at Madam Park's residence. There's one more country that needs to sign on, and that may take a day or two.

Or four."

"Which country is that? Can you say?" I asked.

"I can and I will, Craig. It's the United States of America."

"Holy shit!" Sanjay said. "What does that mean for us? And how the hell did you get China on board with Japan and Korea? That, in itself, is a miracle."

John said, "Common interests are more prevalent than we often know, Sanjay. As for us," he went on, "somebody please tell Monica to zip up her mouth and sit on her ass until she hears from me."

Nana said, "Calling her right now. When will you be back?"

John answered, "The day after the U.S. signs on to what may just be the biggest deal since the Marshall Plan. Except this deal will never be known or reported.

"Keep the faith," John said. "When this is over, you're all coming to Arizona. We're having a *Blessing Way* sing for all of us. Gotta get that hozho back."

Part Five

It's A Wrap!

Chapter Forty

Tragedies Always Come in Threes
Siberia—105° East at the Arctic Circle—January 22

The Iranian convoy, ninety percent of the way to its destination, had managed to cross the Lower Tunguska River when they became bogged down. Their snow plow had to make pass after pass to clear a kilometer of pathway at a time, and they proceeded at a snail's pace. Earlier this morning, the commander had called Tehran on his satellite phone for additional food, fuel, and winter clothing.

They found themselves one mechanical breakdown away from serious danger.

Tehran had promised a parachute drop of the supplies in the middle of the night, which meant the plane had to be airborne already. Members of the nine-man crew had become exhausted. All were affected by snow blindness during the few daylight hours, and that had slowed their progress even further. To keep the crew's spirits up, the commander reminded them that they had less than 1,000 kilometers to go to the target. And that a road lay ahead.

With a little luck and a break in the weather, he said they could make the target by the end of the month—maybe January 30 or 31. After all, that wasn't too much later than they had projected when they set out from Kazakhstan. With the supply plane expected soon, he had called a halt to all forward progress except for the snow-plow truck. It continued to move a path ahead.

Suddenly to their southeast, they saw bright lights approaching. Thinking at first that it must be their supply plane, the commander set off a flare that turned the black sky into a rainbow of brilliant light as its illumination bounced off and through the ice crystals in the air. Too late, the faux Novatek crew realized the approaching lights were far too near to the surface to be their plane.

As the lights grew closer, the unmistakable sound of big diesel engines drowned out the nearby sounds of the Iranians idling vehicles. A loud speaker boomed out in Russian, "Who are you? And what are you doing?" The announcement was followed quickly by a burst of 50-millimeter rounds, aimed over their heads.

Not knowing what else to do, the commander climbed atop the crane on his faux drilling rig and waved a white bed sheet.

The firing stopped, but the lights continued directly toward the convoy. Again the loud speaker spoke, "Stand down. All persons line up with both arms in the air."

The seven remaining crew members followed those instructions, minus the two on their own snow plow, which by now would be several kilometers to the northeast. Grabbing his small amplified megaphone, the commander said to the approaching lights, "We are a Novatek Gas crew, and we are lost."

The answer came swiftly. "Where did you learn to speak Russian? You are not Russian. And you are not from Novatek. Keep your arms in the air."

As the mammoth Sno-cat rolled up to the convoy, the commander saw what he most dreaded—crossed golden swords on a red background. The symbol of the Russian ground forces. *The Suhoputnye voyska Rossiyskoy Federatsii.*

"Allahu Akbar," the commander said quietly."We are dead men."

Salt Desert Underground laboratories—January 22

"Clear!" the psychiatrist yelled for the third time in the last 30 seconds as he placed two paddles onto Haji Khan's chest and triggered the electric impulse intended to start the mad scientist's heart. The resuscitation effort continued for a full three minutes as the monitor above Haji's bed never wavered from its shrill flat-line tone.

Finally, the doctor turned and said, "This man is dead. If we were in an operating theater, I could try open heart massage, though I'm not a surgeon. Nor am I a cardiology specialist. I've done all I can. He's gone."

Instantly, Mahmood Bijahn became terrified. He thought, *What will be my punishment for failing to keep Haji focused? Or even alive? I have failed. Inshallah."*

Seeing the raw fear on Mahmood's face, the colonel and the doctor pulled him aside and walked him down the hall to the canteen, where they ordered three cups of strong black tea. The colonel spoke, "You have done your job, Mahmood, as well as anyone could have done it. This end for Khan is Allah's will. Inshallah."

The psychiatrist tried to explain. "This patient has been semicomatose since the day he collapsed naked in the laboratory. Without an autopsy, which I will refuse to authorize, I can only tell you that repeated dosages of drugs to sedate him may have had little to do with his death. His heart simply quit working. I don't know why, and I will not allow anyone to attempt to find out."

He placed a hand on Mahmood's shoulder and said, "Haji Khan has lived for years with a demon inside of him. As a scientist, I can assure you that demon was biological. As a psychiatrist, I am absolutely certain it resided in his brain. Many such geniuses are tortured—physically, mentally, and spiritually. His collapse in the laboratory clearly represented an involuntary cry for help."

He took a sip of his tea, and then added, "Perhaps his passing is a blessing. A blessing to those of us here in this underground facility, because he might have mistakenly—or deliberately--triggered one of the bombs he was intended to build. Right here. And a blessing to the world, perhaps. Because one more such terrible weapon, even in the hands of our leaders—who are guided by Allah, Inshallah—one more such weapon is not really such a good thing. Do you think?"

The colonel finished his tea and stood. He said to the doctor, "I leave this good man, Mahmood, in your care, Doctor. I should think he will need your skills for some time to return him to a productive life. He deserves that, at the least, for his dedication to the Islamic Republic."

Niavarin Palace—Tehran—Morning of January 23

Grand Ayatollah Ali Khamenei set his cup of tea down and looked at his two visitors. "By your faces, I can see you have not brought me good news this morning. What has happened?"

The general started to answer, but President Hassan Rouhani interrupted. "Thank you, General, but it's my duty as President to tell the Supreme Leader of this colossal failure on all our parts."

Rouhani sipped at his tea and then began, "I am sad to report to you, Ayatollah, that our quest for the Plutonium has come to an unsuccessful end. It is said that tragedies come in threes. Well, the Islamic Republic of Iran has suffered three tragedies within the past 18 hours."

Khamenei said, "Please tell me. Inshallah."

Rouhani began again, "First, I must report that our scientist in the Salt Desert, Dr. Haji Khan, died last night of heart failure. He was a young man still, but our attending physician told me that the stress, over years, of his severe mental problems finally just caused his heart to stop beating. Many attempts were made to revive him, but to no avail. Inshallah. He is in Paradise."

"And our prospect for returning the Persian Empire to its rightful prominence in this world has been put on hold. Again," Khamenei said. "But you said tragedies come in threes. What else has happened?'

This time the general spoke. "Ayatollah, our convoy had reached north central Siberia and was within less than a thousand kilometers of the Plutonium when they were intercepted by ground forces of the Russian Federation. Our men have been detained. We have this morning received word from the Russian ambassador that most likely they will face trial as armed intruders. The big question that remains is whether the fact that they had so few arms with them might reduce the charges to simply illegal aliens and imposters with fake Russian passports and papers."

President Rouhani added, "The big problem there, Sir, will occur if Putin decides to tell the world that the invaders sought Plutonium for the purpose of making nuclear weapons. While our crew did not know the intended use of the Plutonium, it will be difficult to convince other countries—especially the Israelis and the Western powers--that the quest was only for fuel for reactors to make electricity. Especially when we can buy such fuel from Russia and others on the open market."

He thought a minute, and then he said, "We can expect the United Nations and the International Atomic Energy Agency to be all over us like mosquitoes in a swamp. That is most troubling."

"That's two," Ali Khamenei said. "What more could possibly have happened?"

"Our big cargo plane," the general said, "the one that went last night to deliver fuel, food and supplies to the convoy, was shot down by the same Russian ground forces that intercepted our convoy. With a ground-to-air missile. All aboard are dead. The 10,000 gallons of diesel fuel burned."

He thought a moment, and then added, "Also, all our equipment— the trucks and everything in them in the convoy—has been seized by the

Suhoputnye voyska Rossiyskoy Federatsii as well."

A steward come into the office, bringing a fresh pot of tea and clean cups. Even after he'd left, nothing was said for two or three minutes. Each seemed to be waiting for one of the others to break the silence.

Finally, President Rouhani turned to the general. "General, we need to be on our way soon."

Ali Khamenei asked, "Where are you going?"

Rouhani answered, "To Shiraz. Haji Khan will be buried in his hometown before sundown tonight. And he has only one uncle to grieve for him."

The Grand Ayatollah said, "Go with the blessing of Allah. I shall pray for Dr. Khan's safe passage to Paradise at the hour of his funeral."

Chapter Forty-One

False Starts and Bold Moves

Off the Kuril Islands—North of Hokkaido, Japan—January 22

The commander of the KPN's helicopter-carrying frigate concluded what had been a long and tedious radio-telephone conversation with his *Taejang*, or fleet admiral. While he was answering the Taejang's questions about the ship's position, its intended destination and mission, he'd scribbled a note to his officer on deck. It said, *Go find the new vice chairman of the NDC and the minister of People's Security and bring them to me.*

When he'd concluded the conversation, he gave an order: "Bring us to 150° and increase speed to 30 knots." The order would, in effect, turn the ship around on a course back to the North Pacific well east of the Japanese islands.

A petty officer led the two summoned government officials onto the bridge. As the ship swung about in a wide arc and increased power, they, of course, wanted to know why there had been an abrupt change of direction.

Looking at the movement of a large wall-mounted analog compass, the vice chairman asked, "Why are we changing course? We seem to be heading the wrong direction. Is there a problem ahead?"

The *Chungwa*, a lieutenant commander in the KPN and the ship's captain, said, "I know of no particular problems ahead. But our fleet admiral has ordered this ship to return at once to Nampo. And when we are within 200 kilometers of port, I am to send you two by helicopter to Pyongyang."

The NDC said, "Is your admiral not aware of our warrant? The orders from Kim himself?"

The ship's commander said, "I am told your warrant has been rescinded. I'm expecting a telex momentarily confirming that cancellation. When it arrives, it will also contain specific orders for you both."

Puzzled, the two new bureaucrats huddled to try to figure out what had happened. Why Kim had apparently canceled their mission. "He was so adamant," the People's Security Minister said. "What could have changed his mind?"

NDC said quietly, "You know Kim is unpredictable. Whatever his reason, I'm sure it won't be good news for the two of us."

"Why should that be?" People's Security said. "We've followed our orders precisely."

NDC said, "Do you really think that matters?"

His fellow official simply shook his head. "No, not really," he said.

A Lamson tube arrived on the bridge from the communications shack below decks. The ship's commander opened it, removed a flimsy, and quickly read the message. Then he handed it to his two passengers.

To: Minister of People's Security and Vice Chairman NDC
From: Kim Jung-Un, First Chairman of the Supreme People's Assembly
Prior to reaching port at Nampo, you are to return to Residence No. 55
by KPN helicopter. Report to me at once. Questions have arisen that you
must answer before proceeding with the mission you have been assigned.
Your warrant is canceled. Perhaps there will be a replacement. Perhaps
there will not.

A facsimile of Kim's original seal appeared below the message.

NDC leaned in toward People's Security. He asked, "Do you know how to fly a helicopter?"

People's Security nodded. "I learned during my military days."

NDC said, "Then we must be sure to be armed when we get on that 'copter."

They looked at one another and nodded in unison.

Seoul—National Assembly Building—January 22

John Greycloud and Kwak Pum Ji sat quietly talking in a small parlor on the building's first floor. If anyone were to ask, they would say that they were discussing their common Athabascan ancestry. But the subject of their discussion was much more substantive.

Kwak said, "Do you not want to take some notes about what I'm telling you?"

Greycloud answered, "From my youth I've trained myself to remember details. Our language, you see—Navajo—is not written. As a singer,

I've had to learn to remember the exact words to many ceremonials. Some of them last more than a week."

He paused, and then added, "Besides, it's better, don't you think, that nothing we speak about should be written down anywhere?"

Kwak nodded. "Especially if it should include my name. Or the names of any of my potential associates I may have mentioned."

Meanwhile, in another room down a long hallway, Madam Park, three of her ambassadors, and representatives of the People's Republic of China, Japan and The United States carried on a top-secret discussion. The gathering, at the least, was unprecedented. From time to time, brief breaks were called as one ambassador or another placed a secure phone call to Beijing, Tokyo or Washington, D.C.

While the meeting, on its surface, remained cordial, the subject being discussed involved big stakes for the future of the whole Pacific Rim, if not the entire world.

Horse trading went back and forth, with one country demanding something in return for another acceding to demands. Perhaps not demands, but more correctly, perhaps, concessions.

After three hours, President Park stepped down the hall to see Greycloud and Kwak. Actually, she wanted to talk with Kwak, but she wanted Greycloud to listen in. And to either approve, or question, the thoughts she shared with Kwak. It was clear to John that progress was being made, as unlikely as that might seem given the subject being talked about. And the participants involved. As Madam Park turned to go back into her meeting, John gave her a "good-work" smile and a thumbs-up.

While she had been out of the room, additional progress had been made. Lunch had been served. All those present had finished soup, sandwiches, and their bottled water by the time she returned.

The ambassador from Japan asked, "Madam Park, would you like a few minutes to have your lunch?" He added, "We think we're almost finished here."

"No, thank you," Madam Park said. "Concluding a reasonable agreement is much more important to me than food at the moment."

The ambassador from Beijing said, "Can there possibly be such a thing to come out of this meeting as a 'reasonable' agreement?"

All heads in the room turned to him, and he realized he had misspoken. "What I mean is," he said, "that what we're discussing here cannot truly be approached with reason. Can it? By its very nature, whatever agreement we conclude must, by definition, be more than unreasonable. 'Bizarre,' I think, is not too strong a description."

The Japanese ambassador said, "Don't forget 'hopeful.' Twenty-five million oppressed people will be affected eventually . . . if this venture is successful."

The U.S. ambassador said, "I might suggest that the number, forgetting the oppressed part, would be closer to eight billion."

Madam Park then said, "Where do we stand? What did you accomplish while I was meeting with our subject from the North?"

Japan took the floor, moving to a large white-board on the wall. He said, "My country can participate to the extent of one-point-five. Each of the U.S. and China can contribute two-point-five, plus tons of surplus materiel. That leaves another one-point-five for your country, Madam Park. Can you do that?"

"Just a moment," she answered, taking out her phone and texting a quick message. She stared intently at the screen until, about a minute later, a small bell sounded. She looked at the answer to her text's question. "South Korea is in for one-point-five."

The U.S. ambassador said, "Then we have the seed funds. A starting point of eight, plus perhaps another four or five from the U.S. and China in surplus materiel."

He turned to the ambassador from Beijing. "Are you sure, Sir, that your country is actually ready to do this? It flies against both history and ideology. And, frankly, nobody's going to believe it."

"Ah, yes," the Chinese ambassador said. "That's the beauty of it. Who would expect China to be in league with both Japan and the United States? Or South Korea, for sure. But my country has had enough. It's time to cut the umbilical. And to get on with reality. Though I still have one question we haven't discussed: What about the Russians?"

The U.S. Ambassador said, "My country will consider carefully whether to even approach Putin. Right now, it seems like a very bad idea. It might just give him a chance to open his propaganda machine and blow the whole thing."

Madam Park said, "If we are completely discreet, nobody will suspect any of us. Who would be suspect? Except maybe the CIA?" She looked to the U.S. ambassador. "I assume you're prepared to face that heat?"

"Madam Park," the U.S. Ambassador said, "Our Central Intelligence Agency is always the first to be accused when anything out of the ordinary happens anywhere in the world. We're used to it."

The Chinese ambassador felt compelled to add, "With good reason are the eyes of the world often focused on your CIA. They have a 70-year precedent of stirring crap up. And then claiming it doesn't stink."

"Touché," the U.S. ambassador said.

Madam Park said, "Then we are agreed. And we are committed. There will be no record of this meeting. Absolutely nothing in writing or on tape. And we each have the words of honor from all in this room that absolutely nothing happened in this room.

"Today. Or ever.

"I wish you all a safe journey to your homes, "she said. I will speak with Hosteen Greycloud immediately about delivery matters. And remember, we all talk only by secure phone. To one another only. And only if and when it's absolutely necessary."

With that, the meeting ended. Madam Park began to eat her lunch, and she asked that another lunch be brought to her for John Greycloud—with no kimchi.

"Take Mr. Kwak back to his quarters at the presidential palace, and see that he's fed as well," she said.

Chapter Forty-Two

And Then There Were None

White House—Oval Office—January 23

The President spoke to the Secretary of State. "Thank you for rushing over here. Madam Park called me about an hour ago and asked that I receive her ambassador to our country—in person. She said he brings a most important message to us. Do you have any idea what he wants? Or when to expect him?"

"Mr. President, I learned late yesterday something of what he wants. We need to hear him out. And I spoke with him on my way here. He should be here any minute. I hope you don't mind, but what he has to say is significant. I took the liberty of inviting him to come at once. Since I knew I would be here, too."

"So, tell me," POTUS said. "What is this all about?"

"It's about the Plutonium to begin with," State said. "Beyond that, he wants to personally fill us in on an international effort. A top secret effort, I might add. And one that includes his country, Japan and mainland China."

She paused, and then added, "We're in it, too, our ambassador to South Korea tells me. Unless you veto our participation."

"Should DCI and NSA be in on this meeting?" the President asked.

State said, "Please, Mr. President, decide that after you hear out Madam Park's ambassador. This may be a case where you'll want to by-pass the entire cabinet. Including me, I might add."

"But, the Plutonium? Don't tell me the South Koreans have an eye on it."

"Mr. President, from what I learned earlier this morning, the Plutonium's no longer where it was. But apparently the South Koreans know where it is. And they want to see it turned over to some country where it can be useful and not dangerous. Right now, they're looking to us."

"But they don't actually have it?" POTUS said, looking confused.

"They know where it is, and they say it's in safe hands. They refuse to tell us whose hands, though. They just say it's not theirs."

The President's chief of staff buzzed the Oval Office. "The ambassador from South Korea is here, Sir. And he says he's been invited to see you. Madam Secretary, are you in on this? Shall I let him in?"

State said, "Yes, he's expected." She turned to the president and said, "You know what? This job just gets weirder and weirder."

"Tell me about it!" POTUS said.

And the South Korean ambassador came into the room, led by the chief of staff.

The Kremlin—President Putin's Office

"They are Iranians?" Putin said. "Disguised as a Novatek convoy? You're shitting me, Boris. That can't be."

"No, Sir, Mr. President. This is no joke. Here, I have copies of their passports and papers. All fake, of course." He handed a file folder to Putin.

"Where were they again? And what did they say they were trying to do?"

Boris pointed to a map on the wall. "They were here, Mr. President. Just north of the Lower Tunguska River—and right on top of the Arctic Circle." He moved his pointer to the northeast. "As you can see, they were reasonably close to the site of the Plutonium eruption. Our ground force that intercepted them is certain they were headed to claim the Plutonium. Apparently they had with them a lead-lined container of suitable size for the prize."

Putin was incredulous. "They came from Iran all the way up there by land? In January? In Siberia? There are no roads up there, are there?"

"A few. And apparently they made use of the ones that kept them headed in the right direction. But from where they were intercepted, they would have had to travel mostly cross country," Boris said.

Putin sat back in his chair, stared at the map, and reached to press a button on his intercom. "Bring us some tea, please. My special blend." He looked up and winked at Boris, who knew Putin's special blend came from potatoes, not tea leaves.

Putin went on, "So now it's those crazy thieving billionaires and Iran who would dare invade our soil. Who else, Boris?"

"You're not going to like this, Mr. President, but our man in Pyongyang tells of another Kim Jung-Un incident. Apparently he was screaming at the household help to 'get their asses to Siberia and bring back the ball.' The palace guard had to sedate him with a dart. Again."

The vodka arrived. Oddly, Putin gave it no immediate notice. "That little son-of-a-bitch is getting too big for his britches," Putin said. "First he makes a couple of bombs. They don't work right, we think. And he doesn't have dependable rockets. But he's somehow made the underground rumble. And now? Now he thinks he can make a whole lot of bombs if he can steal that Plutonium?"

Putin stopped, poured two tumblers full of ultra-chilled vodka, and raised his glass to offer a toast. "To Kim Jung-Un, the megalomaniac."

He looked at Boris and added, "He's got to go!"

Boris, taking a sip of Putin's special blend, asked, "Is that an order, Mr. President?"

"Putin said, "For now, Boris, it's an idea. But a damned good one, don't you think?"

Boris nodded, raised his glass above his head, and said, "To the former Kim."

White House—The Oval Office—January 23

The Secretary of State walked the South Korean ambassador out of the Oval Office following a 20-minute meeting with POTUS. "Thank you, Mr. Ambassador," she said. "Our President will respond directly to Madam Park, and I will personally relay the content of that message to you. Will you be at your embassy the rest of the day?"

The ambassador nodded and handed State a card that included his direct line number, his residence number and two cell phone numbers. "These numbers are not given out, Madam Secretary. Ever. To anybody outside the embassy. If we are to be working together, you will need them. I'll await your call. And thank you."

With that, he bowed, and left with the usual Marine escort.

State returned to the Oval Office.

The President had just finished filling in his chief of staff. He said, "I want the two of you to stick around for a few minutes. Let's think about this deal together."

He looked at his chief aide, thinking as he spoke. "Roger, quietly find out if one of our Gulfstreams can carry a 5,000 pound payload. I want one three-man crew, all pilots, and I want all three of them to have Top-Secret clearance. Then I want to speak to each of them. In this office. Separately. Sometime over the next two days. Get me a dossier on each before they show up."

He looked to State. "I will be making a previously-unannounced trip to Portland on the 30th of this month. Madam Secretary, find me some political or humanitarian reason to be there. Then, I will be making a purely political trip the next day from Portland to Austin in Texas. Set up a meeting there with the president of The University of Texas at Austin. See if he's willing to chat aboard Air Force One. I'll arrive from Portland mid-morning. Tell him we'll have lunch."

Roger said, "Mr. President, those arrangements are very unusual to be left to State. Don't you want some more normal help from the White House Travel Office?"

"For now, Roger, the three of us have to handle all this stuff. By ourselves. You'll need to clue the Secret Service about Portland as soon as something's set up there. But for Austin, we'll stay on the plane. No big folderol there."

The Secretary of State said, "Mr. President, I genuinely appreciate your confidence in me and my top aides, but do you really intend to carry this out without the knowledge of the DCI, the NSA, and the FBI?"

"I'll tell you what I intend to do, Madam Secretary." He turned to Roger and said, "When you have a few minutes, get with the vice president. I want the two of you, in total secret, to bring me the names and credentials of individuals suited to new positions—one group who could become DCI, and one group who could become NSA.

"And be sure they all have backbones. Look at younger generals and admirals. They didn't get where they are by being afraid to make a decision."

Incheon International Airport—Seoul, South Korea—January 24

John Greycloud, first-class boarding pass in hand courtesy of Madam Park, called the Austin Office of Van Pelt Industries. He was using a special phone given to him "for the duration" by President Park herself.

When Nana answered, John said, "I'm on my way back. I'm on Asiana Airlines to Detroit, then on into Austin on Delta. But I have two questions I need answers to before I board here in a few minutes."

"Go ahead," Nana said.

"First, can we guarantee the USS *Pavlovich's Folly* can be in port in Hokkaido by January 30—that's six days away?"

"What's your second question? And then hold on a minute while I get Josef to answer the first."

"My second question is this: Can you get the entire Austin team together tomorrow evening? I have negotiated a plan with several governments relative to the prize. I need to explain as much as I can about what's going on . . . and then extract some blood oaths."

Nana returned to the call. "John, Josef says 'No problem' getting the new driller back to Hokkaido by the 30th. She won't be able to dock without Japanese Customs looking around, though. I'm not sure we're ready for that yet. Until you know what . . ."

John said, "Don't worry about Japanese customs. They'll roll out the red carpet for your ship. How about the meeting?"

"Sure. Everybody but Monica. Can we phone patch her in?"

"No. She needs to be there. It's critical. Send one of your planes for her if you have to. We all have to sign our names in blood. Including Monica."

"Can I tell her why we need her here?" Nana said.

"You don't know why," John said.

"And you're not going to tell me, are you, John?"

"Tomorrow night. The medicine man dispenses. But only if there's a full house."

Chapter Forty-Three

Now You See It; Now You Don't

Wakkanai Airport—Hokkaido, Japan—January 29

What appeared to be a corporate Gulfstream G-550, long-range jet landed to the northwest and taxied deliberately to a hangar between the runway and the shores of the Sea of Okhotsk. The airport sits on the northern peninsula of Hokkaido where the Sea of Japan meets the Sea of Okhotsk at Cape Boya's Wakkanai Port.

To any observers, the flight appeared to be just another routine bit of traffic at a busy airport. Nobody paid any particular attention to it. If anyone had bothered to look up the letters and numbers on its tail, they would have learned the plane was registered to the State Department of the government of the United States of America.

But it went mostly unnoticed. Which is exactly what the crew and the man who had sent them on this trip intended. The man who had sent them was the President of the U.S., otherwise known as POTUS.

The plane carried only a crew of three, all pilots with Top Secret clearances, as well as two passengers—John Greycloud and Dr. Sanjay Pradeet.

The reason for the light load? They were to pick up a parcel weighing 4,796 pounds in a heavy container, and with three crew and two passengers, the plane would be heavier than its rated load limit of 6,000 pounds for the return trip to Austin in Texas via Portland, Oregon, a refueling stop.

As it rolled into a large hangar, the doors of the building slid shut behind it. There would be no customs inspection. No immigration check.

Cape Boya—Wakkanai Seaport—January 29

Less than five kilometers north of the airport, two ships with U.S. registry put into port. Both the ice-breaker *Josef* and the shallow water drilling rig *Pavlovich's Folly* had returned from an extended, three-week shakedown cruise for the new ship. Their logs would show the two had been on a test of mid-winter exploration and drilling in Siberia, under contract to the Russian gas company Rosneft.

That exploration having been completed satisfactorily, the ice breaker had escorted *Pavlovich's Folly* back to its birthplace in Hokkaido for its builders to make one final inspection before turning ownership over to Van Pelt Industries. All this, of course, would be quite routine. Completely SOP.

Again, largely unnoticed, a Japanese military three-ton truck had rolled alongside the shallow-water driller, and a container had been transferred from *Pavlovich's Folly* to the truck.

Amanda and Josef, Lobo Diaz, and Monica Skrabacz welcomed their two captains and their crews in a private room at the port's headquarters. The gathering was small. No more than 18-20 people total. The crews had cleared passport control, advising the immigration agents that they would be landward for only one day.

They would return to their ships tonight to refuel and re-provision before beginning the trip back to the coast of the Laptev Sea at 105^0 east and $7\frac{1}{2}^0$ north of the Arctic Circle. The geologist's observations made him certain he could find gas reserves within a few meters of a certain glowing mixing bowl along the shoreline. The water, itself, had bubbled regularly with what he'd tested and found to be methane. In the report to engineering officials at Novatek, he'd noted, "Methane is literally bubbling out of the shallow water at the coast."

Besides the celebration and bonuses for all, Monica had serious business to conduct. Following a private meeting, back in Washington, called by the Secretary of State, Monica—as head of the CIA's Russian Desk—had been given the job of securing what amounted to oaths of secrecy from all the crew members. And this was to be done without the knowledge of the DCI.

Monica had reminded State that not all the crew members were U.S. citizens, including one of the two captains. The Secretary of State had replied, "You know, Monica, that these oaths are not enforceable. In fact, in Federal Court, they would be laughed at. The point, though, is to impress on the crew members the dire consequences that would result if any one of them decided to talk. Or, God forbid, maybe write a book. And I can't think of anybody in government since J. Edgar Hoover who is better suited to imparting the fear of God than you."

With that, she'd laughed and invited Monica to consider a career change to the diplomatic side. "At State, we could use your Russian knowledge. It's for damn sure that the Company isn't using it with any intelligence. No pun intended."

So now Monica found herself in Hokkaido with a choice to make: to try to scare these crew members into everlasting silence; or to just level with them and not pour out the BS.

These guys are not roustabouts like you might find on many ships, she thought. *They're professionals—engineers, geologists, specialists in mechanics.*

So she made her decision.

She began, "What you have just done is of immense importance to the safety and well-being of the world. You should be proud. As proud as Amanda and Josef and all the rest of us are of you. And also as proud of you as the President of the United States is. I have for each of you two things—besides the bonuses Amanda and Josef have just announced. First, I have a Presidential Medal of Freedom, awarded to you in secret and in *absentia* by the President. He asked me to tell you each that he is proud of you and what you've done, and also to say to you that you must never speak of the mission you've just finished. To anyone. For any reason."

She went on, informally, to explain the secrecy oaths. Everyone stepped up to sign. There were no questions, and there was no resistance. At the end of the signing, she did mention that the people in the part of the government that she worked for had been known to be "less than understanding" if anyone failed to abide with these kinds of oaths.

Captain Ruggles asked, "What part of the government do you work for?"

Thinking quickly, Monica said, "Department of Agriculture. I'm in charge of making up recipes for healthy, nutritious cookies."

Back at Wakkanai Airport—Two Hours Later

Nobody thought much about it when the doors to a large hangar slid open wide enough to admit a three-ton Japanese military truck. Neither did they notice a half-hour later when the doors opened again—this time wider--to allow the Gulfstream G-550 to exit onto a taxiway and move slowly to the southeast. Lined up with the runway it had landed on less than three hours before, it was soon airborne. Flight plan filed for Portland International Airport on the west coast of the U.S.

The plane carried two pilots and a steward, one nuclear physicist and one Navajo elder—a Shaman. And, oh, yes, a rather large piece of freight.

Austin-Bergstrom International Airport—January 30

Two planes sat on the tarmac at Atlantic Aviation Services, a private FBO on the south side of the airport. A Gulfstream G-550 had arrived about an hour before the 747 that dwarfed it. The smaller jet carried only standard registration on its exterior, but the larger plane bore the seal of the President of the United States.

Both planes sat within a circle of black SUV's assigned to Secret Service and FBI, although none of the occupants of these vehicles knew, or had any reason to know, why Air Force One had landed and was scheduled to sit for a little more than an hour. Right where it was parked.

Four men sat in an office near the front of the big 747: Dr. Sanjay Pradeet, John Greycloud, the president of The University of Texas at Austin, and POTUS himself. They were concluding a light lunch and what had been a fairly brief meeting.

UT's president asked Sanjay, "So, Dr. Pradeet, you have a plan for this gift?"

Sanjay said, "Yes, I do. There are at least two dozen research facilities like our Institute for Fusion Studies with whom we can share the gift. Passing pieces of it around won't be a problem."

UT's president said, "Far too much of my job amounts to raising money. I get to keep my job if I raise enough. So, just out of curiosity, about how much is the monetary value of this gift? I'm a lawyer, not a scientist."

POTUS said, "You know you can't count this one."

UT's president nodded. And shrugged.

Sanjay answered. "We really need an advanced mathematician to answer your question. Here's a start: It's rare. One gram is worth at least $4,000. There are twenty-eight-plus grams per ounce. That's about 454 grams per pound. So, a pound would be worth about $1.8 million dollars. And we're looking at about 4,700 pounds. I'd say it's worth just a whole bunch of Rubles."

Greycloud began counting on his fingers and said quickly, "I get about $85 billion."

POTUS looked at him and said, "I don't have that many digits. Pun intended."

Epilogue

Months Later

Washington Daily News

NSA and DCI Out

President Shakes Up Cabinet

By Edward Wright and Emily Creech

Washington, D.C.—May 15—In an unexpected and stunning move not seen in Washington since the days of Nixon and Watergate, the President today announced a major realignment of two cabinet posts, both related to foreign policy and national security.

Although he used the word "resignations," White House sources confirmed that both the National Security Advisor and the Director of the Central Intelligent Agency have, in effect, been fired.

Word of the shakeup came at an impromptu, early morning press conference in the White House's Rose Garden. The president thanked the two former cabinet members in *absentia*, as neither was present. Sources refused to say whether they had been invited or asked to stay away. The comments by the president were brief and without praise for the service of the two deposed officials.

Asked to clarify reasons for the changes, the President simply said, "New leadership, decisive leadership, is often a good thing."

While nominees to replace the NSA and DCI were not announced, speculation on Capitol Hill is rampant. Those mentioned most frequently include both the present Secretary of State and Secretary of Commerce, along with a Naval admiral and an Air Force four-star general. The mix also includes an unidentified Russian expert from within the CIA, although that candidate is apparently a dark horse at the moment.

The President's remarks were brief. After he left the podium, Press Secretary Anita Upchurch would only say that the search for replacements is underway. "We expect to have simultaneous announcements within the week," she said.

Questioned about other potential cabinet changes, Ms. Upchurch said, "Every member of this administration serves at the behest of the President. It's his prerogative to make changes whenever he thinks changes need to be made."

Both the Speaker of the House and the Senate Majority Leader declined comment.

In his typical jocular fashion, the Vice President simply said, "There's no such thing as 'indispensable' in this, or any other, administration." Both the NSA and the DCI were unavailable for comment. Spokespersons at both of their offices confirmed they had cleaned out their desks and left the premises.

Moscow—The Kremlin—May 16

Russian Federation President Vladimir Putin shared a good laugh with Boris, head of the Russian FSB. "I see POTUS finally got off his ass and canned those two clowns you tried to deal with, Boris. Typical, though, it took him 90 days to figure out what needed to be done back in January."

Boris nodded. "I wonder how many committee meetings he had to call and how many studies he had to commission. And how many senators and representatives he had to counsel with?"

"That's the beauty of our federation," Putin said. He smiled and added, "Can you think of anybody we need to sack today? Anybody?"

Boris said, "I'll give it some thought, maybe have three or four meetings and have six of my assistants independently prepare white papers on the subject. I'll let you know by, maybe, October."

Putin burst out laughing.

Turning serious, Putin said, "What happened to those Iranian imposters we caught trying to grab the Plutonium?"

"Boris said, "You know, Sir, that we're eminently fair. We sent them back to Rouhani . . . with a severe scolding—for him. We did keep their trucks and equipment."

"To the victor go the spoils," Putin said. "Let me ask you, Boris. What do you think really happened to the Plutonium?"

"What did POTUS tell you, Mr. President?" Boris said.

"He said it was their opinion that the earth swallowed it back up. One thing I can tell you for sure, though: we're not going to go digging some big hole to see if that's right. Good riddance to a major nuisance."

Boris's face turned dark. "We could always tell NATO to back off or we'll use it on them."

"I've already done that, Boris."

Tehran, Iran—May 18

Taking advantage of his recently established relationship with the psychiatrist from Tehran, Mahmood Bijahn had voluntarily checked himself into the Roosbeh Psychiatric Hospital at The Tehran University of Medical Sciences. While the doctor could not be sure immediately whether Mahmood really had need of specialized treatment, he was sure that Mahmood had become completely exhausted. He needed a rest. A long rest to shake off the tension caused by month after month of playing guardian to the former Dr. Khan.

Mahmood, too, had no idea if he really had gone "crackers," as he described his condition. But he welcomed the chance to rest his body and clear his mind of the make-believe world he'd been living in for so long. He willed himself to participate, along with others in the hospital, in craft projects, and he'd even become more than proficient at finger painting.

After three months, though, Mahmood was ready to leave the institution's confines—to take on a new assignment. He pronounced himself fit—physically, mentally and spiritually.

President Rouhani, recognizing Mahmood's previous service to his country, offered Bijahn his choice of three different government positions. True to his masochistic tendencies, Mahmood had chosen from the list the one he quickly saw as the most difficult and demanding.

In two days, he would be leaving for Baghdad to become the director of security at his country's Iraqi embassy, even knowing times in Iraq had become tense.

As a dedicated, but reasonably pragmatic, Shiite, his job would involve some serious undercover work. On behalf of his country, he would represent Iran's—and the entire Middle East's—position that the government of Iraq must address the need for a working coalition among Shiites, Kurds and Sunnis.

This is a crazy assignment, he thought. Saddam's Sunnis ran roughshod over the Shiites. Then Al Maliki's Shiites ran roughshod over the Sunnis. The Kurds want their own independent state. And who knows what's going to happen in Syria?

President Rouhani had said to him, "You're perfectly suited for this job, Bijahn. After all, you're very experienced in dealing with lunatics. And you'll have just another set of crazies to whip into shape."

Rouhani had laughed.

But Mahmood wasn't sure the comment had been all that funny.

Although he knew it to be a stone-cold fact.

Say'un Airport—Central Yemen—May 20

A long, black Cadillac limousine moved slowly in total darkness from a small parking lot to the remote airport's tarmac. The need for stealth had nothing to do with the vehicle itself. Cadillac limousines anywhere near the border of Saudi Arabia were as common as Volkswagens on an autobahn. But inside the cavernous back seat of this behemoth, One, aka Ali bin-Salam, lay trussed up in a body bag that was wrapped in duct tape. His head poked out one end just far enough to allow him to breathe.

Two Canadian soldiers wearing night vision goggles sat on the cushy seat across from their prisoner. Both were covered to their knees with the desert sand of Yemen's Empty Quarter. And they stank, as did their guest, of sweat and goat feces. They checked their watches and peered out the darkened windows. The only lights outside came from the corners of a small frame terminal a quarter of a kilometer behind them.

One of the soldiers pointed to the darkness outside and cracked open a side window. Immediately the sound of an approaching helicopter filled the car's interior.

One began to struggle, kicking and moving his body as violently as his new outer-wear would allow. He stopped struggling as the soldier nearest the open window pulled out a jambiya—One's own weapon—and swiped it just above the prisoner's head.

On the remote tarmac, an unmarked and unlit Sikorsky UH 60 Black Hawk helicopter sat down not 20 meters from the limousine. Its rotors continued turning as two doors opened—one on the Black Hawk and one on the Cadillac. The two Canadians grabbed One's body bag and hoisted him out of the car, across the tarmac, and shoved him into the airship.

A U.S. Army Ranger said, "Welcome aboard, mates. Next stop, Riyadh."

One of the Canadians looked at One and added, "And then a long flight for you and us, my friend, to Ottawa."

6⁰ 55' North Latitude—158⁰ 11' East Longitude
Federated States of Micronesia—May 30

Four felt certain the only way anybody could find his new home would be by Googling "Middle of Nowhere." Finished with his project for the Brazilian Navy a month ago, he sat idly in a lawn chair on the beach, watching the beginnings of the construction of his new and forever home on the outskirts of Rontiki, a small village on the island of Pohnpei. Rontiki lay a few kilometers due south of Palikir, capital city of the Federated States of Micronesia.

He'd chosen the location for three reasons: first, it afforded contact with real civilization. The island was home to 26,000 people, assuring him access to whatever supplies and electronic equipment he might need in years to come; second, the village of Rontiki lay right on the Pacific shore, far enough away from the capital city of Palikir to be truthfully described as "secluded." And finally, though two native languages were spoken commonly, English had become the language of business, and almost everyone on the island spoke and understood it.

Four had enough money to build a lavish home, but he chose instead to keep it simple to blend in with the local culture . . . and not call attention to himself. He knew if he became too bored, he could hop a plane at Pohnpei International Airport (PNI) and be in Manila in the Phillipines–3,000 kilometers to the west-northwest—or Port Moresby in New Guinea—1,700 kilometers due south—in a matter of hours. But the international airport was on the opposite end of his island. He would go there rarely. If ever.

He'd never experienced boredom. Anywhere.

Right now, his priorities included finishing and furnishing his small home, maintaining an open corridor to the sky above for his satellite phone and the internet, and watching for news from Canada and Yemen concerning the fate of his old buddy, One.

Desert—East of Shenyang, Manchuria—June 2

So far, Kwak Pum Ji's several personal infiltrations into the Democratic People's Republic of Korea from his makeshift base in Eastern Manchuria had proved to be uneventful. And non-threatening. At this morning's strategy meeting with his leadership team, he had ticked off the things he knew for certain:

- "We are in this cause alone," he'd said. "Our benefactors will never admit to having heard of us. Nor will they lift a finger to assist us if we get into a jam. And only I know who those benefactors are. You will never know. Please don't bother speculating. You'll never figure it out. So, let's not get into a jam.
- "Time is on our side. There is absolutely no reason for us to

rush—on any action or on any planning. If we have to rethink our plans weekly, then we will rethink our plans weekly. Our efforts, maybe for years, will have to be clandestine—a small step at a time. We don't have the power of Kim Jung-Un at our disposal, but we have the brains to overcome his power. One small move at a time. Think of our cause as a chess game. We eliminate one pawn at a time. We bring one of Kim's knights into our cause at a time. Ours is a battle of attrition. And conversion.

- "Never forget that what we are committed to do is right. Kim and his henchmen are a blight on humanity. There should be no question of right or wrong among us. The world is waiting for sanity to overcome psychosis. For truth to replace fabrications. For humanity to replace inhumanity. We are the good guys."

- "If anyone here is not willing to give his or her life as we proceed, please leave. Today."

Boston—Massachusetts Institute of Technology—July 15

Dr. Sanjay Pradeet had finished his visit. He hailed a cab for Logan Airport and a flight back to Austin and his office at the Institute for Fusion Studies at the University of Texas. MIT had been his last stop on a tour of nuclear research facilities across the U.S., Great Britain, and Germany.

In the past seven weeks since the end of UT's spring semester, Sanjay had made 15 stops. Personal calls on peers and associates who were in the same business he was—nuclear physics. His international reputation had made him welcome at each stop even though he'd refused, in each case, to explain why he wanted to stop by.

But, once there, and after he'd explained the reason for his visit, he had been welcomed effusively. When he had announced that UT was willing to offer each of fifteen university's research arms up to 250 pounds of almost pure Plutonium, he had, in fact, been hailed as a hero. The only stipulation for the deliveries was to be that the head of each facility sign an agreement not to divulge either the source or the amount of the gift he was offering. A gift worth $4.5 billion each. After all, Sanjay considered the Plutonium both a gift from the gods of physics . . . and also most certainly contraband.

Nobody turned down the gift. And everybody swore to secrecy.

Contraband or not, he thought, *one thing's for certain. Our little esca-*

pade has not only saved the world from possible mass destruction, but it has also turned 4,796 pounds of a rare and heavy metal into an instrument to actually do some good.

As he waited to board his flight, he called Arizona.

"John," he said, "it's finished."

Navajo Indian Reservation—Near Chinle, Arizona
November-- When the Thunder Sleeps

Gady and I, and my entire team of detectives, had not run into any crimes as bizarre as those we'd been faced with over the past couple of years. I, in fact, had settled in to the routine paperwork grind required of my new position as head of the Austin Police Department's detective division. Of course, in our work, routine doesn't mean assembly-line tedium. Nor does paperwork follow any predictable pattern. Ours is not a job that leads to boredom.

Since the Plutonium had been plucked from the Siberian permafrost back in January, none of us had any idea what finally had happened to it. None of us, that is, except John Greycloud. And maybe Dr. Pradeet. But, whatever they knew, neither was talking. They wouldn't answer one question.

Monica, on the other hand, had proclaimed the entire operation "a smashing success." We'd all noticed that Monica had lightened up. She had even begun cracking a joke now and then. I suspected her new outlook might have something to do with the President canning her former boss—the one she colorfully described as a "weak asshole."

Her only comment to me had been, "Weenies come, and weenies go. We'll see just how much of a weenie this new guy—an admiral—turns out to be."

John Greycloud, true to his word, had commanded the entire Plutonium-catching task force to meet him at the airport in Gallup, New Mexico, three nights ago. He said he had important follow-up work to finish for all of us. "Just get out here," he'd said, offering no further explanation.

Gady, as a half-Navajo, knew what John had in mind. As she explained it to us, she said that John intended to return for two days to his lifelong role as a shaman. We all, she'd explained, had displaced our natural harmony and beauty with nature and the cosmos during the Plutonium caper. She called it our *hozho*.

"It's Navajo metaphysics," she'd said. "We follow a long-ago-established pattern of walking in beauty and harmony with nature, the world around us, including the animals, even the insects and plants. Hozho keeps us in balance. It's not a religion—at least not in the sense you biligaanas think of religion. It's more a way of life. Of living."

"Why did he wait until now to sing to us?" I said, fearing that such a characterization might be offensive.

Apparently it was.

"Craig," she'd said, "my Little Father is going to perform what we call 'The Blessing Way.' Its purpose is to return all for whom it's sung back into their balance—their hozho. But it must be sung during the time when the thunder sleeps. For the uninitiated, those not lucky enough to live between the four mountains of our home land in New Mexico and Arizona, the thunder sleeps from late fall until late spring—a time we never experience thunderstorms.

"That's why he waited," she added. "And don't ask me to tell you why the thunder has to be sleeping. It has to do with First Woman, and it goes all the way back to our concept of the creation. If you're really interested, maybe John will explain it. And maybe he won't. It's not for biligaanas to understand."

Seeing that I looked puzzled, Gady said, "Just go. The Blessing Way lasts two nights. By the time we get back to Austin on Monday afternoon, you will see the effects. Just accept the good it's going to do for you. And for all the rest of us."

So go with the flow I did. Nana loaded us all, except Josef, who was back in Argentina at his new job with the Commerce Department, into one of her two Gulfstreams and flew us to Gallup in western New Mexico. John met us there and drove us a few miles across the Arizona border to Window Rock, where we spent Friday night. Next morning, we all drove to Chinle, Arizona in the beautiful Painted Desert.

All I can tell you about the next 48 hours is that it seemed like no more than a half-day, start to finish. John performed the ritual singing—call it chanting if you want, but it was no chant. He prepared intricate and colorful sand paintings which had no particular meaning to me. And, of course, I had no idea what the Navajo words he sang meant.

But it was all impressive.

Around APD, I'm known as "Mr. Objectivity." Sometimes as "Anal

Craig." I have to tear things apart and put them back together so I know how they work. And what makes them work. Imagine my frustration as I tried to analyze what had happened to me in Arizona. I kept trying to figure it out. I continued to ask Gady questions until I could see she was not just avoiding me, but actually hiding from me.

So I called John Greycloud. I started to explain to him why I had called. That I needed to figure out what had happened and why.

John would have none of it. "Craig, do you feel better about the world than you did last week?" he asked.

"That's what has me confused," I said. "It's like I'm seeing everything through a new set of eyes, John. What did that Blessing Way do to me? And for me?"

There was a long silence on the line before he finally said, "For thousands of years, Craig, members of our Dineé—the Navajo family of clans—have wondered the same things you're wondering now. There is no explanation."

"But," I started to say.

"Craig," John said, "interrupting someone is a serious breach of etiquette among Navajos. But, with apologies, I have to interrupt you. Here's the deal. Shut up and accept what's happened."

The line went dead.

The End.

For now.

What will Detective Lt. Craig Rylander get into next?

**Follow the on-going adventures of the
Austin Police Department's head of Detectives
on the author's website:**

www.CIAcats.com

A Million Thanks

No book should ever be published without the help of dozens of individuals in many organizations working together to produce a worthwhile product. Our books are no different. Except our partners in crime are particularly talented. Here they are. Those to whom we give special thanks.

To Our Dedicated Manuscript Reader Panel

In all our books to date, we have found the input, suggestions, corrections, and critiques of a panel of voluntary manuscript readers to be of invaluable help in the production of a quality manuscript. We offer our sincere gratitude to the following panel members who read the fourth draft of our manuscript, chapter-by-chapter, and helped us improve the story and the writing:

Seattle, Washington

Barbara Ivancich	Vice President, Publicis US
Marion Woodfield	Retired Advertising Executive

St. Petersburg, Florida

Jim Arnold	Retired United Airlines Captain
Barbara Arnold	Grandmother, Burgee Queen, and Church Lady

Houston, Texas

Julie B. Fix, APR	Assistant Professor, University of Houston, Fellow, Public Relations Society of America

Navasota, Texas

Mike Cooper	Author, Martial-Arts Teacher

Dallas/Fort Worth, Texas

Jerry Cooper	Retired Managing Director, Henry C. Beck Company
Marilyn Pippin, APR	President, Hopkins & Associates Public Relations
Matthew Arnold	Creative Manager, The Legacy Senior Communities

Jim Haynes, APR	Author, Teacher of News Writing, SMU Fellow Public Relations Society of America
Sun City, Texas	
Connie Carden	Retired Teacher
Joe Helton, Ph.D.	Retired Psychology Professor
Irvine, California	
Margery Arnold, Ph.D.	Psychologist
Cleveland, Ohio	
Dave Hood	OTR Trucker
New Orleans, Louisiana	
Elizabeth Hood	Broadcast and Film Producer
Fredericksburg, Texas	
Jan Fritz	Radio Broadcaster
San Antonio, Texas	
Ken Squier	Entrepreneur and co-author of several of the Detective Craig Rylander Mysteries

Major Contributors

The author would like to extend special thanks to **Jim Haynes, APR**, who not only read and commented on the manuscript, but also provided extensive proofreading and editing suggestions. And to **Ken Squier**, whose ideas led to the writing of this book.

Thanks, Jim and Ken.

To Our Publisher, Cover Designer and Illustrator

Our thanks also go to **Billy Huckaby** of Eakin Press, the newly-acquired division of Wild Horse Media Group, our publisher; to **Matthew Arnold** for another great cover design; and to **Jason Eckhardt** for his map of the Russian Federation and the drawing of the lethal jambiya.

These incredibly talented people make tasty lemonade every day.

To Our Readers and Fans

Without you, we would find ourselves shouting into a well. Our mission is to create reading enjoyment that we hope inspires, entertains, and sometimes even informs. Thank you for your loyalty and continuing interest in our creations.

To Our Production, Distribution and Retail Partners

We can create manuscripts until the cows come home. But getting those works to our readers requires the tireless work and cooperation of many organizations. And we thank our many friends and followers at **Barnes & Noble Booksellers** and independent bookstores for not only carrying our books, but also allowing us to meet face-to-face with our readers and potential readers in regularly scheduled signing events in their stores. We treasure our association with you. You know who you are. Know also that we could never accomplish our mission without your cooperation and support.

To Sources We Relied on for Accuracy in this Book

Finally, we are most grateful for the maps and information provided by **Doctors Without Borders** for a variety of geographical and cultural references that helped to pinpoint the action. And to the many excellent books of the late **Tony Hillerman,** the master of detective stories set on the Navajo Reservation in New Mexico and Arizona. If you haven't read Hillerman, do it. Today!

Now For the Mea Culpa-CYAs

Any mistakes you may find in this book are solely my responsibility.

George Arnold

Dallas/Fort Worth
2015

Other Books by the Author

Adult Fiction—Detective Craig Rylander Clover—Mysteries
By Arnold and Squier

■ **ENIGMA: A Mystery:** Seven young girls have disappeared from the streets of Austin, Texas, presumably kidnapped by "The Austin Monster," leaving no clues, no trace. APD Detective Sergeant Craig Rylander and Family and Protective Services Psychologist Dr. Amy Clark race against time to find the girls. Will Craig–with his no-nonsense style of catching criminals–and Amy--with her in-depth understanding of the violent criminal mind–find the girls in time? And, if they do find them, will they be alive? Dead? Or something in between? The clock is ticking.

■ **UNDERCURRENTS: The Van Pelt Enigma:** Craig and Amy begin what they think is an investigation of two local cases–an arson murder and a terrorist-like car bombing–only to step unwittingly into an international terrorist ring dating back more than two-hundred years. A ring controlled by the descendants of the Romanoff family, Russia's last Czars. They, along with the FBI, Texas Rangers, Interpol and the CIA, wander perilously into the crosshairs of the assassins themselves. Will Craig and his team solve the arson and car bombing without becoming victims of assassination? Extraordinary measures are called for.

■ **CONFLICTION: A Moral Enigma:** Disappointed in the criminal justice system that somehow can't shut down a ring of international assassins after two-hundred years, Austin Police Detective Sergeant Craig Rylander accepts a leave-of-absence from APD and takes on a privately-financed worldwide hunt to put an end to the assassin himself. Amply financed and furnished with fake identifications and a "black" Gulfstream G-550 airplane, will Craig and his small team—a rookie detective from Tucson and an old, mysterious Navajo shaman and tracker--find the elusive and dangerous Felix Pavlovich, head of the Czarists? Or will Pavlovich and his group of international assassins kill Craig and his team first?

- **ADVENTURES OF THE CHURCH-LADY GANG: A Conspiracy of Crones:** Bedeviled and threatened for an entire year with strange cases involving child abusers, domestic vigilante groups and a ring of international assassins, APD Detective Sergeant Craig Rylander gets himself assigned to a case he thinks will be simpler and provide a bit of a breather–a local gang of eccentric Robin Hood wannabe church ladies. Stereotypical church ladies banded together to help the less fortunate by hook or by crook. Occasionally by crook. If Craig thought tracking down, all over the world, a 200-year-old assassination organization would be the kind of case to try his patience, threaten his life and his often brilliant deductive reasoning powers, he badly underestimated the Church Ladies. No scam is too bizarre for this pious little group, as Craig and his team will quickly learn. Warm, human and funny to the bone, ADVENTURES OF THE CHURCH LADY GANG presents a hilarious puzzle for Craig to unravel. To Craig, Dominus vobiscum, and to Craig's entire team, Et cum spiritu tuo.

- **FIRE AND ICE: BEYOND ALCHEMY:** by George Arnold
Over three or four billion years, a basketball-sized mass weighing more than 4,800 pounds has drifted upward from the earth's molten center . . . through the mantle and the crust to rest, at last, near the surface on the Central Siberian Plateau, seven degrees north of the Arctic Circle. The U.S. Central Intelligence Agency has confirmed the mass is pure Plutonium. Enough to fuel more than 100 nuclear bombs. But who else knows? Monica Skrabacz, head of the Russian desk at Langley, implores Craig Rylander to form a team to recover the geological aberration that could be used to destroy civilization as we know it. Based on past experience, she trusts only Craig for this mission. Based on his own past experience, he doesn't trust Monica, period. But the stakes are high. Too high to ignore. Will he accept the assignment? And if he does, will his team recover the Plutonium before it falls into the hands of terrorists? Or nationalist despots desperate to have "The Bomb"? Hundreds of ticking dirty-suitcase bombs and dozens of big bombs are counting down.

Nonfiction for Readers of all Ages – by George Arnold

- **Growing Up Simple: An Irreverent Look at Kids in the 1950s:** With foreword by Texas icon Liz Carpenter, this multi-award winner has been compared favorably by critics to Tom Sawyer. Winner of the IPPY (Independent Publishers' Association) humor award as the funniest book published in North America in 2003; the Violet Crown Award from Barnes & Noble as the best nonfiction book of 2003 by a Texas author; and a coveted Silver Spur, Growing Up Simple explores the lives of a merry band of overachievers bent on saving the world from itself in the 1950s. Must-read for anyone born between 1939 and 1947–the "In-Betweeners." And for anybody else who enjoys nonstop belly laughs.

- **Chick Magnates, Ayatollean Televangelist, & A Pig Farmer's Beef: Inside the Sometimes Hilarious World of Advertising:** Funny to the bone–both human and chicken–Chick Magnates reports on the world of advertising agencies and their clients during the last quarter of the 20th century, taking names and kicking butt with a series of chronological vignettes that are totally true, but almost unbelievable. It's a tribute to creative thinking down through civilized history—thinking and action that have raised us all out of cave-dwelling and rubbing sticks together to make fire.

- **BestSeller: Must-Read Author's Guide to Successfully Selling Your Book:** The truth, the whole truth, and nothing but the truth about the author's role in the marketing of his or her own books, this book inspires and sometimes frightens would-be authors. Accompanied by free 90-minute workshops in bookstores for writers who want to be published and published authors who want to sell twenty times as many books.

Cats of the C.I.A. Fiction Series
for Readers from 8 to 108—by George Arnold

■**Get Fred-X: The Cats of the C.I.A.** (English only): Meet Buzzer Louis, black-and-white tuxedo cat and retired director of operations of the C.I.A.–Cats in Action–a secret group of enforcers run out of the White House basement by a gray tabby named Socks. Buzzer, his gray-tabby sister, Dusty Louise, their hilarious tiny orange tabby twin siblings, Luigi and Luisa, and Buzzer's best friend and former contract operative, Cincinnati the dancing pig, introduce this fun and educational series by tracking down the infamous international catnapper, Fred-X, a giant owl who grabs cats and tries to fly them nightly to Memphis.

■**Hunt for Fred-X: Los Gatos of the C.I.A.** (English/elementary Spanish): Buzzer Louis, Dusty Louise, Luigi and Luisa, and Cincinnati the dancing pig head to Mexico at the request of the Mexican president to help the Federales (Mexican national police) stop the catnapping Fred-X from grabbing cats in Chihuahua and flying them to the Yucatán to sell into slavery in Aruba. Along the way, they learn to speak considerable Mexican Spanish. You will, too, with a 750-word and -phrase vocabulary and pronunciation guide in Spanish as spoken in Mexico.

■**Fred-X Rising: I Gatti of the C.I.A.** (English/elementary Italian): Our crime-fighting cats and Cincinnati are summoned to Italy by Buzzer's first cousin, Césare Pepperoni Giaccomazza, head of the Rome bureau of Interpol, to again capture Fred-X, who this time has the help of his German girlfriend, Frieda-K, and a greedy cardinal from the Vatican, capturing Italian cats to take to a one-armed ship's captain in Venice who plans to transport them in his old rust-bucket ship to the cat slave trade in Tunisia. As they track down the catnapping owl, they learn considerable Italian. You will, too, with a 750-word and -phrase vocabulary and pronunciation guide in Italian as spoken in Italy.

■**Tango With a Puma: Los Gatos of the C.I.A.** (English/intermediate Spanish): Fresh from capturing Fred-X in Italy, our heroes are invited to Argentina to help the PFA (Policia Federal de Argentina) capture the infamous international terrorist, Carlos the puma, just escaped from a maximum security prison at the headwaters of the Amazon River and headed for Buenos Aires. This time a diabolical, but simple, plan by Luigi and Luisa to corral the ingenious big cat in Los Jardines de Palermo, a big park in the Argentinean capital, Buenos Aires. In the process, they polish up and expand their Spanish. You will, too, with a 750-word and -phrase vocabulary and pronunciation guide in more formal, intermediate Spanish as spoken in Argentina.

- **Eiffel's Trifles & Troubles: Les Chats of the C.I.A.** (English/elementary French): When Carlos the puma again escapes from the headquarters of the PFA in Buenos Aires, Socks' spy satellite intercepts a phone call to his headquarters from Carlos on a ship in the South Atlantic. He's headed for Paris, and so are our heroes. Again they lay a clever plan to capture Carlos once and for all–even while touring the sites and sights of Paris, the City of Lights. And they learn to speak considerable French along the way. You will, too, with a 750-word and -phrase vocabulary and pronunciation guide in basic French as spoken in Paris.

- **München Madness: Die Katzen of the C.I.A.** (English/elementary German): The Bavarian region around Munich is the setting for the final attempt to capture Carlos the puma and return him to the authorities in Argentina, where's he still wanted as a fugitive and for bombing the headquarters of the national police, the PFA–Policia Federal de Argentina. As they track Carlos in Bavaria, they learn to speak considerable German. You will, too, with a 750-word and -phrase vocabulary and pronunciation guide in basic German as spoken in Germany.

- **Kremlin Kerfuffle: Koshki of the C.I.A.** (English/elementary Russian): Fresh from their Bavarian adventure tracking down Carlos the puma, the cats of the C.I.A. and Cincinnati the dancing pig are commanded secretly by the U.S. President (POTUS) to travel once again, this time to Russia. Their mission: capture the infamous international opium smuggler from Beijing, Ar-Chee the panda. Ar-Chee, you see, is the world's most active smuggler of opium from the poppy fields of Afghanistan via secret routes through the People's Republic of China, and he's set his sights on the lucrative Moscow market. POTUS and Russia's president, meeting in secret in Iceland, are determined, rather than sending in the troops, to cut off Ar-Chee's supply lines by simply capturing the big panda as he plies his trade around the Kremlin. Along the way, our heroes learn to speak considerable Russian. You will, too, with a 750-word and –phrase vocabulary and pronunciation guide in Russian as spoken in Moscow.

■ *Coming Soon:* **Beijing Ding-a-Ling: Mao of the C.I.A.:** The President of the United States, at the request of the Premier of the People's Republic of China, dispatches Buzzer Louis and the Cats of the CIA to help track down the brains behind Ar-Chee's opium smuggling ring. You see, Ling Ting Tong, a brilliant, multi-lingual porcupine, is known to be hiding in the Chinese capital. Having captured Mr. Ling's front man, Ar-Chee the panda, in Moscow, it's now up to the clandestine CIA cats to find Ling Ting Tong and put an end to the smuggling of opium from Afghanistan for resale along the Pacific Rim and in Moscow. Join the lovable twins, Luigi and Luisa, their brother and sister, Buzzer Louis and Dusty Louise, as they track down the porcupine with the help of their cohort, Cincinnati the dancing pig. The whole team learns to speak some Mandarin. So will you with the 750-word and –phrase vocabulary and pronunciation guide built right into the story.

For More Information
**Visit the Author's Website: www.CIAcats.com
Or e-mail me at George@CIAcats.com**

About the Author

George was born on the kitchen table in a small house on the family farm north of Kansas City, Missouri. He doesn't remember much about that day. But as a 12-pound, 10-month baby, he gave his mother some lasting memories . . . an entry worthy of note.

His early playmates were pigs, ducks, chickens and a calf or two. Messing with them gave him the rare ability to talk to animals, although they didn't answer him back. Most of the time, that is. Which likely explains a lot about his later life.

At age four, he moved with his family to Texas, where he was educated in the public school systems of Uvalde, Waco, San Antonio, and Austin. Well, really he ran away from school in the first grade in Uvalde, so that probably shouldn't count.

Following graduation from the University of Texas at Austin with B.J. and M.A. degrees, George entered the advertising, public relations, and marketing practice in Dallas, where he rose to become president and chief operating officer of a major office of a national agency at 34. After selling the Dallas agency to that national agency in 1986 and then participating as a director and officer in the sale of the national agency to the French in 1998, he retired. He and Mary, his wife of 50 years, have four children and seven grandchildren. They live in the Dallas/Fort Worth Metroplex.

The admittedly "strange, but quality," author spins a tale in this fifth Detective Craig Rylander mystery, *Fire and Ice: Beyond Alchemy*, a story based on recent major process patents granted The Institute for Fusion Studies at The University of Texas at Austin.

Oh, and he still talks to animals. And they mostly still don't talk back. Other people usually think that weird. That's their problem.

For more information, visit the Author's Website: www.CIAcats.com

CPSIA information can be obtained at www.ICGtesting.com
Printed in the USA
LVOW10s0010180315

430948LV00012B/40/P